TO CLAIM A KING

ALL THE QUEEN'S MEN, BOOK 3

BY CORA FLYNN

CONTENT NOTICE

This book is intended for mature audiences, recommended for readers 18+ years only as it contains profanities, sexual innuendo, and detailed sexual scenes.

This book is my darkest yet. Hillary's story begins to unravel, and with it comes a lot of deeply violent baggage. With that in mind, this book includes:

1. Dark themes and graphic depictions of violence including and not limited to: Severe torture, gruesome deaths involving the use of guns and knives, drugging, genital mutilation (male), sexual assault of a male character, witness of a murder, captivity, guns, child soldiers, murder, removal of body parts (head)

2. Graphic sexual scenes including and not limited to anal sex, tandem sex, misuse of coconut oil, group sex and unprotected sexual activity (all consensual).

3. Mentions of past sexual assault, past addictive drug use, human trafficking, and past death due to overdose, anxiety, insomnia, discussions of depression, emotional manipulation, mentions of dead parents, the deterioration of a parental/child relationship, grooming, child grooming, humiliation.

For a full list of content inclusions, please check my website: www.coraflynnauthor.com.

This is a Why Choose/Reverse Harem romance novel, which means the FMC will end up with more than one love interest and will not have to choose between them to find her HEA. The characters are bi-sexual and will eventually enter an ethical poly relationship.

This novel is written in American English by a Canadian author, and the spelling, terminology, and grammar have been edited accordingly.

This book has been edited multiple times by multiple people, both personally and professionally, but the imperfection of human beings is a beautiful and inevitable thing. If you notice a typo in any form, please choose to contact me so I may fix it immediately at coraflynnauthor@gmail.com with the subject "Typo Found."

Thank you!

xo
Cora Flynn

ACKNOWLEDGEMENTS

I am beyond fortunate to work with the most amazing group of people who support every single aspect of this book coming together.

My graphic designer/PA/everything in between, Megan Butchard. My lifeline. I would be a puddle on the floor without you.

My dear friend and incredible book coach, Jen Larkin. Your guidance strengthened my words and this story in ways I could not have imagined.

My Alpha team: Paula, Megan, and Brandi. Your insights made this story as engaging as it is.

My Beta team: Kristie, Emmi, Nikolette, Marina, and Van. You make me snort laugh and sweet cry.

My editor, Lara. You continue to bring out the best in my work, and you're so damn good at it.

My cover designer, Artscandare. Once again, you designed a show-stopping cover to do this story justice.

My friends, colleagues, and family, who nod along when I drone on about these made-up characters in my head. I love you so much for indulging me.

Finally, my husband. Another book has come and gone, and you've supported all the other areas of our lives I ignore when I get deep into the writing cave. I couldn't have chosen a better partner in life and in love.

To you, my readers. Thank you for reading my book baby and allowing me to write more words with every purchase. Because of you I get to continue to write, and because of every one of the people above this story is coming to an end.

In my humble opinion, Hillary, Lucky, Aaron, and Kellan truly get the HEA they've been so desperately searching for.

I hope you think so, too!

XO

Cora

For every woman with a broken smile and a
brittle soul:

You weren't born this way. You were made.

You were forged in fire. Hazed through hell.
Darkened by the damage of someone else's
despair.

...

May you get your own vengeance one day.

CHAPTER 1

Hillary

Coagulated blood would be a beautiful nail polish color. It was brighter than I would have thought—a rich burgundy with blackened edges, captivating and ominous. The pool fanned out in a bulbous pattern against the clear glass backdrop, the drying whorls and eddies once the vibrant flow of a woman's essence.

All thoughts of finding my men here and strategizing what to do about the shocking Mutilation Mistress news Joey and I had heard over the radio twenty minutes ago was temporarily on pause while we figured out what to do with the severed head on my coffee table.

I drew in a deep breath through my mouth and closed my eyes, but the blood vessels permanently held the image of the dulled stare on the familiar face, no longer seeing this side of the living. I fought through the waves of nausea that threatened to drown me in their despair.

Blackbird was more than a professional acquaintance; with the private information we'd shared—including my truest nature behind the shielded window of a computer screen—I could have called her a friend.

Joey shifted beside me and gently placed a strong arm around my shoulders. The move forced my attention back to reality. We had to clean up this mess and get out of here as quickly as possible.

Icy spiders dug their spindly legs between my shoulder blades as I regained consciousness from my temporary fugue state. My condo, my primary shelter of safety, had been compromised. My place of peace had become the drop zone for the true computer brain behind my operation, and I couldn't trust I wasn't still being watched.

Joey's voice broke through the deafening silence, her voice barely above a whisper, but abrupt enough to sound like a shot in a metal drum. It jolted me to life. The bile in my stomach and stiffened spine took a back seat to the very necessary job of risk assessment.

"You check the cameras—I'll get rid of this." She nodded in the general direction of our guest and released me from her grip. Stumbling without her hold to keep me upright, I barely stopped from pitching forward into the present.

I'd seen a lot of depravity in my lifetime, from rich goons down to basement-level thugs, but I had never, ever, come face to face with detached body parts. Staggering toward my panic room, my legs wobbled and my guts roiled at the colorful image now boldly painted like neon graffiti on the backs of my eyelids.

I'd be lucky if I slept tonight—or ever again.

My room was as pristine as when I'd left it this morning —not a single rumple in the duvet or a hair-clip out of place on my dresser. The subtlety of my intruder's violation sent another shudder through me. Without Blackbird left...there, I'd never have known someone crossed my threshold without permission.

I entered the code into the security pad behind my closet door and was relieved to see the hidden room untouched. The quiet hum of the air filtration system and the steady whir of the monitors belied the heaviness of the moment— as if the woman I'd spoken to hundreds of times over these very screens wasn't lying in pieces in my living room.

These systems were active at all times, and while I wasn't a hacker like Blackbird or Lucky, I could navigate the software that protected my office and buildings. I brought up the cameras to review the footage from the last twenty-four hours and multiplied the speed to scroll through the images quickly.

Whoever had made me their target today had the technical skills to circumvent my entire security system. The cameras discreetly installed around my building went dark for approximately fifteen minutes—by a quick calculation—just enough time to take the elevator up to my condo, deposit the head, and leave. I cycled through the video feeds three times, but it showed nothing more than a grainy picture of a white van parking on the periphery of the farthest camera before the whole system went down.

It didn't matter what the feeds said. The only person I knew of with the motive and intel to kill Blackbird was Alvarez.

I saved the complete set of footage in backup files protected within hidden folders and transferred what I could to an external hard drive before deleting every file on the computer entirely. Lucky's skills would have been useful; I was knowledgeable enough to know nothing ever truly got erased from a hard drive, but didn't know how to make the data disappear entirely. A thought for later. For now, we needed to get out of here as quickly as possible.

Joey appeared in the doorway, the single micro-crinkle in her brow letting on she hadn't been aware of my secret space. Her stoic features remained devoid of emotion, however, as her gaze swept through the dark room, as if scanning for threats.

"I have the head"—she grimaced—"all packaged up, but we're going to need to dump it immediately. Where are we headed afterward? You're not coming back here."

She made the declaration as if challenging me to object. Joey took her job of protecting me seriously, and I was never more grateful for it than I was right now.

I'd always felt safe in my home, but I also walked along a dangerous ledge between two worlds, and had to prepare for every eventuality. I'd had the foresight to have a Plan B, though I could admit I never thought I'd be using it this quickly.

Acquiring Aaron's warehouse when I'd taken over his company was part of the asset transfer. The building had been outfitted with maximum security in mind—satellite cameras, bullet-proof windows, a fireproof panic room... I'd even gone so far as to install a fail-safe in the walls that would implode the building with the press of two offsite buttons, like the old buildings in Manhattan in the seventies.

"The warehouse." My voice was thick with exhaustion. "It's the only place I can trust right now."

I hadn't finished the interior, but it had an office, a bedroom, and a kitchen area—with a few sparse furnishings besides. I had hoped it would one day serve as the most secure women and children's shelter in the state, but for now it would only get the chance to serve as our shelter while I figured out our next moves.

Our shelter—it finally dawned on me — I hadn't gotten a single response from the men. *My* men. Where in the fuck were they?

Joey dipped her head in acknowledgment. "Leave everything behind. They could have tracers buried in anything, and we won't have time to check for bugs. Better just to start fresh."

If I was right, and I knew I was, the man we'd put behind bars was behind the tortured gift on my coffee table. He would just be getting started. He'd pull any strings he could to be my puppet master, and a weaker person might bow on his stage.

Hillary Lane would never dance in his show. *Never.*

I followed my protector through the once warm hallways. The light of sunset now struck the cream paint with malice, turning light hues into bleak, somber shades.

I had kept nothing of high importance here except the painting, which was now traveling to the other side of the country, and a few of my mother's and Isabella's trinkets, which I kept in a safe deposit box three towns over. There were no incriminating paper files to speak of. But the necessity of leaving my home because it had been poisoned, likely by the very man I'd dedicated my mission to destroy, brought an unfamiliar feeling of failure to burrow deep into my belly like a snake.

As we descended in the elevator to our waiting car, I brought up the tracking app on my phone to find my partners in crime. Wherever they were, they'd better be in one piece. My body couldn't handle another surprise.

My already roiling stomach sloshed a fiery wave of acid. My number was up. Years of planning, executing, and administering revenge had now come to a head. The media had discovered my actions, and it was just a matter of time before they discovered me.

Mutilation Mistress. The shock of the news announcement over the radio was still present, even in the aftermath of our severed head cleanup. The clever title underscored the many women and children I'd saved from cycles of abuse. I circumvented the useless justice system that protected so few by removing the predator's weapon and destroying their pride. Caught or not, I would apologize to no one.

Care and concern morphed into irritation when three flashing dots showed up on my screen. At the warehouse.

Fury flooded into the hollow marrow of my bones at the realization they were blatantly ignoring my many calls and messages, sitting in *my* shelter while I panic spiraled from my world collapsing around me.

Joey brandished her gun beside me as the elevator doors slid open, on her guard as I stalked through the concrete underground with a renewed vengeance in my heart.

"Mother fuckers," I growled as Joey ushered me forward and I tossed my phone into the waiting front seat of one of my newer, less noticeable vehicles—a simple black Audi Q8. "I hope you have extra ammo in this vehicle, Joey, because we have three men to kill."

I only half meant it.

CHAPTER 2

Lauchlan

I'd seen the bargain basement dregs of humanity as a con man, but I'd never watched a man bleed out in front of me.

A thick layer of the red sticky stuff surrounded me; on the floor, on the smock the Doc had made me wear before she'd had us load Aaron on the hospital bed she'd stolen from God knows where. So deep beneath my fingernails, a thousand showers probably wouldn't take it away.

I conned a high-profile surgeon once—a secret baddie who'd dabbled in some French gambling ring. Luckily, I'd held onto some of that medical training. Unluckily, that meant I was the man to help the Doc with the bleeding wounds all over my Colombian's body.

Tan men weren't meant to look like ghosts, not like the pasty skin of my Gaelic blood. I swallowed the swirl of panic back into my guts as he lay in front of me. The whisper of breath and the chirp of the heart monitor she'd left behind were the only real confirmation Aaron was still alive.

Nothing left to do but wait and hope something with more power in the universe would show us some mercy.

Worth a shot.

I sat down on the hard office chair beside the bed and put my hands together in prayer.

If you're there, gods or goddesses, please don't let this stubborn, sexy, scary-as-fuck man die. Please allow him many more years of flaying and fucking, if anything, to keep our little family of misfits together.

How did you end a prayer again? Ahh, right.

Amen.

I wasn't a religious man—wasn't even sure I believed in God in the traditional sense. If there was a God, he would be she, and she would be an all-knowing, all-seeing woman like my *Epona*, not a surly man in the sky like a more impressive version of my Conan.

Still, when the world was going to shit and your Colombian crush lay on the table like a barely there cadaver, saying a prayer to the Sky Daddy certainly couldn't hurt.

He was more than a Colombian crush. He was a good man with a shyte family who needed us as much as we needed him. Well, he probably needed Blondie more than he needed any of us, but he wasn't going to have her, if he let himself drift off to the mafia version of the afterlife tonight.

If Aaron died today, a piece of Blondie would die too, and then Kellan would lose the tiny amount of hope he had that wasn't scrawled in ink across his knuckles. And I... well, I'd have nowhere to go.

The realization hit me like an anvil over the head, like I was Wile E. Coyote in the children's cartoon. Without this group of fuckery... what did I have?

I still didn't have a solution for The Six—not without Aaron's forger at least, and I wasn't rushing back into the arms of my opportunistic Mumsy. Never had, really. And now she was salivating for a coup with my head on the chopping block, not ever. My friends in Dublin didn't have a clue who the 'real' me was.

Without these three, I was just a lonely wandering conman with a decent bank account and a grand car.

Scratch that. My car was long gone, abandoned in Club 7's parking lot. I'd shed a tear for my lost baby when our whole day had gone arseways, before I shed more tears for my Roboto on the makeshift operating table.

I carefully wiped my clammy hands on the cotton of the hospital blanket the doc had brought with her and draped over Mr. Roboto's sleeping form.

Aaron Rodriguez was a scary, stubborn sap with a bleeding heart and a bunch of bleeding orifices. Doc had given him a transfusion and patched him up as best she could, but he'd lost too much blood, and he had to make it through the night. Only three hours had gone by, but it felt like an eternity.

Doc had said the incision *just* missed Aaron's liver and his stomach, by a millimeter on both sides, at most. I don't know what we did to deserve that miracle, but a word of thanks could probably get me in the Almighty Creator's good books.

We were in what was supposed to be an office. A barren desk with two chairs had been pushed into the corner to make room for the hospital bed and monitors Kellan's contact had brought with them. The rest of the room was empty—nothing on the walls, no lighting but the crappy fluorescent tubes overhead. I had no idea what Blondie was planning for this place, but it wasn't cushy or expensive like any of her other spaces.

Kellan was confident it was the safest place for us. State-of-the-art security, planned for things like this, blah-blah-blah. Hadn't been paying much attention to him with a bloody body in the backseat, but I trusted him. And I most definitely trusted Hillary's security measures. Her condo was a feckin' fortress.

The barbarian was out in the main lobby area pacing the floor, and had been on his phone for the last two hours. I had no idea who he spoke to, but I knew it wasn't Blondie by the lack of shouting. When she found us, she was going to murder us. Not with her fists, though I knew she could do it.

No, Blondie would chop all our dicks off with a few chosen words spiked with cyanide. I should have kept the doc on standby for the inevitable tongue-lashing we were all about to receive.

I wanted to call her, but I'd lost my phone in the shuffle, somewhere in the Brothel of Betrayal between killing a scary assassin chick and racing like hell to save the life of the sleeping fucker in front of me.

Luckily, it was encrypted, and only a hacker as good as me or Blackbird could get into it. Unluckily, I wasn't leaving this place anytime soon, so I wasn't able to pass the time with anything but counting tiles on the ceiling or praying to gods that may or may not exist.

No phone, no car, no apartment. I was completely beholden to two sexy, murderous bastards, and a sexier vengeful Queen.

Not exactly how a little boy pictures his life going, but I couldn't say I was all that sad about it. Honor among thieves, and all that. We were a cantankerous bunch, but the loyalty they'd shown me in the last few weeks was more than I'd ever received among my band of *actual* thieves.

Looking at Aaron now, paler than a sheet with sweaty dark hair plastered to his temples, I could say with certainty I'd be sad if he was gone. We needed him to make this group work. Hell, *I* needed him.

Please don't die, you bullish twat.

As if the comatose man could hear my thoughts, he shifted beneath the blanket, brow furrowing in sleep. The doc warned us he might awake sooner than if he'd been put under at a hospital, but I hadn't expected he'd come to right in the middle of my "sacred" prayer time.

Except he wasn't coming to. He was coding. The heart monitor beeped out a harsh rhythm and the spiky mountain of his arrhythmia lapsed into the straight line of doom.

"Kellan!" I yelled sharply, rushing to the med kit the doc had left with the AED paddles. I grabbed them and threw off the blanket, ripping open the hospital gown to expose Aaron's bare chest.

"Kellan!" I screamed again, peeling off the strips of sticky backing to tape the two pads to his pecs. Aaron was a hairy fucker, and he'd hate me when I had to tear them off later, but I'd risk his wrath to keep him alive.

My barbarian friend barged into the room as if it were on fire, surprise overtaking his features when I pressed the shock button. Aaron's chest heaved upward with the burst of electricity.

"We're going to need to do CPR," I told him, surprising myself with the cold calm in my voice. "Get ready."

He did as he was told for probably the first time in his life, settling immediately on the other side of the bed. The paddles pulsed one more time before I barked out the order.

"Now!"

I fought the urge to hurl while Kellan blew air into Aaron's lungs. I waited with the paddles, hoping like hell I wouldn't need to use them again.

Chest compressions. Breaths in the mouth. Chest compressions.

If I thought the wait through his surgery had stopped time, that had nothing on the black hole I was trapped in now.

Please, Epona, Gods, and Goddesses—let this man live and I'll never pull another con again.

More chest compressions. More breaths. It wasn't working.

Fuck, fuck, *fuck.*

I hit the shock button again, knowing it was the last time I could feasibly do so without risking his heart.

Please, please, please.

I held my own breath until Kellan blew out the last of his air into Aaron's lungs and raised his gaze to mine. The blue in his eyes dimmed to a terrifying black as all hope drained out of them.

Pain exploded in my chest as if I'd been the one to get a zap with the paddles. This was it. Hillary was going to have a broken heart, and Conan and I wouldn't be able to pick up the pieces with our own hearts broken too.

The room was deathly silent until we were both jolted by the electronic chirp once again.

Beep. Beep. Beep.

I'd thought a woman's orgasm was the most beautiful sound in the world, but it now took second place to the sound of the heart monitor singing the tune of a steady rhythm.

Setting aside the pads, I leaned over his body, placing my head to his heart, needing confirmation with my own ears.

Thump. Thump. Thump.

It was barely there, but it was real.

Thank the fucking gods.

I drew up and raised my eyes to the ceiling in silent thanks, determined to work out my payment to them later. My gaze dropped to our patient's silent form, staring hard at every stoic wrinkle lining his face as if it would tell me when he'd wake up.

Hopefully, the gods weren't cruel enough to dangle this hope in front of us and then take it away once we accepted the gift, like tricky little pixies.

"Thanks." Kellan broke me out of my fixation, his voice gruff and gravel, layered with exhaustion. Our fierce, self-appointed leader was an unraveling mess.

I turned to assess the Viking impersonator. Sweat covered his brow like he'd just come out of battle and barely survived. Disheveled. Dirty. Bloodshot eyes and sallow skin. His suit and pants criss-crossed by Aaron's dried blood.

Tasty, yet terrifying.

"Thanks, back." I scrubbed the back of my neck with a soiled palm, my blood still buzzing with the major hit of adrenaline. We stared at each other across the bed, the air between us thicker than a Guinness. Without thinking, I reached for the back of his neck and hauled our heads together, closing my mouth over his in a desperate kiss.

I'd expected him to pull back or push me away; too fucking aloof on the best of days, but he fisted my hair instead, forced my lips open with his tongue, and thoroughly tasted me until I was dizzy.

He felt like passion, and protectiveness, and home. A wee bit more than a casual fuck.

More gently than I expected, he drew away, but the emotionless tulip wouldn't look me in the eye again, turning his attention back to the man lying between us.

"Doc said if he made it through the night, he should be okay. I'll keep an eye on him." I gestured toward the door. "Maybe you should lay down too, ya? You're cooked."

Red-tinged navy eyes squinted into slits. "I'm not the problem here. Worry about *him*." He thrust a large hand toward Aaron dressed only in boxers and two AED sticker paddles.

Moving carefully to peel the padded tape from Aaron's chest, I winced when I ripped out a good chunk of hair. He barely stirred, the monitor still humming softly in the background.

"I'm more worried about *her*." I lied through my perfectly straight teeth, shooting him a meaningful glance across the bed. "Have you talked to Blondie yet?"

Kellan squirmed. "No. I tried calling her back, but she didn't answer. She'll find us." His tone was tired but confident, as if it were only a matter of time.

Ahhh, yes. Everybody was stalking everybody in this little group. Well, in cases where our lives were on the line and we needed to hide out in super-secret quarters, that toxic trait was useful.

Despite his manly protests, he slumped into the chair where I'd been sitting and leaned over the bed with uncharacteristic care.

I was definitely right; something more was between these two than a relationship of convenience. Kellan's eyes were solemn—almost tender. A stupid little flick of jealousy pricked my heart. He'd kissed me back and denied me in the same breath.

I didn't want to almost die to have him look at *me* that way, but...

Fuck, this little foursome was complicated.

We sat in silence for what had to be an hour—too tired and anxious to even try a conversation. When I was about to fall asleep in my hands, a masculine whimper jolted me upright.

A dark-lashed lid eased its way open, and I fought every urge in my body not to pounce. Aaron stared straight ahead through that one window, slowly opening the other until a two-eyed brown stare fixed on the ceiling above him.

The relief that flooded my bloodstream was so strong, like I'd taken a hit of ecstasy from a beautiful woman's mouth. Fucking euphoric.

"About bloody time, you bastard!" I leaned over the bed, my face hovering right above his. "You fecking scared us, Roboto!"

So much for giving him space and keeping calm, but there we were. I'd gone through too much terror in the last few hours to contain myself any longer. This broody fucker was awake, and alive, and—

Kellan forced me back by the shoulders, then leaned beside me a few feet above Aaron's face too.

"Can you hear us?" he asked somberly, as if speaking to a mourner at a funeral parlor.

Our Colombian not-cadaver slightly nodded, his eyes squinting at the effort of the movement.

Kellan's nod was quick and decisive. "Good. The doctor left some ice chips for you. You're not going to eat or drink for a little while."

A crushing groan pierced the stale air as the mangled man shifted his weight on the bed made for someone much smaller. Our Viking King hesitated just a second too long, relief written on his own features, before turning on his heel and leaving—presumably for the ice chips in the cooler by the entry door.

I leaned forward again without a responsible adult in the room to hold me back. "Don't mind him." I placed a light hand on his shoulder. "He's allergic to feelings."

Aaron's lip twitched, but whether it was from pain or my superior humor, I couldn't be sure.

Still, the sheer relief at seeing the whites of his eyes gave me the smallest taste of hope. We'd made it out of the impossible alive.

Now I just had to pray Blondie wouldn't murder us.

I had a feeling there weren't enough gods in the universe for that.

16

CHAPTER 3

Aaron

The Irishman stared at me through tired eyes, and I was surprised to feel relief at his presence.

The disbelief of my attendant's betrayal and the blade piercing my skin had been far more potent, so perhaps my judgment was off.

A bitter taste lay thick on my tongue from apparent sedation. I had no way to know how long I'd been unconscious, but the relief in *Rojo's* eyes told me it had been long enough.

"Thought we lost you there, mate." The usual cheeriness that laced his tone was absent, his expression pained at the admission. "Thanked a few gods to get you through."

That statement meant nothing to me, but I took comfort in his concern. I'd been considered dead for many months. I was grateful to still have people to mourn me at all.

My body was tender, but my chest felt as if it were on fire. A quick sweep of my gaze confirmed the bleeding had stopped, but two large patches of skin lay bare where I'd previously had hair.

"We had to revive you," Lauchlan said, rubbing two palms over his face to cover a grimace. "But you made it through."

So, my heart had stopped. I blinked as I processed this information.

I'd endured many years of my father's slow lessons in torture, but none of his teachings had prepared me for this level of pain. When I shifted on the mattress to relieve the burning itch across my abdomen, Lauchlan settled a palm on my shoulder to assist my adjustment.

"It is I who should thank you, *Rojo*," I returned, once I was in a manageable position. "You saved my life after my actions risked yours. It was not my intention."

He rested his fingers along the pulse point of my wrist, as if to confirm I was truly alive.

"Eh, you're more noble of a man than I am." Lauchlan shook his head, a gentle smirk softening the sadness that sat in his eyes. "Dunno if I would have risked my life for the same. But I can't fault you for bein' a decent human being."

I snorted in response, no part of me ever being so disillusioned as to think I could be 'decent'. I was paying penance for the sins of my parents. Had I not been set on a different path with their betrayal, I could not claim to be any better than Vicente.

I owed my father a debt for my newfound conscience. It was his misfortune I was not a forgiving man.

He settled back into the chair next to the bedside but did not remove his hand from my wrist, keeping the warm contact of skin on skin. It was too much of a comfort for me to remove it.

I had thought little of this man before now. He intrigued *Mi Reina* and had a set of skills that had proven useful. She trusted him, and I had put my faith in her judgment. He could have abandoned me when I'd failed to return. Instead, he'd remained. I was not immune to the charms of loyalty. Perhaps Hillary had seen something in this man I had not.

I examined him through a fresh lens. Long red lashes fanned bright green eyes, though the spark in them had dimmed from the darkness of our day. High cheekbones and the faint lines of a permanent smirk made him attractive, but his tousled auburn hair gave him the boyish air of a man yet to mature. His body was molded but not sculpted; approachable; a safe energy. Through these eyes, I could understand the attraction.

And he'd just saved my life and was not bragging from rooftops about his heroism. Perhaps I truly didn't know him at all.

His voice broke through my assessing thoughts.

"But you're going to want to give Kellan a big kiss later."

I searched the Irishman's face for the joke, but it held a deadly serious air. "Without him, we'd both probably be strung up in someone's meat locker somewhere."

A visible shudder vibrated through his body and into my arm. I did not know this thief well, but it was unlikely he had the same violent upbringing as my *compañero* and me. It would be a painful initiation to remain in our company.

"I will express my gratitude when he returns," I vowed. Kellan Carlos was intended to be my ultimate end; instead, he had saved my life twice, at great sacrifice to his own.

An unforeseen enemy had struck us, but we remained. We would work together to rid him of the scourge that was Antonio, and bury my father with the same dirt. The two men would share a burial plot under unmarked headstones —a fair tribute to their vile legacy.

"Where is the woman?" I stared into the green sea of his eyes, needing closure for my attendant's betrayal. We'd shared our bodies, and I'd protected her from my father, only to discover it was all a ruse to bring me to my knees.

"Dead." He croaked the word out as if he were ashamed. "I shot her while Kellan carried you out."

So, he was my savior as well. I felt a twinge within my heart that could not be attributed to my injuries.

He tore his gaze from mine in obvious discomfort, choosing to crack a joke instead of feeling his pain. "We're going to need another tailor, by the way. None of our suits survived."

As if summoned, Kellan returned with a whiskey glass filled with ice chips, his suit a painting with what could only be my blood. I accepted it gratefully, eager to rid my mouth of its metallic coating.

"I am sorry for the trouble I've caused you, my friend." I dipped my head in deference as the swirling storm of his stare thoroughly assessed my bandaged torso.

The blond man said nothing to accept my apology, choosing instead to fixate on my wrist, where Lauchlan's fingers remained, now caressing the underside of soft flesh. I'd done nothing to stop his touch. The warmth of it reminded me I had lived another day.

"You're in your old warehouse. In case you didn't recognize it," he said instead, moving to stand at the foot of the bed and folding his arms across his chest. "Hillary fixed it up and made it another fortress. Given the circumstances, we figured it was the only place that was safe. I had a friend of mine patch you up."

He and *Rojo* exchanged a dark look, but neither rushed to explain what it meant. They turned their attention back to me.

"Then I am in your debt twice over," I mused, wishing he were closer to clasp his hand, to demonstrate my gratitude in ways my words could not. Softer, I spoke. "I am not sure I am worthy of your loyalty, *compañero*."

"It was my decision to make," he returned gruffly, his attention on the wall beside my head instead of my face. "But we can talk about the consequences when Hillary gets here."

Mi Reina. It was a great gift she had not been near us when Antonio sent his assassin. She was more trained in combat than I, but to test her abilities meant she'd also put her life at risk for mine.

I felt the large man's scrutiny on me once again. Turning into the penetrative stare, I observed the layers of darkness imbued in his irises. I could not read his emotions, but I felt his intensity sear into my skin. His eyes narrowed.

"Do you trust me with those consequences, *Guapo?*" he said, his tone deathly serious.

Guapo. Another nickname of endearment. This man was becoming much more than a trusted ally. I respected him. I cared for him. I recognized his need to exert control to feel safe. I could give him this, as he'd given me another chance to live.

"I do."

We exchanged a look, many words within a quick gaze. Loyalty. Attraction. Trust.

Before I could say anymore, a harsh feminine shout came from the corridor behind us. My heart leaped at *Mi Reina's* voice, knowing she was safe and sound, then returned to my chest with a vicious drop.

Kellan immediately turned on his heel and left the room to address the woman I was certain we all loved. I braced myself for my inevitable punishment and Lauchlan held his breath beside me.

We had endured hell today, four demons preparing to face our devil.

But first, I had to face her.

22

CHAPTER 4

Hillary

Stupid, infuriating *fuckers.*

It had been hours—*hours*—since I'd heard from any of these men, and here Kellan was, looking like he'd barged his way through an apocalypse, staring at me through bloodshot eyes like a stunned deer in headlights.

"What in the fuck are you three doing here!?" I hissed, my voice hovering on the border of mania after the living hell of the last few hours.

Imagine my surprise when I finally had a moment to track these three idiots; their glaring blue dots had all congregated in the same place—*my* place.

They weren't dumb men. Mostly. Kellan and Aaron had proven their loyalty to me, and Lucky—well, Lucky had been given an open opportunity to walk away unscathed and pledged his allegiance to me instead. While his options were limited and it didn't exactly scream 'undying devotion,' it meant enough to keep him within this exclusive club. Seeing as Aaron and Kellan hadn't killed him yet, he had to have some value to them too.

So, I would allow the three of them an explanation *before* slowly removing each testicle from their whimpering bodies. If this was because of one of Lucky's tricks or because Kellan went overboard on protection duty, I was going to—

"Oh, thank fuck." The graveled timbre shocked my anger into temporary submission. Kellan's broad body dwarfed mine in a crushing hug, burying his face into my hair. He smelled of copper and ash, and the vicious tangy scent of fear.

For the briefest moment, I collapsed into him, letting his heat and tight hold absorb morsels of my grief for Blackbird, and the visceral dread that coated my skin. Before I could escape into the comfort, I pulled back, the geyser of my rage erratically bubbling to the top of my forehead.

"What the fuck, Kellan!? What in the actual fuck?"

His brow creased into a hundred lines—his own anger sparking in the little flecks of blue remaining in his eyes. I took him in—the visage of a bullish man about to tear through me—when I noticed his clothing for the first time.

Thick burgundy streaks of what I knew had to be blood created a hatched pattern all over Kellan's signature FBI-issued suit. It was torn in three places; the stitching coming apart at the seams along one shoulder.

What the hell had happened to him?

Aaron. Lauchlan. Why weren't they out here in the common space too? My already butchered heart felt as if it was about to cleave into ten pieces, the muscle palpitating out a staccato rhythm.

"Whose blood is that?" I whispered, my eyes flicking all over his body in search of other injuries. Other than a ruined suit, I couldn't find any.

Foolishly, I didn't have biometric scanners to track them with. Aaron's new tracer—placed in the ring I had given him—could only tell me his location within a few yards' accuracy via satellite. Lucky's was a similar model, buried deep inside the muscle tissue of his arm.

Kellan's was a digital signature in his phone; the least secure of the three. After this mess was sorted, everyone was getting new versions, so I could monitor their vitals at all times.

Unless ... Panic flared in the base of my belly, its acidic bite gnawing away at my organs.

Was one of them ... *dead?*

Swollen, tattooed knuckles flashed as Kellan rubbed the back of his neck, looking uncomfortable. He breathed out a long-suffering sigh and beckoned me to follow him.

"You'll want to see for yourself."

Instead of tearing him apart with my nails and my words, I pursued him to the office space I hadn't had time to properly furnish yet. The barely concealed fear nearly exploded from my rib cage as I took in Aaron's bandaged body on a makeshift hospital setup in the middle of the room. Lucky's green eyes cast a haunted glow as he peered up at me from a perch beside the bed. His crumpled white dress shirt was also marred with streaks of dark dirt and bright blood.

"Aaron!" The shriek left my throat before I could process its sting. I flung myself to his bedside, tempering my frantic energy while removing the flannel blanket to scan every part of his body like I had Kellan. This time, though, my worst fears were confirmed.

Judging by the heavy layer of gauze and medical tape, Aaron had sustained severe injuries. His normally tanned skin was ashen, significantly paler than mine; the pallor of a corpse. Thick bandages wrapped around his abdomen and thigh; the crisp, dark patches of hair shaved away to clear the skin for proper sutures. His chest hair, normally thick and groomed, was patchy in two places, as if ripped from his skin.

They'd had to revive him. He'd very literally almost died today. Fiery tingles of sharp emotion collected in the back of my throat as I held back my tears.

"Oh, Aaron." I breathed out his name in a whisper as if in prayer.

Whoever had done this to him was going to die a *very* painful death. Interlinking our fingers, I stared into the slitted caramel eyes of the man I loved. My need to punish him for nearly stopping my heart warred with my need to make him whole again.

"What happened?" I demanded as terror crawled through my abdomen like a parasite. A tired but smooth tenor with an Irish accent spoke up beside me.

"Internal bleeding but missed the organs. Had a blood transfusion, and he's on a whole cocktail of painkillers, but Doc says he'll be alright."

Aaron shifted his position on the bed with agonizing slowness, his eyes never leaving mine. "*Mi Reina*," he rasped, the words tinged with pain and contrition. "I am sorry you must see me this way. I—"

"My fault, really." Lucky's lilting words rushed to interrupt him. "See, I rescued this fucker with a savior complex, thinking he was joking. Turns out he wasn't, and really did need saving after all. Although we can thank Conan here for that."

He dipped his auburn head toward Kellan, whose hulking frame remained in the doorway behind us, as if guarding our group from more potential threats tonight.

His falsely cheerful bravado forced its way through the somber air, but it did absolutely nothing to relieve the tension.

"What do you mean *rescued?*" My eyes narrowed as I searched Aaron's face for any sign of dishonesty.

"Vicente." Aaron spat his father's name with a vicious sneer, which quickly morphed into a grimace of pain. He squeezed my hand roughly before starting again.

"Vicente has allowed the raping my staff, *Mi Reina*. I was sent videos of the crime. He had to be stopped."

The rage I'd been holding between my shoulder blades melted through my chest cavity into my stomach. Of course, my knife-wielding warrior with a penchant for bloodletting also had a bleeding heart for those he considered within his protection. I wanted to pound on his chest, tear at his hair —make him *hurt* in the same way I was hurting to see him in this state, but I couldn't.

Aaron held a ravaged soul, but he carried a beautiful heart. He wasn't just a dark knight for me—he was a dark knight for justice, a defender of the downtrodden. What kind of monster would I be to tear into him for that?

A practical one, apparently.

"Aaron, we have *people* for that. You have a price on your head!" I bit out through gritted teeth. My insides were at war. The pride for his insistent heroism and the hurt he'd willingly risk his life without saying goodbye were locked into a confusing battle of emotions.

I released his hand and delicately cupped his cheeks between my palms, the dark, rough stubble pricking my skin. "What would I have done if I had lost you, *Cabellero Oscuro*? How would I be whole without you?"

My eyes grew hazy, filled with tears. These men—*my* men—were making me a sloshy, soppy, sap. Holding onto the hot, liquid wrath flowing through my veins was easier than letting it dissipate into the ether. I needed to mold it into a weapon, not melt it into a pile of goo every time these criminals decided to play the hero.

I wanted to unleash hell onto all of them, but how could I punish the men who leaped into the fray to save the man I loved when I wasn't able to? I was a bitch, but I wasn't heartless. It was impossible to be when they kept finding ways to prove I had one.

A large hand, the one without the IV drip, came up to cover mine, its warm and calloused skin a slight balm to the sting of his decision.

His raspy voice grew stronger with each word, and the liquid honey of his irises became more molten as he stared into me.

"*Mi Reina.* It is you who makes me brave—who shows me what it is to stand up for something bigger than myself. I need to be this man that you are making me. We need to save them."

Well… fuck.

"I'll take responsibility." Lucky piped up behind me, uncharacteristically eager for his own lashing. "Roboto asked me to drive him to the club, and I said yes, although it wasn't necessarily in that order. And if I had known he was going to wear and ruin my favorite suit, I'd likely have reconsidered. And I lost my car too. So, poor decisions all around. Not sure who got it worse, to be fair."

Aaron snorted into my hands; Lucky's attempt at humor only hit the mark with him, while Kellan and I remained silent. If Aaron was willing to see the humor in the situation, I held onto the hope he felt better than the story his bandages were telling.

Our conman was rambling, his accent thicker with each sentence. Seeing Lucky so off-kilter would be amusing in any other circumstance, but I imagined he wasn't used to seeing much blood in his line of work. Then again, he was a true enigma even thousands of dollars worth of hacking hadn't been able to explain.

"Conan really saved the day, though. Truly the hero of the hour. Both of us would have been deader than dead from the supermodel assassin if we didn't have the Cartel baddie on our side."

I released my hands from Aaron's face and whipped around, staring up at Kellan's guilty expression.

"Supermodel assassin?"

Another neck rub, but this time, his shoulders deflated, the visage of a massive man collapsing like a loose helium balloon. His stare held a litany of emotions. Flickers of grief, anger and fear cycled through like the flames of a fire. He broke eye contact, choosing instead to look at the wall before breaking his silence.

"My father hired an assassin to kill Aaron as a failsafe, and it almost worked. She'd infiltrated Club 7 long before now—I guess I'd fallen out of Antonio's favor a long time ago, and he forgot to tell me."

Bitterness laced his tone, tasting like bile on my tongue.

"She was my attendant," Aaron admitted, forcing my attention back on him. "We can only guess that Antonio placed her as a contingency plan several months ago, if my parents no longer honored their agreement. He is a wise man."

"He's a heartless, miserable *sadist*," Kellan spat. He lumbered into the office space and plunked himself down on the single leather chair. "But you're not wrong. We're going to have to be ten steps ahead to beat him."

So, Antonio was now after Aaron and Kellan's heads. They were in more danger than they'd ever been in before. And Alvarez was no doubt responsible for Blackbird's head on my table, which meant Lucky could be next on his list.

Frozen tendrils of fear pierced through my heart like an ice pick. They were all at risk. I needed to protect them, and I needed their protection. We were now officially connected through mutually assured destruction. A perpetual butterfly effect of good intentions and wicked deeds.

I couldn't lose anyone else I loved. Losing Isabella had cracked open my soul, but it hadn't broken me. Losing Aaron... losing any of these men...

I'd be shattered forever.

Fuck, fuck, fuck.

Stepping away from my perch by Aaron's bedside, I turned on my heel to face my three co-conspirators: worse for wear and weary, but alive. Thankfully, so alive.

"That's not our only problem." My solemn tone held their attention as I recounted my day.

The Mutilation Mistress announcement. Blackbird's decapitation. The break-in at my apartment. This nightmare was just beginning.

The empire I'd worked so tirelessly to build, the people I vetted with Black-Ops level precision to maintain privacy and separation from the two worlds I traveled; everything I had hoped to achieve in Isabella's memory, in her honor, was crumbling to ash beneath my feet.

We had to act fast, or we wouldn't be alive to act at all.

Lucky was the most emotional, his eyebrows dancing with his hairline for most of the conversation, coupled with an impressive array of whistles under his breath. To his credit, he didn't crack a single joke or attempt to make light of our situation. Nothing was light about it, and he had the sense to accept the depth of the darkness we all sat in.

Aaron's face remained passive as I spoke; chillingly blank and unsettling to anyone but me. I took comfort in the calm, detached way he listened, knowing he'd unleash his anger when the timing was right.

Kellan, despite his stoic facade, held the stone stiffness of a gargoyle, and the blazing red eyes to match. He held himself so neutrally in public, but he could never turn off his protective rage around me. It too was a comfort, knowing the only people who could unravel the Viking were sitting in this room. We would need that energy to shield us —hopefully using his FBI status and his mafia connections.

They interjected occasionally, voices thick with incredulous rage and dispassionate ire, processing the layers of indelible shit we now found ourselves trapped between.

Lucky stepped up to my side, dispelling the quiet, as I wound down the last few details of one of the worst days of my life. Wrapping an arm around my waist, he tucked an errant strand of hair behind my ear with his other hand before settling it against the small of my back.

"I'm so sorry, love. That must have been horrifying." The most earnest expression filled his gaze.

His breath tickled the shell of my ear. No ego, no humor, just... empathy. It was soul-settling, this look. Lucky himself was soul-settling when he tucked the conman persona away and allowed the real man out for a change.

He said nothing more, only brought his hands up to cup the back of my neck and pulled me forward, pressing a gentle kiss to my forehead. The sweetness of the single gesture sent tingles down my spine, despite the circumstances.

Lucky was the light amid our triad of darkness. We were going to need it more than ever.

"You won't be left alone again. From now on, we'll be the American version of *The Human Centipede*, yea?"

Ugh. Moment ruined. *Classic Lucky.*

"I am going to have to rise from the dead." Aaron's gaze fixed on Kellan's, a meaningful look passing between them. "It is the only way, *compañero.*"

"It is one way," the brooding Viking admitted, ignoring the look of confusion on Lucky's and my faces. "We'll have to consider all the angles—especially since I wasn't informed of this fucking Mutilation Mistress disaster." He shook his head emphatically. "Trish should have told me the FBI was being brought in. We're missing something."

We were missing a lot of things. On the small spectrum —who had hired Lucky to con me? On the large spectrum—

who was about to kill us first? We wouldn't be able to hide here for long, not with so many questions left unanswered.

"I'm going to need a lawyer, and Lucky and Kellan are going to have to lie low right now. Alvarez knows way more than he should, and Antonio won't let this betrayal stand for long." I circled the room so I could address all of them at once. "I can't think of a more secure place in the state right now, and we have people to protect, so I don't want to be too far away, anyway."

Kellan's eyes slanted into angry slits. "We're not going anywhere tonight, or tomorrow." He dipped his head toward Aaron, whose eyes were already shutting with exhaustion. "He needs to heal, we need rest, and we need to fucking eat something more than the damned protein bars I have in my gym bag."

Piercing blue eyes turned from the group as a collective to stare directly at Aaron. Kellan stood tall and broad, calm confidence announcing his status as a leader of men, and it settled the unease roiling in my gut, if only for a moment.

With a thick blond eyebrow raised in challenge, the steel in his gaze turned the navy coloring to pure ice. "Tomorrow, we plan. Tonight, we're resting."

With a note of finality, he stalked out of the room, leaving us behind in his wake. My gut roiled anew.

CHAPTER 5

Hillary

I awoke from a restless sleep, held hostage by the strangest dream.

That I'd fallen asleep against Lucky's chest on the only king bed in the entire complex was its own miracle. Joey had discreetly dropped off a box of groceries with some takeout, but I hadn't remembered to request my sedatives or the noise-canceling headphones.

My condo was no longer a place of safety, and this shell of a building was the sole sanctuary in the state where I could feel some level of security. Or maybe it was the warm chest and calm heartbeat of the man who had held me in his arms. The man who was no longer holding me, his side of the bed empty and cold.

We'd wheeled Aaron's hospital bed into the sparse bedroom after eating lukewarm Thai food. Lucky and Kellan took turns showering in the tiny acrylic corner shower in the bathroom. Then the three of us settled beneath the sheets with me in between them.

I rolled sideways to see Kellan splayed out a few feet away. The sheet shoved down below his abdomen exposed the colorful painting of tattoos across his skin.

My Viking was a beautiful portrait in sleep, slow breaths a stark contrast to the intense energy of his waking personality.

Who would he have become if he'd been raised in a normal family? Who would any of us have become?

Somewhere along the path of our twisted fate, I knew I'd fallen for him, just as I had Aaron. Probably sooner than Aaron. Years of distance and denial had kept him deep in the recesses of my heart, but he'd always been there. My words hadn't made it that far, but my body begged to tell him in its own way every time he ordered my submission.

His bulky arm shielded his eyes. He hadn't reached for me in the night, keeping his distance on the other side of the mattress.

He wasn't the warm and fuzzy type on the best of days, but his lack of touch after such a dangerous day left me feeling... empty. Our connection had never been just sex, even though it would be far more convenient for both of us if we could leave it at that.

After everything we'd been through, from the first time we'd worked together to save Winter and her family from Georgio to now, I could finally admit he was a central point in my life. I wasn't willing to lose him. I loved him.

I would do anything to protect him. To protect all of them.

Regardless of his lack of intimacy, he was right—we'd been in no condition to decide anything last night, but time wasn't on our side, and I couldn't spend another minute waiting for someone else to blindside us.

I crept out of the covers, careful not to wake him, and turned my attention to Aaron fast asleep in the hospital bed. His face was a neutral mask, etched frown lines smoothed by the peace in his dreams. My breath caught in my throat at the sight of his bandages, and my heart clenched painfully at the thought of losing him.

Before I let the tidal wave of emotion swallow me, I tiptoed out of the room in search of the third man of our cohort.

It didn't take long to find Lucky. He'd planted himself at the other end of the building, in one of the few finished seating areas in the grand hall—the original space where Kellan, Aaron, and I had sparred—a lifetime ago.

"Hey, Blondie," he mused casually, holding a lit joint in his hand. "Care to join me?"

Dressed only in boxer shorts, he was a languid form of lazy elegance draped across one of the brown leather barrel chairs in front of an unlit fireplace. He'd thought to crack open the piano window above it at least, but a thick, potent haze floated above his head.

I glared at the smoke coming off the blunt. "Put that out," I chided. "This place stinks enough already."

An indolent smirk crossed his features. "You probably need it more than me. Can't sleep?"

I sighed and moved toward the matching chair beside him, taking a seat beyond the cloud of smoke.

"Can't sleep," I echoed, the swirl of emotions from the previous day finally hitting me over the head with a sizable wallop.

I hadn't gotten high in years—not since the days Isabella and I would lounge on my rear balcony, shrouded by large fir trees where no one could see us. We'd smoke weed in our pajamas and make out for hours, lost in the absence of time and each other's company. The memory brought painful tingles to my chest, but the smallest of smiles too.

My world had fallen apart today—my failsafes and protective measures all destroyed by a man I hadn't considered smart enough to best me. That alone was a poison pill to swallow, not including Aaron's escapade and all that came from it. An hour or two of levity could be exactly what I needed to feel like less of a fuck-up. I wouldn't be able to save my empire with anything less than Queen energy.

I was in my most protected building, with three men I trusted with my life. Hell, two of them I trusted with my heart.

Despite my reservations, I reached for the offered joint, and took a long puff, holding the smoke deep within my lungs.

When I returned the joint to him, liquid calm filled my veins at the appreciation in Lucky's gaze.

"Knew you had a little rebel in ya." He grinned triumphantly as if he'd won a prize. I couldn't return it, though the smoke was slowly softening the tension in my body as it settled into my bloodstream.

"I'm glad you're alive, Luck." I practically whispered the words as I melted into the soft leather of the seat behind me.

He didn't respond, choosing instead to stand and lift me off the seat, pull me into his body, and hold me in the tiny chair.

"I'm happy to be alive too, Blondie."

He spoke the muffled words into my hair. His lips brushed the top of my forehead as he held me tight to his chest. He didn't smell like his usual cherry cola. The familiar scent had been masked by the generic soaps Joey had brought, but it was still his somehow.

Raising his head, Lucky took another long inhale, then blew the smoke behind the chair and spared it from my face. I reached for the pre-rolled parchment between his fingers and brought it to my lips, sucking in another lungful of sweet, earthy air.

"I haven't gotten high in a long time," I admitted, enjoying the floaty feeling in my limbs as I relaxed deeper into his arms.

"Ah, am I a bad influence, love?" Lucky's tired eyes sparkled with mischief. "Do I make you want to do naughty things?" He held the blunt between his lips as he spoke, mimicking a bootlegging gangster straight out of *Boardwalk Empire*.

I giggled as the weed fully saturated my brain with a comforting coating of cotton.

"You make me want to beat you with a mallet," I said instead of the words he likely wanted to hear, but the teasing softness of my tone gave me away. "Don't ever do that again, Lucky."

The shiny glow in his eyes dimmed to a dark forest green. "Promise, Blondie. Although, you might want to have this conversation with Roboto too. I was just the passenger princess."

"You were the driver," I corrected, dancing my fingers along the crest of his knuckles. "You're no innocent man here."

"I'll never claim to be innocent, love." His tone turned somber as he stared straight into my soul. "But I'll be your devil, if you'll let me."

My mouth turned dry at the look of pure devotion in his stare. Despite the welcomed emotional reprieve from the THC, his look stirred something uncomfortable inside me. I knew my feelings for this man were growing into something more, but the strength with which they were forming made me wary.

"What happens if I let you, Lucky?"

My stomach housed a million butterflies as we stared into each other's souls. I had to look away. The intensity of emotion in his eyes was too much. Two men had already taken my heart. I wasn't like Winter, with enough love in my heart for five men.

Shit. Winter. My floaty brain wasn't willing to think about any of the words I'd have to say when I reached out to her. *Hey, bestie, just wanted you to know I'm kind of a killer, and I may be in the news sometime soon, but don't worry about it, okay?*

Lucky cupped my chin, turning my attention back to his face, but he never got the chance to respond. A lumbering shirtless Viking bear stood just ten feet away.

I hadn't even heard him in my Lucky-laced haze.

"You shouldn't be out here," Kellan admonished, wearing a surly frown more directed at Lucky than at me. "And why the fuck are you smoking weed in here? This isn't a frat house."

"Lighten up, Kell-Bell," Lucky drawled, accentuating the 'L's' with lazy flicks of his tongue. It was oddly erotic. He removed his palm from my cheek and gestured toward the now empty seat beside us. "Join us."

"I don't smoke that crap," Kellan growled, shooting us another disapproving glare before flopping into the chair in an angry huff. "I'm an FBI agent."

Lucky burst into drugged hysterical laughter, his entire chest vibrating into my own. "You're with the cartel, mate! Don't you guys sell the hard shyte? Honestly, where you're willing to draw the line is fascinating."

As if to accentuate his point, he drew one last toke of the blunt and cupped the remnants in his fist, blowing Kellan a kiss with the residual smoke.

I giggled through my high haze and flashed my Viking a lolling smirk. "He's got you there, Kellll-Bellllll."

I got an angry eyebrow in return. This man had mastered the look better than a haughty runway model.

"You too?"

"Oh, bugger off, Conan." Lucky's tone turned serious, pulling me tighter into his chest and stroking a finger down my spine. "It's been a rough one for all of us, yeh?"

The Viking muttered something under his breath, but did not lecture us anymore. Instead, he stretched out his long body in the tiny chair, every ripple of honed muscle on display for us to enjoy.

"Where'd you put the snacks?" I asked abruptly, the inevitable munchies forcing several cravings to hit the back of my tongue at once.

"The kitchenette cupboards," Lucky answered, having been the one to complete that task while I spoke privately with Joey and Kellan showered. "You craving some wheatgrass, Blondie? Some kale chips?" He screwed up his face in disgust.

"Actually... I could really go for some Skittles right now." My mouth puckered at the thought of the saccharine sweet candy. "I like the orange ones."

"Oh, ho!" Lucky crowed, as if he'd won something important. "All I had to do was get you high for you to get some tastebuds, hey, Blondie?"

He turned his attention to Kellan's unimpressed form. "Conan, can you grab that bag of Skittles for us by the sink? I would go, but we're a wee bit comfortable." He pulled me in and gave my lips a quick peck, then shot a sassy wink at the buff man, goading him the way only Lucky knew how.

We sat on the receiving end of a lengthy warrior's glower before Kellan stood to his full towering height and stalked toward the kitchen.

"They all taste the same," Kellan retorted gruffly.

"Nice bum!" I called, watching his glutes flex and pull in the tight black boxers, every back muscle rippling with each step.

Lucky wolf-whistled beside me, but our sexy partner refused to take the bait, ignoring us as he rounded the corner to the other room.

I heard a long-suffering sigh between my fits of giggles.

Kellan returned in moments, handing us a family-sized bag of Skittles, then excused himself from our "frat party" and retreated down the bedroom hallway. We tore into the candy with renewed vigor. Lucky dug through the entire bag and sorted out all the orange ones in a neat little pile on the coffee table for me to snack on.

"You like a little sweet when you put all your walls down, do yeh, Blondie?"

Lucky's rust-colored hair was adorably mussed, the green in his eyes brighter than I'd ever seen it. His lips pouted in a pretty pink puff, and I felt the need to pulverize them with mine. He was cunning and devious, and far smarter than I'd ever give him credit. And he was mine. A deep chord plucked in my heart at that acknowledgment. In whatever moments came next, Lucky O'Donnell was *mine*.

He didn't break eye contact and placed a single orange Skittle between his teeth, lobbing it with grace onto the tip of his tongue. "Wanna see how sweet I taste, Blondie?"

My stomach did a little flip that had nothing to do with all the sugar. I leaned in, swirling my tongue over his in a deliciously citrus-flavored kiss. I shifted positions in his lap, swinging my legs around to straddle him, our tongues fused together in a breathtaking dally of passion and escape. When I finally came up for air, his glazed eyes and flushed cheeks brought a deep satisfaction to the pit of my belly. This effect Lucky had on me—the hold on my body and my heart—well, he wasn't immune either.

"Let's try that again with a green one." When I wrinkled my nose in distaste, he grinned before reaching to grab a single lime Skittle off the tabletop. "Come on, Blondie. Betcha it tastes better with a little Lucky in it."

Another fit of giggles came over me. I laughed so hard little tears trickled onto my cheeks and into my hair. A triumphant smirk filled his features before he wriggled his eyebrows at me and popped the second candy onto his tongue.

I leaned in for another taste. Of this man, of temporary freedom, of this single moment in time. The weight of the world was temporarily off my shoulders, and I'd enjoy the lightness of Lucky and high fructose corn syrup until our destruction at dawn.

Whether it was the weed or the man sandwich that put me back into a stupor, I couldn't be sure, but I woke several hours later from the most comfortable sleep I'd had in weeks.

Once the Skittles were gone—every single color consumed between sloppy, delicious kisses—Lucky had carried me into the bedroom, gently placing me next to Kellan before bundling me into his arms from behind.

My Viking let me touch him this time, laying close enough for me to wrap an arm around his waist. I'd drifted off to sleep within seconds only to wake up to the sounds of Kellan helping Aaron off the hospital bed to go to the washroom.

Our patient had been in such a deep sleep from the painkillers, he hadn't stirred once from our antics. I'd felt Kellan get up to check on him twice before morning.

It was heartwarming to see our bear cared about us more than his words would ever say. But when he returned to the bed, he put distance between us again, and the chasm seemed farther than the physical space on the mattress. Kellan's insistence on space was unsettling in these circumstances, but I was trying not to read too much into the actions.

We'd all suffered a wealth of trauma. We had enemies on all sides, and today was the day we set a plan into motion.

Lucky still lay beside me, his limbs tangled in the sheets like a ginger-furred spider monkey, snoring quietly into the crushed pillow beneath his face. The picture of innocence, if only in sleep.

I crept out of bed in need of bladder relief and a strong coffee. After noting we'd need more towels in the bathroom for the four of us, I padded out to the kitchenette area, where Kellan had rolled Aaron's bed out next to the small kitchen island. My ravaged Colombian was chatting to Kellan about his favorite Spanish breakfast rolls as the Viking scrambled some eggs on the stove. It was an oddly domestic picture, completely out of place given our circumstances, and it warmed my heart a few hundred degrees.

"Good morning, *Mi Reina*." Aaron's attention turned to me, his warm brown eyes far more alert than they had been yesterday. "How was your sleep?"

I moved to him, pressing a light kiss to his forehead, and then pressed another chaste peck on his lips, careful not to jostle him.

"Good," I responded, bringing a palm up to cup his stubbed cheek. "How are you feeling?"

"Sore." His full lips pursed in a thin line as he shifted his weight slightly upright on the hard mattress. "But I am fortunate to be alive, so I am happy to be sore."

I brushed a few errant hairs off his temples and kissed him again, a little harder this time, relishing the warm, soft velvet of his lips.

"I'm happy you're sore too," I murmured before pushing upward to seek Kellan. He kept his back to me, but he didn't resist my arms wrapping around his waist from behind, only stiffening slightly before leaning into my hold.

"I'm glad you're safe, Viking." I spoke into the hard muscles of his back, which tensed and bunched beneath my cheeks while he plated the eggs. Without warning, he turned in my arms. I looked up to see a fierce furrow of his blonde brows, the blue in his gaze a violent shade of indigo.

"As long as you're safe, Killer. That's what matters." He leaned down to kiss the top of my head, then gently nudged me out of his way to grab another plate from the cupboard.

So, still keeping me at a distance. I allowed the slight, ignoring the pain of his dismissal by busying myself at the coffee machine in the corner, pulling the bag of beans off the shelf and burying my nose in their comforting roasted scent.

I didn't need Kellan's warmth this morning. A fresh espresso would perk me up far more than his hold ever could.

"Didn't know you could cook, Conan!" Lucky chirped a bit too cheerfully as I ground the beans for my latte. He padded into the kitchen area on light feet, still wearing the boxers from the night before, his hair sticking off in twenty different directions. It was an irresistibly boyish look, pulling a grin from my previously pressed lips.

Kellan only grunted in response. Lucky pulled out a family-sized box of Lucky Charms from the cupboard, reaching around me to get into the apartment-sized fridge for the milk. His bare chest brushed against my shoulder blades, and he leaned in to nip the shell of my ear.

"Morning, Blondie," he whispered. The stubble along his jaw brushing my sensitive skin caused me to shiver. "Perks of having the world of baddies after yeh is getting to sleep beside the world's most beautiful woman." The nip turned into a soft kiss on the side of my neck, just below my earlobe. "I look forward to having you in my arms again tonight."

"Margot Robbie is the world's most beautiful woman," I retorted with a small laugh, pouring the foamed milk into the espresso to form the shape of a pine tree. I handed the mug to Kellan in silence. He looked up at me with raised eyebrows, but accepted the coffee with a dip of his head. I got to work on the next drink, knowing Aaron preferred his espresso straight.

"Aye," Lucky said, a sneaky smirk lighting up those beautiful green eyes as he poured a heaping bowl of crunchy sugar. "But can Margot Robbie kick Kellan's ass? Because that, my love, is part of the attraction."

The snicker that escaped me was grossly unladylike, but I was too amused to care. I handed the straight espresso to Aaron with an encouraging smile. "Sip it," I cautioned. "Only liquids today, right?" I turned a quizzical eye to Lucky, who'd become our resident medical expert.

"Yup." He smacked his lips, taking a dramatic bite of cereal. "Onfy likkids til Monday," he said with a full mouth, making it hard to take him seriously. It was *very* telling I'd started to take Lucky seriously at all.

Today was Saturday, a blessing in disguise. Saturday meant I didn't need to be in the office to keep up appearances, and incredibly, I had no functions to attend this weekend. We'd been forced into a corner to regroup, but fate had given us a gift by throwing us into chaos right before the week's end.

I started on my coffee, knowing Lucky wouldn't touch the adult beverage without twenty teaspoons of sugar in it, and it seemed he was getting that dose given the size of his cereal bowl. Kellan placed a plate of eggs in front of the empty stool beside him, then dropped his own plate on the round four-person table next to the kitchenette.

It was impossible to miss his intentional separation, with another stool on the other side of Lucky, but once again, I ignored it. Whatever demons Kellan was wrestling today, we had far greater problems.

I'd learned firsthand how completely Kellan pulled away when I pressed him on things he didn't want to talk about. The last time I'd pressured him to leave his father and pursue another path, he'd distanced himself for an entire year, swearing he'd been caught up on a secret assignment and didn't want to put me at risk. Bulls themselves couldn't produce purer shit than that excuse, but it had done the trick. I'd fight Kellan in hand-to-hand combat and battle his brains any day of the week, but a stranger on the street could see he was walking on a razor's edge. I wasn't willing to be the one who pushed him off the ledge.

I was being selfish, as well as my version of kind. If Kellan left now, I knew I'd never see him again. He had the self-control and disposition of a martyr, and he'd convince himself we were better off without him. I didn't have the words in my heart to persuade him I didn't need his protection. I needed his presence. Whatever came at us in the days ahead, I needed *him.* A deep ache registered within my chest, knowing he wouldn't believe me, even if I found the proper prose on a page.

"Okay," I announced with finality once my cappuccino was perfectly poured. I leaned against the counter to face the men, addressing the mammoth in the room. "Order of operations. It looks like Alvarez and Antonio are equal threats now, so we'll have to take a two-pronged approach. What's first?"

"We need to throw more shadows on Alvarez." Kellan slowly chewed his eggs and stared into his coffee, as if lost in his own thoughts. "Rodriguez and I have a plan for that, but he needs to heal up first."

"Is that what you meant by 'bringing him back from the dead?'" I mused, taking a deep draw from the delicious coffee, relishing the burn down my esophagus.

"Yes," Kellan stated. "But first, I have to meet with Trish. With Antonio after me, I'm a liability. And I'm being left intentionally out of the loop on the Mutilation Mistress file, which means something else entirely. I need to talk to her before I can make the best plan to protect you."

"To protect *us*," I corrected, shooting him a severe frown. "This is an *us* now, Kellan. We can't hide for longer than the weekend, but we're either in this together, or every person for themselves. You're not in charge here. This is a collective. Is that going to be a problem?"

His glower rivaled mine, and he stared so hard at me I felt transparent under his gaze. "Fine. *Us*," he amended, not bothering to expand on his thoughts.

"I'm hiring Weston Williams," I declared, having given this notion a good deal of thought on my drive over to meet these three fugitives last night. Marty's husband was one of the best criminal defense lawyers in the state.

"Wait until I talk to Trish today." Kellan stood from the table, grabbed my untouched eggs from the counter and sat back down, taking a hearty forkful. "We don't want to announce your guilt if they haven't linked the two." His tone didn't match his words. The dubious inflection matched my own internal reservations.

If the details of my many escapades had already leaked to the press, my name couldn't be far behind. My notoriety as an heiress, a business mogul, and the daughter of a disgraced man would be a curse, not an asset. The media would leap at the opportunity to burn me alive, regardless of the crime. I would definitely need Weston Williams on my side.

"Another silly, wee problem." Lucky slurped the last of his cereal milk like an obnoxious child. "My work visa's up soon, and given my employer is now an arrested prick, I doubt I'll be getting a renewal. Not that immigration is the worst baddie of the bunch, but I'd like to avoid that group of arseholes too."

I swallowed the final dregs of my coffee, then set the mug in the sink, shooting a pointed look at Lucky. "Looks like you're having a shotgun wedding," I mused. "Better find yourself another willing victim."

"You won't marry me?" He stared up at me through round, hopeful eyes, the very picture of a puppy dog in search of a treat.

Cackling, I shook my head. "I'm never getting married again, Lucky. One marriage of convenience in this lifetime is enough for me." Turning my attention to Aaron and Kellan, my expression morphed to utmost seriousness. "We need to be vigilant—hypervigilant, everywhere. Trust no one but Joey. Guns and knives at all times. We need to keep up appearances and pretend that life is business as usual. We're not afraid."

"I'm afraid," Lucky piped up, swinging around on his bar stool. "I'm very, very afraid."

"I am fearful as well, *Rojo*," Aaron admitted quietly. "I am no longer willing to die when I have so much in this life to live for."

His honey gaze locked on mine. The sheer depth of the love in them stuttered the beats of my heart. I walked over to him and squeezed his rough palm in my own.

"We all have something to live for," I countered, my gaze first on Lucky's in reassurance, and then to Kellan's in challenge. "So, let's make sure we're the ones who live."

48

CHAPTER 6

Kellan

I fucking hated this cloak and dagger bullshit.

I tapped my fingers along the steering wheel in irritation as I weaved through Carlisle traffic in the black Dodge truck I hid in a private garage as a contingency plan years ago. The truck stuttered as I drove after sitting idle for all that time. With my hoodie, sunglasses, and trucker cap, I looked like any other tradesman driving through town as I headed to Trish's rendezvous point.

It was beyond necessary now that everyone in Sequoia County wanted a piece of my flesh, but I loathed the constant need to watch my six with every action and reaction.

My brothers now hunted me, with authorization from our father to kill on sight. It was highly likely Alvarez had put the hit out on Blackbird, which meant Lauchlan wasn't far behind—and there wasn't a chance in hell my father had canceled the hit on Aaron. If Carmen reported back to him before we took her out at Club 7, we were all wanted men with massive targets on our backs.

The twins were idiots, but they were crafty idiots. They lived, breathed, and would eventually die in this world, thriving on the thrill of being little anarchist soldiers under my father's reign.

Luckily, Carmen was out of the picture. Of the three of them, she had been the greatest threat, and it would be easier to hide without her on my heels. The fact she'd infiltrated Aaron's sex club of all places for months spoke to her dedication. How many men had she fucked to keep up the ruse she was a high-class prostitute, while lying in wait to assassinate Aaron? That level of commitment was disgusting, but admirable. She'd just chosen the wrong side of this war and lost her life because of it. I wasn't shedding any tears.

And this Mutilation Mistress business... I had no regrets putting a bullet into that filthy predator's brain, but who the fuck had been looking a little too closely into Hillary's vendetta? As far as we knew, her name hadn't been mentioned—yet—but if the media had this much information already, it was only a matter of time.

And why the fuck had Trish not informed me? If the FBI were involved, I should have known. Trish had feelers everywhere, ensuring my interests were protected while walking on both sides of the fence. Anything to do with a potential sex trade qualified. Falling out of my father's favor and my director's communication channel on the same day was a hard punch in the face. I didn't have the energy tonight to decipher what it all meant—besides the glaring indication, at this moment, we were all royally fucked.

She was meeting me at a diner on the other side of Kensington, an hour west of Carlisle. After twenty-two years of walking the line between the FBI and the cartel life, I was finally completely compromised. She wouldn't be happy, but it was a risk we'd prepared for.

Gaze trained on my mirrors for any signs of a tail, I deliberated my choices in life. More accurately, my lack of choices. At ten, Antonio had brought me to my first "clean-up." The man rarely got his hands dirty himself these days, but back then he got off on the bloody mess that was cartel living. His men had dismembered three of our own guys—stupid saps who'd skimmed a few hundred thousand from drug profits—and he'd ordered me to clean it up while he supervised. I'd puked on myself three times, and each time, he'd laughed, telling me I would have the "*estomago de hierro*"—the iron stomach of real men—when he was done with my training.

He was right. By the time I'd turned sixteen and was staring down the barrel of the gun into Trish's pale face, I could barely feel anything at all. A boy molded into a weapon, both in brains and in brawn. Another year, and I'd have succumbed to the life of a psychopath, just as my father intended. It was a miracle Trish had gotten through to me, and even more so she'd undertaken to mentor me.

I remembered that day more clearly than any other day in my life. Trish hadn't just changed my path; her offer had obliterated my father's trajectory for me.

I stared into the eyes of the unfamiliar woman, the kindness in her gaze something I had never really seen. Why would this stranger give two shits about a kid like me? I'd held a gun to her head moments before she got the drop on me, yet she hadn't begged for her life or tried to goad me like a lesser man would. Instead, she held me captive with the tiny gun held two feet from my crotch, with a lightness in her expression that confused me.

"'The greatest good can be born of the greatest evil,'" she whispered calmly, her hands steady on the pistol as she held me captive with her words. "I can get you out of here, Kellan. And I can keep you safe."

King Lear. *Of all the things I'd expect from someone about to lose their life, a mediocre Shakespeare quote wasn't it. My hand sweat against the cool metal of Old Faithful, and the surety in my stance waned the longer she stared at me.*

"No one can keep me safe," I countered, "especially not some agent spouting bullshit poetry as her last words."

"I can." Her soft voice didn't waver, her stare now the color of steel. "I can, Kellan. Trust me."

The FBI didn't fully trust me—but Trish did. My "arrangement" was the only one of its kind, but the bureau wasn't willing to turn down the opportunity of an inside man in a position of power in the largest cartel operation on this side of the country. Since I was a child when they'd found me, there was little they could do to threaten me to work for them; so, they had a young woman coerce me instead, under the promise of protection.

I arrived at the diner with three minutes to spare and sent off a quick, cryptic text to Hillary. She was sourcing clothes and more supplies for us at the warehouse, while Lauchlan and Rodriguez worked on a plan for Alvarez. I left them to it. Today, I had enough to worry about.

Scanning the parking lot for anything suspicious and finding nothing, I stepped out of the truck and strode inside, Trish already waiting for me in the corner booth at the rear.

She wasn't perfect, but she'd taken care of me this long. She didn't have the manpower to pursue Antonio legally, which was why she had brought me in, but she had resources. I'd have to protect myself, but I trusted she would do what she could to take care of me today too.

"You look like shit," she greeted me as I slid onto the bench across from her.

Grunting in response, I reached for the full coffee pot and poured myself a mug of tar-like liquid that was a poor substitute for Hillary's latte, and looked up at my mentor, who was staring through my large frame like it was nothing but plastic wrap.

"Antonio has decided I'm a liability." I didn't mince words. Taking a sip of the coffee, I grimaced at the bitterness, but took another sip anyway. "My brothers have been assigned to kill me. I'm effectively cut out of all operations."

A general numbness accompanied that statement. My brothers killing me wasn't my greatest fear. It had been more of an inevitability. Who would kill whom first depended on who fell out of Antonio's good graces first. As fate would have it, I was the lucky fucker who'd won.

Truthfully, I was more concerned about Trish's response. We'd planned for this probability, though I'd thought I'd have at least ten years to dance along the fine line we'd created. When Antonio demanded I take over the sex trade, I should have connected the dots he was leading me to this end. He'd known all along how much I detested that branch of the business, and I'd failed his test of loyalty before I'd saved Aaron's life.

"Do you have any men loyal to you?" Her hawk eyes didn't blink as she assessed me, missing nothing as usual.

"Possibly," I admitted, reaching for the sugar container to pour a heaping stream into the cup of dirt. "But that will take time, and time's not on my side at the moment. You'll want to get any double agents out, if you can. He's going to be cleaning house."

Trish had a handful of agents infiltrate Antonio's operations at various levels, but I had no idea who they were—for their safety, and for my own. We all played a dangerous game when we sat on both sides of the fence, but I didn't need more dead men on my conscience.

"I'm still working my cases. I'll just be underground for a little while, with your help." I stopped fiddling with the sugar container and held her stare. "I have some information on The Six, and I need more information on the Mutilation Mistress case. Why wasn't I informed of this?"

Her steel-gray eyes widened before settling back into a carefully crafted neutral expression.

Uh oh. I knew that expression all too well. She reserved it for delivering the most sensitive information that could make or break a case. Which meant they knew about Hillary.

"The Mutilation Mistress case is too close to you, Kellan. You're known to associate with the primary suspect, who already has enough power and influence without your help. That's all I'm going to say about that one. And The Six is no longer your concern."

Fuck. No doubt in my mind now she was referring to Hillary. Animalistic fear pierced my chest, and the icy tendrils of adrenaline burst through my veins in warning my life was about to be compromised.

When it came to Hillary, I *was* compromised—hell, I'd spent the last two years covering her tracks to ensure she never got caught with her little vendetta. Now, I knew I'd failed to protect her.

Somehow, someone had discovered what she'd done, and everything she'd built was at risk because of it. A stone sat in the base of my stomach, its weight dragging down every ounce of hope I'd been foolish enough to have, dissolving in the sea of my raging acid.

Fuck, fuck, fuck.

"Are you implying my judgment is compromised?" I tamped down the anger swirling in my gut, swallowing it before it breached the surface.

"I'm implying your career is compromised," she said carefully, breaking eye contact to browse the menu. "We're going to have to move you out of operations."

I choked on the next sip of coffee, the burning liquid scouring my throat on its way down. "Excuse me?"

Antonio had put a price on my head, and now Trish was putting me out to pasture. I clenched my jaw, registering this meeting for what it was. Brutus was about to stab me in the back, and call it a kindness.

For several seconds, she sat silent. Then she looked up meeting my gaze. Her expression was stoic, but borderline apologetic.

"If Antonio is after you, there is no place in the world I can protect you. You know this. Antonio's allowed certain graces for the FBI because of your status, which is most assuredly gone. I'd rather maintain our other agents' positions and remove you from the picture—we'll have a far greater chance at keeping tabs on drug and weapons runs."

Her explanation was a rational one, and knowing Trish, I shouldn't have expected anything less. Still, it was an elbow to the gut, the knowledge she'd sacrifice twenty-two years of my life and working career without a second's hesitation. The numbness I'd walked in with dissolved into bitter, vile anger. I swallowed the acrid flavor of bile building at the back of my throat and stared back into the cold eyes of Trish the Fish.

I worked hard to maintain a blank expression, but it wasn't good enough for her assertive stare. She reached over the table and placed a small hand on my arm, her tone kind.

"This is about upholding the law. It always has been."

The bile hardened into a stone. I swallowed it down, burying it in the lava of my stomach. I avoided her gaze and stared at her pale hand, delicately holding onto the thick fabric of my borrowed hoodie. The dismissal hurt, but the betrayal of my mentor, of my *friend*, was a far greater knife across the throat. Whatever the luck of the draw was, my parental figures in this life were Antonio and Trish. Now both had cast me aside because I hadn't bent the knee to the angle they required to prove my loyalty.

"This isn't about the law." I laughed bitterly, the bark louder than I intended. I leaned forward, shrugged off her hand and lowered my voice, but suppressed seething fury leaked out with each word.

"This is about power and control. I can no longer give you that, so I'm out. Let's be honest with each other."

A brief flicker of hurt flashed across her face, disappearing as quickly as it came, replaced with the steely gaze that had spawned her nickname.

"Honesty? Here's honest for you. It will take more resources to protect you than I'm willing to give. You've been a great asset, and a good agent, but your time has come. I can't sacrifice more people because you've fallen out of your father's good graces. Your job was to maintain that relationship, so we could leverage it to protect the American people. You failed to do that. The gift I can give you now is that I won't come after you. We'll give you immunity, and you can go on to live your life."

This woman had given me an opportunity. I'd built a life outside of a dangerous family, and avoided the inevitability I'd become a miserable sadist like my brothers. And now, she was taking away that opportunity. Discarding me because I no longer held the position she needed. Abandoning me when I needed her most.

My relationship with Antonio had always been transactional. From the time I was born, to the time he'd discovered Trish's offer, to now—I was only of value if I could strengthen his empire. Trish had her faults, but my protection was never in question, nor my loyalty. Until today.

She wrenched the knife through my chest from behind, and I was expected to fall just as Caesar had.

"Immunity?!" The wrath seeped to the surface of my skin. My cheeks heated and fiery red crept across my face.

"Immunity from the crimes you coerced me into committing?" I scoffed, the guttural noise dripping with poison. "You were right."

Sliding my large body across the bench and outside of the booth, I stood at the end of the table, towering my frame over the older woman. "The justice system I just spent my life fighting for is fucked." I dug the FBI badge out of my pocket and tossed it on the table. The photo of my face stared up at us both.

My fists clenched at my sides. It was a younger face; less broken, more hopeful. The man I used to be. Certainly not the man now ruined by two entities who'd groomed and trained a soldier to be their connected patsy.

"Consider this my resignation," I spat venomously before stalking out of the diner and across the parking lot, not caring in the moment if my brothers took me out with a sniper rifle.

I'd spent my life believing I was the master of puppets, when my strings were just a little longer than anyone else's. My strings had been severed, and Antonio would die for the privilege.

"I need a face to fuck," I announced, growling the words through gritted teeth as I stormed through the side entrance door to our new compound.

Lauchlan popped up from the couch forty feet across the warehouse main area.

"Oh?" he quipped, wearing that stupid, goofy grin of his, but the moment he saw my face, his brows crinkled in concern. "What's wrong?"

I didn't need his concern. I needed him on his knees with my cock down his throat, suffocating as he took me deeper than he could handle.

Stalking over to his position on the furniture, I palmed the back of his neck and forcefully rose him off the couch.

"Everything is fucked." I glowered down at his pretty face with those pretty sea-glass eyes and pretty pouted lips and felt the animalistic desire to make him a lot less pretty.

I was a risk to everyone around me, and the only way I'd ever have a life on my own was to kill Antonio myself. But I wouldn't get that opportunity today. Today, I just had Lauchlan's fuckable body at my feet to bring a brief, but blissful, reprieve.

"But you can make it better." I released my grip on his head, and he flopped backward onto the couch like a rag doll, catching himself at the last second. I fumbled with my zipper, yanking my navy suit pants down, exposing my stiffening erection at the thought of making this man submit to me again and again.

He quirked an eyebrow, taking in the hard cock now leveled at his face. "Need to work out some aggression, do ya, Conan?" His eyes sparkled with amusement, taunting me. "Gonna have to ask me a bit nicer than that."

"Fuck you." I palmed his neck again and forced his lips a hairsbreadth away from my tip. His hot breath caused a deep shudder to wrack through my entire body, standing every hair on my thighs on end. "Suck."

Instead of giving in to my commands like the good little subbie I needed, he closed his teeth over my head and nipped it with sharp incisors, driving a blister of pain through my shaft and up into my balls. I lurched back in surprise and released my hold on his hair. More hot anger flooded my limbs.

Lauchlan scrambled to his feet and stared me right in the eye, apparently unafraid of the raging giant in front of him.

"Wait a goddamned minute, Conan. I'm not your bitch boy. You want to work out some aggression? Don't threaten me with a good time." Crossing his arms across his chest, he raised his chin in challenge. "But you're not forcing me to do feck all."

He spun on his heel quicker than I could react, and before I registered the movement, he was behind me, jumping up and wrapping his arms around my neck and his legs around my waist.

The hot breath that had just hardened me to stone now fanned against my ear. I brought my hands up to release his hold around my throat. *Sneaky fucker.*

"I know yeh don't know a whole lot about me, Kell-Bell, but I was wrestling champ in college."

With another quick motion, his foot released from my waist and wrapped around the inside of my leg, knocking my knee out and toppling us both to the hard floor. My pants were still halfway down my leg, barely protecting my stiff shaft from getting snapped.

I let out a grunt of surprise at the quick takedown as mild pain radiated through my knees. Lauchlan was always surprising me, challenging me at every turn. It was irritating and exasperating, but begrudgingly intriguing. How was I hornier at this man who kept defying my every order?

Flattening me to the floor, his body completely covered me like a weighted blanket. He'd wrapped his thighs around mine in the fall, immobilizing the bottom half of my body completely. The feeling of being trapped beneath him fueled my fire, my need for dominance only slightly more powerful than my need for sex. I went limp in his hold, waiting for my chance to roll over him to punish him properly.

"Guessin' you've never been topped before, eh, Conan?" That Irish brogue was harsh in my ear. "Why don't I pound some of that hate right out of yeh? Expel it through your dick with a come of a lifetime." He leaned in, biting the soft skin underneath my earlobe. The nip spread more heat across my skin, except it was vicious lust instead of rage.

Fuck, I wanted to come. *Needed* to. And he wasn't walking away from this room without my thick dick eight inches into his ass, pounding his greedy hole until it split apart for me.

His lips on my neck were just enough of a distraction to buck my torso, flinging him off me and onto his back three feet away. In two quick shuffles, I was on top of him, pinning his flushed body to the hardwood. My pants had ripped in two with the motion, freeing my legs to straddle his hips. His thick shaft strained against his sweats, the only separation between us.

"I don't bottom," I retorted, offering a violent grin as I looked down at his pliant form. "But you do."

I tore at his sweats, raising only to drag them down his legs, and exposed his heavy, fuckable cock bobbing against his pelvis. He did nothing to stop me, grinning maniacally, like tackling me to the ground was his best version of fun.

"Say please, Conan." Lauchlan licked his lips, his green eyes darkening. He stared up at me. "Say please and you can use me as your cum dumpster until I scream."

Fuck. All I wanted was this sexy, irritating man's asshole to grip my cock and take away this pain for one holy moment before the rest of my world collapsed around me. My whole life was pain, the "hope" inscribed on my knuckles only a naïve prayer somehow, I'd eventually find my way out of the fuckery I'd been born into.

He gazed up at me expectantly, waiting for the words that would hurt me to say.

Please. I didn't say "please." I ordered. I demanded. I took. But, fuck it all, I felt compelled to say them. The sexy Irishman was lying beneath me, willing to give me what I needed. I could give him the same.

"Please, Lauchlan, I need to fuck you." I grit out through clenched teeth, disliking the taste of the words on my tongue.

His eyes lit up with triumph. Sitting up, he gripped the sides of my jaw and slammed his mouth over mine in a deep, drugging kiss. His force matched my own as I leaned into him, stealing every breath and tasting every corner of his mouth as my tongue battled with his for dominance.

Abruptly, he pulled away, leaving me wanting another taste of him. His wide grin exposed two rows of perfectly straight teeth. "Coconut oil's on the table." He nodded toward the end table at the side of the couch. "Joey didn't bring lube, so I've had to make do."

Eyes widening at that insinuation—had he been fucking his hand earlier with *coconut oil?*—I shifted my body weight to reach for the tub , eyeing it dubiously. A shudder rose through my shaft and through every limb. A cock coated in coconut oil was the least of my concerns with Lauchlan's exposed hole waiting for my entrance.

Unscrewing the lid, I rubbed the thick, cream-like substance all over my shaft. It melted on contact. I pushed apart his thighs and scooped a blob onto my fingers, rimming a generous coating along the puckered skin. My needy little victim shuddered beneath me, his body tensing when I pushed one finger inside of him, intentionally massaging his P spot.

"You like that, don't you, you little cumslut?" I murmured and added a second finger, scissoring them in a practiced rhythm. "You're going to let me fuck you full of my cum, aren't you?"

Lauchlan groaned deep in his chest, bucking against my hand, and reached down to stroke his cock. His thick fingers gripped himself so hard, his tip turned a bruising purple.

The need to brutally fuck the man beneath me abruptly halted my teasing. I took out my fingers and lined up my coated erection, then I placed both hands on either side of Lauchlan's hips, gripping so tight I could feel the shift of bone beneath my palms.

Sweat beaded against my brow as I tried and failed to enter him slowly. My desperate need to rid myself of my demons took precedence, and I thrust into him hard. The walls of his ass held me so tightly, stars blinked behind my eyelids. We both let out a rough grunt of want, and the vibration echoed through our chests while Lauchlan stroked himself with jerky movements and I took up my own relentless pace.

"You're such." *Thrust.* "A fucking." *Thrust.* "Brat." *Thrust, thrust, thrust.* The frenzied rhythm and his grip on my cock washed heat over me in a wave. I shut out my own desperate need for a moment to focus on him.

Glassy, lust-laced eyes stared back at me. Lauchlan's flushed cheeks rose upward in a brazen grin. "Yea, and you love me."

Snorting dismissively, I tweaked his nipple instead, grinning in satisfaction when he writhed in pleasure. This fuck was going to be short; My body was too tightly wound —every muscle cramping with need and anger—to savor the feel of him releasing me every time I pulled out, and welcoming me every time I thrust deeply inside. I searched for my salvation in his body, between his cheeks, and within the frantic way we kissed, all teeth and tongues, messy and manic.

Electricity shot up my spine as my balls tightened. I sped up my movements and shifted one hand to Lauchlan's cock. The two of us jerked him off as my entire body stiffened, releasing thick jets of hot cum into his body. Within seconds, he covered my hand in his own release, the sticky fluid exploding all over the "hell" across my knuckles.

The release was euphoric, an exorcism of every bitter thought and burden in my brain and body, like a balloon releasing all of its air and finally resting wherever it landed. This man, apparently, was my resting place.

I held myself still for another second more, leaning down to bite the puffy pink skin of his lips. He laughed into my mouth, his erratic breathing softly fading into deep, satisfied gulps of air. Gently pulling out of him, I flopped down by his side, sweaty and sated, the rage beneath my skin quieted to a light pulse. He interlaced our fingers as we stared up at the ceiling, our heartbeats in sync as we came down from the high.

I turned on my side and looked into the face of Lauchlan O'Donnell, the man I couldn't get out of my head. His arrogance, his silliness—like he'd never held the weight of the world on his shoulders. He was light and easy, and despite his own shitty hand in life, he'd never let it ruin him like mine had ruined me. I envied it as much as I loathed it. I craved him as much as I wanted to despise him.

He was too damn… likeable.

Before I pulled myself up to grab a washcloth, I heard rustling on the far side of the room, followed by the click of footsteps across the hardwood floor. Hillary's surprised blue eyes hovered above us in seconds, her appraising stare one of amusement, and light distaste.

"I'll be ordering more coconut oil, boys," she announced, before the click of her heels retreated toward the kitchen. "I'm pretty sure that's *not* what it's for."

Lauchlan snickered beside me, and despite this shit day, and this shittier life, I laughed too.

64

CHAPTER 7

Lauchlan

Bellamy: Time's up, Locke. Clients want closure on this one. What's your status?

The text interrupted a riveting game I was playing, and I scowled at my phone screen for the rude intrusion. 'Course, I hadn't forgotten about Bellamy and The Six, and the mission that'd brought me into this sorry mess in the first place, but it hadn't been on my list of priorities.

Not to mention I hadn't come up with a plan, exactly, for the priceless painting now on the other side of the Atlantic —or wherever my beautiful Blondie had shipped it to. But, plans could be written in a moment, and I had a semblance of one brewing while my sexy mafia man healed up on the couch beside me.

"Do you still have your forger bloke?" I asked Aaron casually as I threw a potato up in the air, catching it with the ease of a well... well-practiced potato thrower.

This place was empty of all entertainment. No TV, no magazines, not even bloody romance books, and the phones Joey had sourced for us were basic as feck. So, I'd found the closest thing to a ball within the confines of the kitchen cabinets—a potato. I'd been tossing it up in the air for what had to be a good hour; my wrist was cramping, but I hadn't dropped it in over 200 throws, and I'd be gobbed if I stopped before gravity finally made me her mistress.

Aaron looked up from his crossword; he'd snagged the games section in today's paper before I could, so at least he had some entertainment. "I do not believe they have gone missing, *Rojo*," he remarked dryly as if I'd asked a dumb question. "Are you looking to make a copy after all?"

"Of Blondie's painting? Yup." I nodded, snatching at the rogue potato as it spiraled a bit too far to the right. It danced along my fingertips, threatening my perfect score.

Not today, my pretty potassium.

I turned my attention back to the healing Colombian, who was looking far better today than he had since Club Assassin; his lips were no longer parched and starched, instead looking particularly plump and pink. *Nice and kissable, Daddio.*

He eyed me expectantly, back to the healthy, rich color of amber. Aaron was very pretty, in a "don't fuck with me or I'll flay you" sort of way. I was quickly discovering that pretty and particularly murderous was exactly my type—or it seemed to be. All three of my companions happened to fit the description, and I just so happened to want to fuck them all.

Hell, I'd actually bedded two. Although, if you would hear them tell it, they would say *they* bedded *me.* Potatopotahto, really. In either scenario, I was getting freshly fucked, so the semantics hardly mattered.

Why was Aaron looking at me like I had three heads? Right. Forgery.

"I was just thinking," I mused idly as I balanced the lumpy spud on my index finger, "when we get out of this mess, I'll need an out with The Six."

"I can admire your foresight." My prickly companion set aside his crossword and swung his legs down from the couch, turning to face me. "But you are perhaps putting the cart before the horse, no? Or are The Six equally murderous as the likes of Antonio and Alvarez?"

I considered that for a second, but a second was all it took. "I mean, I imagine they're less bloody about it than the likes of you, mate, but they're not people I'd want a mark on my head for crossing."

That they weren't. Bellamy wasn't a killer, but the higher-ups would certainly take a piece of me—likely my heart out of my chest—to send a message to any other squirrelly conmen looking to bow out of a contract. I liked being on a pedestal for certain things, but that wasn't one of them. I stifled the shudder creeping up my backside, not willing to lose my potato-winning streak for a bit of fear.

He nodded curtly, as if taking my words to heart. I liked when Aaron took me seriously. He was a serious man, so for him to do so meant I was part of the serious club instead of the group joke. I eyed the spinning potato in my hand and quickly palmed it. It pained me after all that effort—and the very literal pain of my spasming wrist—but it was hard to be part of the serious club when playing with potatoes.

"I will connect you." Aaron nodded thoughtfully. "But they will need access to the painting to forge it. You must compel your 'Blondie' for that one."

Right. Well, surely Blondie didn't want me to die a right sorry painful death at the hands of another criminal organization, so I'd make my appeal soon—with a few administered orgasms to sweeten the deal. I wasn't above bribing her with my tongue in both ways to secure the forgery. Such sacrifices had to be made when a man's life was on the line.

Speaking of—I looked at my watch. Hillary and Kellan had been gone most of the day, and their absence was *felt* in this cavern of a warehouse. I could think of a million ways Daddy Roboto could have entertained me today, but I'd chickened out each time I had the urge to kiss the feck out of those delicate lips. It wasn't often a man could make *me* nervous, but shyte.

Flayer McFlayerson just might be my undoing. I wanted to pounce on that tight, slightly damaged body of his and suck on every square inch of bronze skin until he creamed all over me from pleasure.

"Wanna play a game?" I asked instead, nodding toward the kitchenette behind us. My Colombian god raised one eyebrow in question, but he didn't say no. So I leaped at the opportunity before he'd decide his crossword was more entertaining than I was.

As if.

In my exploration of the place yesterday, I'd found a small bottle of Scottish whiskey in the office cabinet, unopened, and coated in plasterboard dust. Some sneaky little carpenter had likely stored it for a nip and had left it behind. Their loss, my gain.

Dropping my potato pal, I led the short distance to the kitchen with Aaron slowly following on my heels. Taking out the pint of whiskey, I eyed him with a grin. "We're going to play a drinking game."

Stone-faced, he shook his head. "I am recovering from surgery, *Rojo*. That is unwise."

Right. Feck. Stupid little thing to forget. "Right," I agreed, as if Aaron was just stating the obvious and everyone in the room—he and I—knew that little fact.

"Which is why I'm going to drink, and you're going to play along."

Another thick eyebrow went up, like a well-manicured, judging caterpillar. I didn't like the way it taunted me. "I have a revision for this plan."

"Lay it on me, Roboto." I swung my arms open wide, inviting him to suggest anything in this world he wanted. Anything was better than counting the ceiling tiles for the sixth time, even a mediocre *not*-drinking game with the sexy robot.

He moved to the right and removed a pad and paper from one of the kitchen drawers. "How are you at tic-tac-toe?"

An incredulous snort escaped my lips before I could stop it. Tic-tac-toe. Here I was, about to suggest an invigorating, sexy little game of drunken Truth or Dare, and this man wanted to play tic-tac-toe? A children's game?

"I thought you were a man of strategy, *Rojo*," Aaron goaded, a shining gleam in his eye I'd never seen before. "Are you not a smart engineer? Let me show you my version to see how smart you are."

Oh, ho, this man did know how to get my goat. A face-puckering smirk took over my mouth.

"Alright, Daddio. Teach me."

Fire lit up his eyes, and it was definitely the sexiest look I'd seen on him by far. Still slightly pale, his dark hair less sleek without all of his expensive products, but those eyes could take me out with one targeted glance—like they were now.

He lingered over the small circular table, and I quickly maneuvered around him to pull out the chair. Settling into the seat, he started drawing a huge tic-tac-toe grid. I drew up the chair beside him, curious about his version.

"If I had coins, I would show you Trique," he intoned as he drew precise lines I could only achieve with a ruler. "But this version will do."

Fuck, he was cute. An adorable little man-child in a scary, sculpted meat suit. I needed to keep seeing the light in his eyes.

"What do we need for *Trique*?" I asked, eager to learn more about his Colombian heritage. "Could something other than coins work?"

A flicker of surprise crossed his face, but it quickly melted into that excited, childish look again. "I can draw it if you find something to use as pieces. We need eighteen; nine of each."

I flipped through the kitchen cupboards, finding a box of Froot Loops. What was Aaron's favorite color? I took a stab at red and shook out the cereal on the countertop, counting out nine red rings and nine blue ones, then shook out a side bowl of dry cereal to munch on. I whistled a tune and sauntered over with my colorful cereal pieces.

Aaron had drawn a small square inside a big square, with lines cutting the squares into eight equal triangles with the tips cut off. He shook his head when he saw my chosen game pieces, but I swear I saw a curl of amusement on those supple lips.

He patiently explained the rules—similar to tic-tac-toe —and we played several rounds, him beating me every single one.

"You are not wise enough to beat me, *marica*," the Colombian crowed as he finished his last move, actually besting me at a children's game after all. I wasn't fazed. The silly triumphant grin on his normally stoic face riled my insides with equally silly little butterflies.

Curiosity was getting the better of me about this zombie super-secret plan he and Kellan were cooking, and he seemed relaxed enough to chat, so I gave it a go.

"What have you and Conan been planning to bring you back from the dead?" I asked as we cleared the board for the third time. He separated the pieces by color and handed them back to me slowly, as if considering his answer.

"Long ago, before we arranged my end," he started cryptically, "we put in place a contingency plan, should I ever need to return. We recorded Marco Alvarez threatening me and ensured a witness overheard a useful conversation. Kellan planted evidence in the car that will point to Alvarez once they remove it from the water. And we confirmed that the night we made me disappear, Marco's whereabouts were suspicious—he was bargaining women's lives with a human trader. He will struggle to produce an alibi."

I whistled through my teeth. The plan caught me completely off guard. It had been a useful gamble to put these layers in place before Aaron's disappearance, and yet...

"You know," I mused aloud, working through a scenario in my head as I played with my Froot Loops poker chips. "Sometimes the best solution is the most obvious answer. The easiest cons are the ones where the explanation you give the mark is so nicely packaged with a bow, they don't even consider any other answer. It's easy. They like that it's easy. You've taken the hard work out of it for them."

Aaron turned his full attention to me. I preened under his notice like a wee kitten in the sunshine, but I didn't care. My mind was working a mile a minute. There was a way to weave more than this story together.

"What if..."

I wove a grand tale, one where we could tie Hillary's and Aaron's stories together with a neat little package for the friendly police force of the city of Carlisle, with enough planted evidence the FBI would dig elsewhere for the dirt they needed to close the case. It would connect Alvarez to Hillary, Sandra to Alvarez, and lean into the media-spun narrative something was afoot, but not in the ways they thought it was.

It wasn't foolproof—no con was—but it was pretty near perfect.

Aaron grew more interested as I talked, and by the time I'd gotten to the end of my epic con proposal, he'd shifted so close to me in his seat, our thighs were touching. His hot, thick muscle just rubbing against mine on a carbon-fiber seat, like the softest porn I'd ever watched. Didn't matter though—the heat of him and his close, spicy scent made my heart rate pick up and my palms sweat.

Since when did I simper for anybody?

"That is quite brilliant, *Rojo*." His voice was low and his eyes now set in a dusky stare, an intense liquid gaze of impressed... lust?

Please let it be lust.

"I must admit, you are quite... surprising."

He leaned in closer still. The lips I'd been fecking dreaming to kiss brushed over the top of my earlobe and forced a zing of electricity down my spine. I jolted in the seat, and he chuckled darkly against my skin.

"Do I make you nervous, *Rojo*?" A large hand with long, strong fingers slid down to my thigh and gently squeezed the tense muscle, creating another zing, though this time it went right to my dick. It twitched painfully in my sweats, standing at attention like I was fourteen again with a PornHub password.

Aaron's mouth retreated from my ear. "Or perhaps this is not what you want?"

He started to remove his hand from my skin, but I clamped my palm over his in a death grip.

"You're a bit of a scary brute, Roboto." The words I whispered were a little pitched as I turned to face him properly. "But, feck, I want you to kiss the fucking shyte out of me right now."

Amber eyes flashed gold, and that was the last I saw of them before he gripped my chin tightly with one hand and leaned in, pressing the softest lips I'd ever felt against mine. He maintained steady pressure, coaxing me to open my mouth up to him, slipping his tongue against mine in a commanding caress that made me putty to mold in his hold. He was so hot and wet and...

Christ, I was explaining the kiss of a lifetime like I was tonguing a cup of coffee, not the delicious tempting taste forcing pre-cum to weep from the tip of my painfully stiff cock. I reached both hands up to cradle his neck, careful not to jostle his torso, and let him take complete control of my mouth and my body. Whatever he wanted in the moment was his. He could take any piece of me, flay skin off my arse, it wouldn't matter. I'd do whatever he asked with a goddamn grin.

With Kellan, I thrived on being a brat, worming my way under his skin until he couldn't help taking me. With my Blondie, I loved being whoever and whatever she needed—a sex toy to punish, a pleasurer to take away her pain—I didn't care, as long as she was using me in whatever way pleased her.

But with Aaron—I wanted to be the one he took care of. The baby doll to his Daddy. If sex with him was anything like this kiss, I was going to die a *very* happy man.

Before I could crawl into his lap and grind the shit out of him, he slowed down the kiss until it came to a complete and gentle stop. Leisurely pulling away, he bowed his head to touch mine, like we were seasoned lovers instead of onetime kissers.

"I am tired, *Rojo*," he admitted with a light chuckle, but there wasn't a hint of regret in his expression. Just the cutest flushed cheeks and bright eyes—looking nothing like the robot I knew—and something settled into place in my heart.

I wanted a seat at Kellan and Hillary's table—I'd known that for months. I wanted to slide into their lives as a permanent fixture and never look back. And now, I was sure I wanted Aaron there too.

If the may-or-may-not-exist gods and goddesses were smiling down on us, I hoped they gave us the family we'd never had as our present, once we worked our way through the shittiest set of circumstances known to man.

I smiled back at the still-scary-but-incredibly-cute crush of mine and stood. Leaning down, I guided my hand to his lower back and pulled him upward.

"Then let's go for a nap, Roboto. I'll get you into bed."

CHAPTER 8

Hillary

"If you could kindly return my calls, *dear daughter.*" My father's voice sneered through the voice message forwarded to my new phone. "I need to speak to you."

I couldn't stifle my eye roll as I listened through the remainder of the message. My egotistical sperm-donor felt the need to remind me of my family duty a half a dozen times before hanging up, with Marcie's simpering voice in the background at the end.

What a gold-digging tramp.

The pair of them, really. By my calculations, Daddy would have run out of his monthly stipend by now. He always did by the third week and had somehow determined a lecture was the best way to get me to pour more money into his bank account. Truthfully, I'd done it a few times just to shut him up, but I'd be damned if he got another red cent out of me outside of our original agreement.

As it was, I was looking into the legality of ripping up that arrangement. Since the audacious Christmas request, I no longer felt indebted to the man who insisted on using me as an ATM instead of learning from his own poor choices. Especially when my assets, like my paintings, were suspiciously missing. Sold for cash, no doubt. I couldn't trace cash like I could all of his other transactions, and Camden Lane was getting craftier as he continued to screw me.

The irony was not lost on me. I was spending valuable time listening to my selfish, pitiful father complain while I was evading the wrath of two dangerous men.

A call came through the line the moment I deleted his third message. I didn't recognize the number, but picked it up on the second ring.

"Hillary Lane," I answered with authority, my gaze catching on the bleak buildings covered in a drab coating of late February outside the car window. Joey was driving us in our new rented Audi to Tracey Williams Law for my first appointment with Weston. After Kellan's meeting with Trish, I needed to arm myself with strong legal counsel to prepare for whatever came at us next.

"Ms. Lane." An equally authoritative female voice addressed me coolly. "Excellent to hear your voice. I'm Agent Smith with the FBI. I've been trying to reach you through your office, but it seems you haven't been there these last few days. We'd like to bring you in for questioning on a particular case."

My breath hitched in my throat, heart rate skyrocketing. It was the call I'd been expecting, but I was nowhere near prepared for it. Through my crusade, I'd convinced myself I was untouchable. The work I was doing could be rectified legally if it came to that. I'd pay Tracey Williams Law a small fortune to pad my gamble, but that's all it was. A heavily fortified gamble.

Calm, Hill. Calm.

I drew in what I hoped was a silent, deep breath to settle my nerves. It barely registered.

"Yes, I'm a busy woman, as I'm sure you can understand." My tone was casual, despite the fiery heat coursing through my veins. "You'd like to see me regarding... what?"

"It's best to keep those details to a private conversation, Ms. Lane. We'd like to see you today, if possible."

Today. Of course they did. A typical law enforcement response was to catch their perp off guard. Fine—if today was what they wanted, I would control the parameters, at the very least.

"I can meet you within the hour, but I'll be bringing legal representation. I'm sure that's not an issue?"

My voice remained cool, borderline icy, maintaining the knife's edge of arrogant and professional. No matter what evidence they thought they had, they would not catch a single pitch of guilt in my tone.

"Wonderful," Agent Smith replied, her tone equally unflappable. "Here's the address."

I repeated the directions aloud for Joey's benefit, then hung up the phone without another word, rapidly dialing the law firm instead.

Weston Williams, Marty's husband and my latest lawyer on retainer, would be thrown into the fire immediately. Hopefully, his skill set was truly as strong as his reputation as the best criminal defense lawyer in the state. He answered immediately.

"Weston? Hillary Lane. Change of plans. I'm going to need you to meet me at the 78th Precinct. I'm being summoned."

"Understood." The rich baritone echoed through the tinny line. "What should I know before I arrive?"

"I have my suspicions, but I'd rather see what they say first. Let's schedule a meeting afterward."

I hung up the phone and immediately sent a text to the group chat I'd started with Kellan, Aaron, and Lucky.

Kellan walking away from the FBI was terrible timing, but by his gruff and short explanation, Trish wouldn't back him or choose to protect him anymore. My blood boiled when I'd caught the flicker of pain in his eyes. This thirty-eight-year-old man cast aside like an abandoned child. Agent Smith wasn't to blame for Patricia's failings, but she would get the bare minimum of cooperation from me today for the FBI's shitty history of taking advantage of their people.

HL: Summoned to the 78th Precinct. FBI. Weston joining me. Will update when I'm out.

It took all of three seconds for a response. The burner phones Joey had provided were advanced in terms of security, very limited in extra capabilities, but they could send texts well enough.

Lucky: Fuck! Hang in there, Blondie. Channel your inner Kellan and just grunt every few sentences.

Aaron: Please be safe, *Mi Reina*. We'll await your return.

Kellan: You know your rights. Let Weston do the talking for you, as much as possible.

HL: I'll keep you posted. I'm feeling feisty today.

I stared out the window again, the heavy clouds on the rare gray day taking on an ominous sheen.

"78th Precinct, Joey," I directed. Without question, she effortlessly changed course through four lanes of traffic to head eastward to the precinct.

Contingencies, ten steps of separation, never showing my face... My hubris was now besting me in a battle I hadn't even known we were fighting. Thankfully, I had one weapon on my side. Possibly the only thing standing between me and a jail cell. Money. It worked for men all the time. They avoided consequences for their selfish actions with a well-timed partnership and the selective padding of pockets.

Why couldn't I do the same? My actions were to protect people. I executed justice when the misogynistic system failed to do so at every turn. Surely, I could leverage my wealth to walk away from lasting consequences like the hundreds—thousands—of men before me?

A light, disbelieving chuckle escaped me at that thought. That same misogynistic system would nail me to the cross as quickly as they could if they found me guilty. It wasn't even a question, but a simple reality of being a woman of power. I didn't need to hear the rumors to measure how many of my peers would happily throw me off my pedestal at the first chance, never believing I deserved to be there in the first place.

To hear I was complicit, the director of brutal castration, exacting real justice on those who deserved it? Sequoia would have its first witch burning, and I'd be the one at the stake.

"We're here, Ms. Lane," Joey reported. The car slowed to idle in front of the towering white marble building in the center of the city. I was pleased to see Weston's tall, dark figure waiting for me on the curb, his black pinstriped suit and rich, ebony skin a beacon against the somber backdrop.

"Thank you, Joey." We locked gazes through the rearview mirror, her slate-gray eyes peering into mine. Wordlessly, she expressed her concern and questioned my next steps.

"Please wait for me here," I directed, stepping out of the vehicle without her help. I caught her quick nod before turning my attention to Weston Williams, formidable attorney at law and my new legal shield.

Every tiny hair on my body stood on end, electrified by nerves. I discreetly wiped my clammy hand against the back of my skirt and stuck it out for a perfunctory shake. I gripped his thick, warm palm in mine in a firm hold.

"I'd rather not be blindsided going into this, Hillary. Can I at least know your suspicions?"

My gaze scanned our surroundings. I no longer trusted any space that wasn't my own—and even then, I'd been proven quite wrong recently. "I've heard from an inside source that I am a suspect in a series of violent crimes against men in the county."

Weston's booming laugh ricocheted against the stone and surrounded us with its echo. "That was not what I was expecting. Disgruntled employee? Sure. Not violence."

The velvety brown of his irises appraised me with open curiosity, but he said nothing more. Weston's reputation preceded him; whip-smart, ruthless, and imperturbable. Whether he believed in my innocence, he'd fight for the best verdict possible and get it, if it came to that.

We walked side by side up the granite steps and through the large double doors of the precinct. A thin, stern woman with her brunette hair pulled back into a harsh bun greeted us in the entrance.

"Ms. Lane, welcome. I'm Agent Smith, and this is Agent Arnold."

She gestured to the older, silver-haired man beside her, who thrust out his bony hand. Once the perfunctory introductions were out of the way, she beckoned us forward through the powdered blue hallways of the building. She led us to a stark, private room with a single rectangular table and four metal chairs in the center.

"Please sit." It was not an invitation, but a thinly veiled command. Channeling my most practiced nonchalance, I walked to the farthest chair and waited for everyone to take their seats before sitting down.

"Thank you for coming on such short notice," Agent Smith said, her severe expression trying its best to form a welcoming smile, and failing miserably. "Ms. Lane, I'll cut to the chase. Given your influence and wealth, it'd be useless to play games with you, and I'm not one for theatrics."

Agent Arnold let out a light snort beside her, as if this were an understatement.

"Where were you on September 19th of last year?" Agent Smith asked.

My eyebrows rose, surprised by the specificity of the request. "I would have to consult my calendar. I'm a busy woman."

Except, I knew that date. That was the night Sammy and Anita's team rescued the twin girls from Judge Cowan, and we removed his cock. I'd orchestrated the evening within the privacy of the panic room in my condo, but I'd entered my building through the underground garage and bypassed the doorman. Still, there would be camera footage of my entrance and lack of exit, which could be enough to justify a strong alibi.

My hands shook in my lap, and I clasped them tightly to stop the vibration, ignoring the sweat collecting in my palms. Better my hands than my brow. I grit my teeth, fighting a vicious battle with my facial muscles to remain neutral.

"I imagine you are," replied Agent Smith coolly. "How about November 22nd? Or December 10th?"

My mind cycled through the information in quick succession as my stomach pulsed upward into my chest, pushing acerbic bile into the back of my throat. I cleared it once, as if considering her statement, and controlled the flow of air through my nostrils.

Slow and steady. Slooooooow and steeeeeeeeady.

Two more castrations—specifically orchestrated through my heavily fortified online back channels with Blackbird's help. The men we'd mutilated weren't connected—they hadn't even run in the same social or professional circles—so it was highly unlikely they'd corroborated their stories. I couldn't imagine Sammy getting caught. The man was a seasoned expert at evading all law enforcement and hand-picked members of his team were the same.

Who had fucked me over? And what was their endgame?

"Again, my calendar," I repeated, narrowing my eyes at the shrewd woman in front of me.

"Enough with the cryptic questioning, Agatha." Weston's strong voice cut into the stillness of the tomb-like room. "What are we here for? My client is a busy person, and we don't have all day to play 'guess the date.'"

If I thought Agent Smith had looked stern before Weston's consternation, she injected steel into her expression now. Ignoring Weston entirely, she faced me, eyes full of emboldened determination.

"You've been specifically named by a victim as a culpable party to a series of violent mercenary-style crimes in the Carlisle area. Power or not, Ms. Lane, the FBI doesn't take too kindly to mutilation. In the interest of clearing your name, you could give us full access to your computer files—you know, to speed up the process." Her eyes shone with triumph, as if she'd already caught me in her snare.

I fought to control it, but my entire body stiffened. My firewall was excellent, and after Blackbird's head had graced my coffee table, I'd deleted all hacking information from my desktop. Blackbird and I had used the dark web to facilitate our conversations and transactions, but nothing ever truly was eliminated online.

I knew with the right people on their side, they would find something incriminating.

Weston shifted in his seat beside me, speaking up on my behalf. "Ms. Lane is in possession of highly sensitive business information that is not intended for the public. We will contest the FBI's unfettered access to her files, based on —"

"Ms. Lane's business files will remain exempt for now." Agent Arnold interrupted, finally contributing to the conversation. "All personal files, including laptops and cellphones, however, are fair game should the evidence support their necessity."

My old cell phone was smashed into tiny shards of lithium and cobalt, the SIM card shredded and destroyed. My laptop was scrubbed "to the nubbins," according to Lucky, who'd done the work himself. That left my system in the condo building—the same condo I hadn't returned to in over a week.

"What evidence?" Weston asked, his piercing eyes hardening on the two agents across the table.

"Written testimony and computer files from another source." Agent Smith's bitter stare washed over me, the contempt rolling off of her in waves. "Stay close, Ms. Lane. We won't hesitate to come after you."

"Until you offer your evidence and your warrant, my client can go wherever she damn well pleases." Weston rose from the table, and I followed his lead. "Unless you have anything further, you'll escort us out of here."

We weren't making any friends here today, but I preferred honest enemies to fake friendships. Without another word, the two agents stood and opened the door, bracketing the pair of us between them as they led us back to the front entrance.

"Stay close, Ms. Lane." Agent Smith's mouth curled into the semblance of a smirk before she turned on her practical black heel and stomped back toward the bullpen of desks. Agent Arnold followed close behind her, his attitude far less snarky, but no less imposing.

Weston turned to me, eyes full of concern. "I need you to go home, search through your calendar, and send me your whereabouts for the three dates they mentioned. I'll also need anything you can tell me about their suspicions without incriminating yourself. We need to be aggressive and offensive on this one. Asset seizure is messy, and they'll take their time to fuck up your life as much as possible just because they can. We'll need to play ball, but we'll do it on our terms, okay?"

Nodding slowly, I blew out a long, staggered breath, cleansing my insides from the unexpected attack. Joey still waited in the rental vehicle at the curb, and I was eager to cocoon myself in the safety and familiarity of her presence.

"Let's meet tomorrow," I suggested, already walking toward the mobile sanctuary. "I'll send you those details later on today."

Before he could respond, I was descending the steps, my Louboutins clacking noisily across the stone. Joey stepped out of my waiting chariot and silently opened the rear door for me. I cast her an appreciative, tired smile before ducking my head inside.

A plan brewed in my mind as we looped back several streets and side streets on our way to the warehouse, in case we were being followed. It would require one of Lucky's many skill sets, and I'd take a substantial financial loss, but what was one building in the grand scheme of things?

HL: I need your help tonight.

Lucky: Blondie needs me! Been waiting for this moment. Pleasure or pain, love?

HL: Both. Joey's going to pick up what we need. Make a list.

I explained my plan both to Lucky via text and to Joey via conversation. It was risky, messy, and an act of desperation. I no longer had the upper hand in any area of my life, and it was time to take a little of my power back.

One raging fire at a time.

CHAPTER 9

Aaron

"**W**here are you going, *Rojo?*"

An abrupt noise woke me from a fitful sleep and I peered through the weight of heavy eyes. When I'd finally fallen asleep, *Mi Reina's* soft body had been nestled between Lauchlan and I. Kellan slept on the sofa in the great room, the wrestling thoughts of his mind disallowing him the luxury of rest once again. I now lay in the king bed alone, Hillary nowhere in view, with the Irishman's shadow dressed in all black in the doorway.

He brought his ghostly finger to his lips in a shushing motion. "Go back to sleep, Daddy. I'm on a mission tonight."

I shot out of bed at the quiet declaration. The quick movement tore at my stitches, forcing hot sparks through my stomach. I glared at him through the pain, my body now on full alert.

"What is this mission and why are you going alone?"

A brief smile twitched across the lips I had kissed just two days ago. I had not expected it, yet, it had felt as natural as kissing the lips of my queen; supple and sweet. I did not know where the kiss would lead, but I did not want this man risking himself unnecessarily. For *Mi Reina's* sake, if not for my own.

"From Blondie's own lips, I swear." His slight smile morphed into a devious grin. "Don't worry, I'm taking Conan with me."

Frowning, I slowly twisted my body on the bed. He was in front of me before I could get a foot on the floor. Gently placing a palm against my shoulder blades, he took my weight and lifted me to my feet, his hand lingering on my bare skin before stepping back.

"Ask for help, Roboto," he chided. Green eyes leisurely roamed over me, ogling my flesh as if it were one of the fine paintings he thieved. "You're looking damn good for a patient, though."

My tanned skin flushed as his gaze roamed all over my naked skin. I was covered only by new bandages and a small pair of silk boxers. The stitches were healing well, and my muscles no longer felt the heat of a thousand suns each morning. I was still slow to move, and my strength quickly waned. My impatience was winning in the battle of wills, while I begged my body to keep up to the task.

The conman nipped the crux of his bottom lip and winked long lashes at me, sending delicate shivers up my spine, before slowly turning toward the door again.

"Come on," he called as he walked out into the hallway. "Might as well see us off."

Confused, I trailed behind him, silently wondering why I was the last to know about this late-night endeavor. The four of us were now a cohort, and with Lauchlan's plan, we would be tied together for the rest of our lives, should we be fortunate enough to live so long. My impulsive actions had caused me to become a liability, though I'd mostly hidden in the shadows as a docile pup these past few months. I was considered a dull paring knife in our stack of tools until my body healed, but I did not like being the last to know information.

Kellan too was dressed in all black, a cotton ski mask rolled up above his eyes. His stance was wide and guarded, arms folded across his chest in irritation as *Mi Reina* spoke softly to him, unaware of my presence.

"Where are you going?" The command escaped me before I could soften the words, my weariness fading as I took in their appearance. Determined. Disciplined. Ready to report for whatever duties *Mi Reina* had ordered.

Lauchlan's forehead rose at my order, but he relented. "We need to destroy some evidence, Roboto!" There was no fear or hesitation in his tone, just cheerful joy to be useful. I too needed to be useful.

Hillary stepped up to me and wrapped cool arms around my hot skin. "The computer systems in my condo need to be destroyed before the FBI issues a search warrant. Lucky's going to rig up a fire. That's all." Her warm smile melted the ice forming around my heart from being excluded. "Why don't you wait here with me?"

"I would like to go." The words escaped me before I could stop them, but I could not take them back. My actions had caused my injuries. I couldn't deny it, but I had more value to this group than Lauchlan and Kellan's plans for our future.

Hillary's tender smile dissolved into a firm line. "Aaron, you aren't able to…"

They doubted my ability to contribute. To be useful. I would prove otherwise.

I shrugged out of her hold and stalked over to Kellan, removing the gun clipped across his back in the holster. He allowed me the action, watching me curiously, saying nothing. I was grateful I did not need to explain myself to this man. We'd been forged in the same fire, and had our positions been switched, I was confident he too would be as restless as I.

I checked the barrel to ensure it contained bullets, then reached into the Viking's pants pocket for the slim, cylindrical silencer he always carried. He didn't shrink from my touch, choosing instead to lean into it. I brushed the sensitive bulge as I withdrew the steel device, noting his subtle shift in posture. It was not a time for distractions.

Screwing on the silencer, I held the gun steady in front of me and aimed for the vase on the fireplace mantel over forty feet away. With a sharp *pop*, the crystal shattered in an explosion of shards, littering the floor and furniture in front of it. The kickback was admittedly sharp against my side, but not excruciating, a humble reminder of my mortality. I had not trained in months, but the honed skills of youth were difficult to erase.

My companions simply stood back in total silence and allowed me this demonstration. I held out my hand to Hillary, who now stood directly behind me.

"Knife, *Mi Reina*." I ordered. The familiar authority seeped into the facet of each individual syllable. She stared at me with muted disapproval before pulling out a small dagger from her thigh sheath, something she only removed now to shower, and handed it to me.

The knife felt like an old friend against my palm, its warmth and smooth exterior an extension of my body. I welcomed it back into my life as I sought out the victim for my demonstration. I was damaged, but still powerful. My use remained. I would show them.

Lauchlan's sneaker lay carelessly by the side entrance door twenty-five feet away. I held the dagger by the hilt and threw it on an outward breath. The blade effortlessly pierced the leather skin of the tongue.

"Aye, mate!" the Irishman exclaimed indignantly. "Grand aim and all, but ruin your own shoes, yeh?"

Hillary ambled over to the dagger and pulled it out of the executed trainer, sliding it back into its sheath before turning to face me, hands on her delicate hips.

"I get it." She blew out a long breath through her nose and eyed both men before saying anything more. "You're tired of being cooped up. But you're still injured, Aaron. It's not safe for you to go."

"What is Kellan's purpose tonight?" I demanded, in search of more validation before I would drop my desires. "Is he to enter the building or remain in the car? I am just as able to protect in motion, if it is necessary."

I reached for her again, gathering her feminine frame between the hard body of my own. Gripping her hips, I bent my head low, seeking salvation in the deep blue of her eyes. My domineering tone flattened into a soft plea. "Please, *Mi Reina*. I need a purpose. I cannot atrophy under the tenderness of kisses and softness of pillows. I will do as you ask, but I need you to say yes."

Heart pounding in my chest, I listened to the violent drumbeats as I awaited her reply. My father would mock me for my compassion toward this woman, the way I yielded to her. My father failed to understand the power of a true joining of souls, as I had with *Mi Reina*. From now until my last breath, her wish was my command.

"I hear you, *caballero oscuro*." She buried her nose in my chest, her lips brushing against the hardened skin along my pecs. I basked in the delicate touch, the cotton of her skin softening my resolve. When she pulled back, her cool stare slid to the men awaiting instructions by the door.

"Aaron will go with you." The firm command of a leader. Her disposition brooked no arguments. Neither man looked happy with this development despite my demonstration, but they did not say anything to contest *Mi Reina's* will.

I gripped her chin within my palm, pulling her to me in a forceful kiss, my gratitude passing between our lips.

"Allow me to get dressed."

Without fervor, I walked as quickly as my body would allow toward the bedroom, determination feeding my limited strength. I would prove my worth to this group of formidable allies. I would be a burden no more.

"Why is the solution to set fire to the computers, *Rojo*? Why can we not just remove them from the premises?"

I was seated in the rear cab of a black truck Kellan had been using as an alias vehicle. The trip to Hillary's condo took far longer than usual to ensure we weren't being followed. I wasn't accustomed to the secretive games Kellan played. All my life, I had people for these sorts of things. Surveillance. Clean-up. They were simply a call away, not a trained skill set like the many other traits Vicente had beaten into my flesh.

Lauchlan turned in the passenger seat to face me, index finger raised.

"One, Hill's got a state-of-the-art setup. There's a small hacking army of equipment in there. It would take several trips to bring it all down to the vehicle, and this one doesn't have the capacity."

He held up another finger.

"Two, this shit's fucking heavy. You're not exactly helpful there in your condition, mate, and Kellan's too bulky for any kind of stealth mode with a whole boatload of computers in a crammed elevator. It'd take too long and be too noticeable."

The air between us had shifted since we had shared our first kiss. Every so often, I could feel the weight of his stare against my back, or the heat of his gaze along my skin. He had not escaped my notice either.

"What about the sprinkler system?" Kellan asked, continuously scanning our surroundings in all the mirrors. "Wouldn't water destroy the electronics?"

"Maybe, maybe not," Lauchlan replied, his voice taking on a gleeful edge. "Can't count on it, though. Those hard drives need to be fried, and it can't look like we're intentionally tampering with evidence. So, we're going to cause a wee fire in the elevator on the opposite side of the building, pull the alarm, and get the nice, very rich people out of there safely, while I'm upstairs, rigging up the actual fire that's going to burn everything in sight on the penthouse floor."

"According to Hillary, half of the building is unoccupied for most of the year, anyway." My *compañero's* words were muffled as he turned into the rear parking lot of a public park, near to our targeted building. "Foreign nationals, that sort of thing." He raised a critical eyebrow in Lauchlan's direction. "You're sure you can rig it to stay within her residence? No other casualties?"

"Pretty sure." The Irishman grinned and pulled out a series of supplies from the backpack at his feet. "Can't say I've ever rigged a job this size before, but I'm excited for the opportunity."

Wonderful. *Rojo* was a pyromaniac, in addition to simply being a maniac. Kellan and I exchanged a meaningful stare through the rearview mirror. We were allowing this man to execute this plan unattended. Perhaps a bigger risk than the FBI.

Once Lauchlan had organized his supplies, Kellan drove out of the parking lot and toward our mission. *Mi Reina* could still access the building's camera system, including the exterior feeds. Nothing suspicious had been noted in the time since her hacker's decapitation, but our tactical agent continued to be cautious as we approached the underground parking garage. Hillary had given him a device that would open the doors into her private bay.

The rumble of the vehicle between layers of confining concrete was obnoxious in the tomb-like structure. We waited in silence for a few minutes in the dark, listening for any sign of activity before opening our doors.

The plan was simple, as I would expect it to be from *Rojo*. Kellan had obtained a camera scrambler during his time in the FBI to fully cover our actions when the authorities analyzed the recordings in the coming days.

Armed with the codes to get inside the condo and the panic room, Lauchlan would set up the mechanisms to start the fire remotely. Once the fire was set in the elevator, we would reconvene in the underground garage, then pull the trigger, setting off a minor explosion in the panic room, kitchen, and living room to look like a coordinated attack instead of a cover-up.

I could admire the elegance and simplicity. The man pretended to be the least intelligent person in the room, but I was now certain he was often the smartest. Most clever, certainly.

"Off I go!" Lauchlan exclaimed as he tugged on the heavy pack over his broad shoulders. He pulled down the ski mask over his crown of thick hair, and winked a glowing green eye at the pair of us before stepping out of the vehicle.

It felt useless to be idle when he was setting fires to protect *Mi Reina*, but I'd joined the mission as an observer and had to accept that fate. Kellan remained in his seat, pushing the lever to lower into an inclined position. He scanned the parking garage before shifting to face me, navy eyes scrutinizing me for weakness.

"Are you hurting?"

The question was abrupt, but not sharp, genuine concern for my well-being. Nodding, I touched the portion of my abdomen still bandaged to protect the stitching beneath.

"It is not comfortable, but there is no pain tonight," I assured him, relieved it was not a lie. "Are *you* hurting?" I volleyed the question back, no longer speaking about physical ailments. "Betrayal is the most brutal of hurts. You have faced many these past few weeks."

As expected, the formidable man simply grunted and closed his eyes, as if this were a worthy response to the question. I did not push him, waiting in the cab's silence for a proper reply. When I said nothing for several moments, he cracked open one eye, and blew out a breath of annoyance at my expectant frown.

"Yeah, it sucks." He placed his tattooed knuckles over his eyelids and rubbed hard, as if scrubbing the thin skin could erase his sins. "But not unexpected. I didn't expect it to be this soon, or in this way, but I've always had one foot in each world, without belonging to either. There's not a whole lot of loyalty in the cartel." He huffed out a bitter laugh. "Or law enforcement, apparently."

"Are you able to kill your brothers?"

I was curious about this answer. I did not have the burden of siblings, and I could only consider it a luxury. Veronica and Vicente did not need more children to ruin. The connection came from growing up with other children was unknown to me.

He cocked his head, the usual waves of blond hair plastered tight to his forehead with the aid of the ski mask shoved over top. "I'll know when the time comes, I guess. I want them dead, but not by my hand." He stared at his knuckles, the "hell" and "hope" still vivid in the gray light of the parking garage. "There's only one good man in my family, and he's tucked away. Antonio doesn't even know about him. I've already had to kill one brother, and it was the bureau who killed my other one. Neither of them were good men, and these two... they're all that's left. But they don't deserve to live either. They'll both dance on my grave if they get to me first."

I didn't like the churn within my belly at that imagery. I would not allow a burial plot to be dug for this man.

"Then I will be the one to kill them, so you may save your energy for your father," I announced, knowing as soon as I'd uttered the words they were a solemn vow to a man I cared for. "You have my word, *compañero*. They will not have to die by your hand."

The brutal Viking's hard mouth slacked at my declaration. The smooth lines of strong lips buried within the groomed beard turned up into a softened smile. "I appreciate that, *Guapo. Estoy agradecido de tenerte como amigo.*"

I am grateful to have you as a friend. The words were pleasant, but not the words I wanted from him.

"Is that what I am to you, Kellan? *Soy más que un amigo.* I am more than a friend." I stared into the richness of his gaze, the sea of dark blue capturing me in its depths. He did not turn away, instead holding me prisoner within the intensity of his stare.

The gaze was a siren's song. Unwittingly, I had shifted closer to his enormous frame still lying in the seat, and the heat of his body casting a warming glow against my skin.

"It is dangerous to be my friend, *Guapo.*" The low words barely registered as I remained caught in his commanding presence. "It is even more dangerous to be... more."

I could now smell the spicy cinnamon scent on his breath, the bristles of his wiry beard tickling the skin of my chin.

"Don't let my appearance fool you, *compañero*. I, too, am a dangerous man."

My mouth muffled the gruff snort by covering his. The press of our lips was neither gentle nor kind. It was the kiss of desperate men succumbing to the solace of a similar spirit, abandoned men tasting forbidden fruit and relishing its flavor. Two hands cradled the base of my skull, forcefully pulling me even closer to shipwreck. I welcomed the reckoning as he tore my mouth apart with his tongue.

My erection pressed painfully against my trousers, this inevitable moment between us rising at the most inconvenient time and place, but I could not regret it. Kellan fulfilled a need in my soul I wished to keep. And I would fulfill my vow. I would kill his brothers to keep him.

The electronic sound of the garage door rising halted our kiss, our eyes widening at its implications. Kellan shot up, and peered into the side mirror to see two SUVs barreling inside.

A moving target caught my sight-line in the opposite mirror, Lauchlan's frame racing toward the truck from behind. He hauled open the passenger-side door, expelling ragged gasping breaths.

"We've got company!" he yelled and pulled into the cab and slammed the door shut.

Without pause, Kellan stepped on the gas, veering around the line of Hillary's parked luxury vehicles in the center, toward the SUVs now blocking the garage entrance.

I reached for my gun tucked beneath the seat for safekeeping, already loaded, and prepared to fire. I peered through the center glass at two similar-looking men staring through their own panes of glass. Their dark features hardened into severe masks of steel. Several men occupied the vehicles alongside them.

Kellan's brothers had arrived. Perhaps I would fulfill my oath to him today, after all.

CHAPTER 10

Lauchlan

"I'm a maniac, pyromaniaaaaaaaaac, on the floor..." I sang to my rendition of Michael Sembello's classic 80s jam as I unraveled the tiny firebomb that would trigger the building's fire alarm. There were two sets of elevators, but only one went up to Blondie's penthouse suite. I was in the opposite set, holding open the door jamb with an extended toe as I shoved the small box into the far corner.

It would take about ten minutes to ignite, then it would smoke for a good five before the flames were strong enough to trigger the alarm. Better still, the fire would completely engulf the entire apparatus and leave a pile of ashes in its wake, making it one hell of a challenge to determine the source. Bit of genius on my part, but I couldn't take all the credit. Fire was a fascinating mistress, and I worshipped at her altar.

I lit the tiny fuse and then flicked the button to bring this set of elevators up the shaft. It was three a.m., so doubtful anyone would rightly see it on their travels and try to play the hero. Could just pull the fire alarm myself, but for one, that was a very unfun mission, and for two, that could be traced. Better to keep the mystery alive and frustrate the living hell out of the FBI agents looking for clues.

They want to come after my Blondie? This was my passive-aggressive anarchist response. Way better plan.

First job done, I jogged over to the other set of elevators to take me up to Hillary's condo. So far, so good.

Given it had been all of three minutes, and I was carrying the camera scrambler with me to hide from the visual feeds all around the building, that was the most likely outcome, but still... Celebrate the small wins and all.

I was a giddy little schoolboy, in truth. I hadn't felt the buzz from a mission in a good while. The endorphins ripped through my veins like I was riding the high of a great bender. Nope, I was high on life, fulfilling my role in a modern-day misfit Musketeer squad. Blondie needed us, and we would deliver.

I entered the passcode when the elevator arrived at the top of her penthouse and entered my home away from home. The faint scent of bleach clung to the air as I entered the living room; I wrinkled my nose as my gaze hit the glass coffee table in the center, grateful Joey had a much stronger stomach than the likes of me. Not that I'd been expecting it, but no evidence of the chopped-off head remained. The place was still a pristine little palace cleaned by house-elves.

I would have helped Blondie get rid of the body if she'd needed me to, but I was a much better fire bloke than a disposal bloke. Probably would have spewed my guts up a few times before I was done.

I surveyed the main living area of the condo outside of the scene of the crime—nothing amiss to the naked eye. It struck me odd there was nary a boot print on the rugs, or a single speck of spatter, despite Hill's place being mostly done up in boring cream colors. Whoever had been up here was a professional crew, not some chainsaw-wielding mafia hack job.

An icy shiver struck me between my shoulder blades. Best not to think about that.

I removed a handy little gadget from my backpack and turned it on, scanning for the tiny transmitters in audio bugs and GPS trackers. A skin tracer was the thickness of a piece of human skin, and virtually unnoticeable—it would take a few showers to wash it away if they placed it anywhere a person would naturally pick it up, like a light switch or a door handle. The scanner was a hard bugger to source, but Jediah was a pretty handy contact for these kinds of things.

I'd paid him a lot of money for three of them, but when the screen lit up like a Jackson Pollock painting, it was worth every single American penny.

I whistled through my teeth at the sight. Tracers and bugs fecking *everywhere.* Every light switch, every lamp. I made my way toward the panic room inside her walk-in closet and caught one on the shower taps.

Sneaky, kinky fuckers.

I wouldn't *endorse* such behavior, but the immediate punch of anger in my gut was a helluva surprise. When it came to my Blondie... no one got to get a peeksie of our billionaire's beautiful body but *us.*

It was a good thing she and Joey had the sense to leave and never come back, but bad news bears for me, because all those bugs were transmitting somewhere right now, which meant *they*—whoever *they* were—knew I was here.

Time to get a move on, Locke.

I input the code I'd memorized and when the door slid open, I grinned like I was a techy *James Bond* in black cotton sweatpants. *Feckin cool.*

No time for grinning. Evidence tampering first, then I had to get the fuck out of dodge. An interesting American saying I had no idea the origins of, but I liked it. It was cheeky.

Firing up her systems, I looked around the room for any outward clues of its purpose. Other than the state-of-the-art set-up, nothing—no bulletin board with red strings attached to a bunch of scary photos of creepy pedo bad guys. Just a genuine panic room for a scared billionaire princess to the untrained eye. That was good. The incriminating stuff was in this bad boy.

Plugging in the flash drive with the program to eat the data from the inside, I started my work. Hard drives couldn't just be wiped. The new ones couldn't be erased with magnets or reformatting, making them tasty little nuggets to crack. We didn't have the ability to shred the metal into teensy little shards so the data was unrecoverable, so fire today would have to do.

The malware was just a way to scramble all the files on the off chance the fire didn't destroy the system. Another little failsafe because I was a destructive fucker, but a thorough destructive fucker.

I soaked the floor with a tiny bottle of propane—a special blend with no odorant added, undetectable by any fire-sniffing dogs if the FBI used them. Agent Smith evidently had it out for Blondie, so I wasn't taking any chances. Another little treat from Jediah that had cost a pretty penny, but my billionaire girlfriend could pay me back later with kisses and another pegging.

My girlfriend—was that what I was calling her now? Seemed a bit amateurish, like we weren't criminal baddies with two other boyfriends taking on the mafia underworld, but what did I know? I'd never had one before.

Enough chatter in my head—I had to speed up this process. I opened up the back of the computer tower and doused the last of the system with the propane and took out the lighter. This beautiful setup wasn't going to take long to become a blaze of glory, and I had a beautiful woman's bed to return to.

I grabbed a fresh sheet out of the linen closet that likely cost more than my bloody apartment back in Dublin and rolled it tight into a rope, leading it into the panic room from the closet. Luckily, it was Egyptian cotton and not silk —silk was a bitch to burn. I tucked the detonator in the sheet, which I'd flick on once safely in the elevator, and admired my handiwork for a quick moment before leaving it behind.

Walking out of the bedroom on quick feet, I halted at the reflection of tiny headlights headed down the condo drive through the twelve-foot windows. Two sets, speeding down the lane toward us, screeching into the condo building parking lot.

An esteemed resident getting home late at night?

At three a.m. on a Wednesday? Bloody unlikely.

Running back to the panic room, I struck a match and lit the sheet manually, then I raced to the double doors leading down to the garage. We were officially out of time. I launched into the elevator, pounded the button, and willed it to go fecking faster than two kilometers an hour.

Come on, come on...

Kellan and Aaron knew how to handle themselves, but I had no idea who was down there—the FBI? Alvarez's men? Kellan's fucked-up family? Some unknown party we'd pissed off just by breathing funny?

Adrenaline returned like a fresh hit of fun, and I let it sweep through me like Superman on red kryptonite. Whoever they were, the bad guys were here.

Time to show the pecker-heads what we're made of.

CHAPTER 11

Kellan

*T*hey'd been watching the building.

It was the only way my brothers could have found us in this position. I made sure we weren't followed on our way here. So, they'd been laying in wait, hoping for... What, exactly?

The claws of fear dug into my chest when I realized why. They'd been watching for Hillary to return. My tenuous relationship with her over the last six years hadn't been announced, but it wasn't a secret, either. Antonio had known she was someone of importance. A person they could use to get to me. Here they were, finally hitting the jackpot —had they bargained they'd get two of their actual targets?

Or was this a lucky coincidence of fuckery we'd now have to fight our way out of?

The abrupt metallic grate of a pistol being cocked resounded through the cab of the vehicle. I shifted my weight only slightly to catch Aaron in my periphery, positioning his gun against the window behind me.

Lauchlan's gaze hadn't left the group in front of us, a calculating gleam in the sea-glass of his eyes. I scanned our surroundings. Two SUVs, three men in each, no other way out but through. At least, no other way out in a vehicle, and I wasn't risking our men in here by commanding them to leave our protective cage. None of my vehicles were ordinary models—bulletproof glass and reinforced steel made them harder to penetrate. But only for so long.

It wouldn't matter, anyway. The muffled, tinny sound of the fire alarm several floors of concrete above us would rouse the entire building. Lauchlan had to set the explosion in the condo before the fire department showed up, or we'd have more than our capture to deal with—my Killer would be compromised too.

My brothers *were* intent on capture, no doubt—Antonio would have already set up a torture chamber with our names on it. He wouldn't lose the opportunity to make Aaron and me suffer for our insolence. Lauchlan would be dead before we made it out of this building. Just another casualty in Antonio's many battles for ultimate power.

We could play a game of chicken and see if they'd back down. Jonah would be smart enough to save his own skin and try another day, but Mical would leap at the chance to knock me down a peg, even at his own peril, driven by bloodlust and the undisguised envy he'd harbored for me all these years. As if being the prodigal son was a position anyone actually wanted, instead of being cursed with.

I reconsidered my thoughts about leaving the vehicle. We all had guns, and Hillary had ten of her personal vehicles in this garage—we could use them as cover and hope the fire department showed up in time to rescue us from an actual fire. Lauchlan assured us the fire in the elevator was just to trigger the suppression system, which would immediately put it out, but the fire department would show up anyway as a precaution.

It would be pointless to make it out of a gunfight alive, only to get burned to a crisp in the moments after.

Without blinking or looking down into his lap, Lauchlan dialed a number on the cellphone and pressed the call button. A light click resonated through the line, followed by dead air.

"Explosion activated," he declared nonchalantly, as if this was our most pressing concern at the moment. "One job done for the night."

I drew my attention back to my brothers and their men. No movement yet on their part or on ours. My brothers' beady little eyes assessed us through the mild tint of their windows a good hundred feet away. I couldn't see them clearly, but I could feel the laser beams of their stares burn through me even at this distance.

Lauchlan's rustling beside me captured my curiosity. He jutted his ski-masked chin toward our guests, who were no doubt getting restless at our lack of movement. "Why don't we play a little fire with fire with them too?"

Before I could ask what the fuck he meant, he held his backpack tight to his chest and crouched, opening the passenger side door and rolling low to the ground. Terror gripped my heart in its claws, but I couldn't stop him—he was already outside of the mediocre protection of our vehicle.

"Cover me!" he yelled as he ran toward the nearest vehicle, Hillary's prized Jaguar.

"Fuck!" I shouted, ducking down as gunfire echoed across the cement landscape. A spray of bullets rained down over Lauchlan's previous position beside the car and riddled the still open door with holes. The abrupt pings of metal on metal added to the cacophony as Antonio's men continued shooting at the Jag instead of my truck.

I couldn't keep my eyes on the crazy fucker and still protect his ass from becoming my brothers' newest shooting dummy. The acidic scent of fear-tinged sweat dripped down my brows and soaked into the mask covering my face, distracting me and forcing my well-aimed bullet to veer too far to the right. *Fuck!*

"COVER ME I SAID!" Lauchlan screamed through the noise, and I mentally castrated him before lowering both Aaron's and my windows so we could return fire. If he died tonight, he'd rob me of the chance to kill him myself. That thought spurred me on, improving my aim to distract Antonio's goons long enough to get Lauchlan some cover.

The vehicles didn't come any closer, my brothers and their crews choosing instead to open their doors and shift their positions, shooting at us now as well. Three bullets embedded into the modified glass windshield.

Fuck, fuck, fuck. Stupid, fucking cu-

"To your left, Kellan!"

Aaron's warning came just in time and I leaned into my years of training, hand blindly shooting leftward while pivoting my torso to the right. A bullet smashed through my driver's side mirror, just as my own bullet sunk between the eyes of the man who'd shot at me.

One down, five to go. Resolve flooded into my bloodstream like a potent hit of the many drugs my father sold. We would not let ourselves get killed here tonight. Aaron, Lauchlan, and I would make it out to hold Hillary in our arms once again, and hopefully we'd be wearing the blood of my brothers as a trophy.

Pulling open the center console, I grabbed the cartridge stockpile to reload my weapon and tossed two back at Aaron to do the same. I caught Lauchlan's head bobbing between the Jaguar and another one of Hillary's vehicles, what looked to be a clear plastic hose dangling from his mouth.

When we made it out alive, I was taking a page out of Aaron's book and skinning the fucker alive for this stunt. *Stupid, fucking cu—*

Sirens pierced the night air, barely making a dent in the chaotic sound of the parking garage, but loud enough to know they were close. We needed to get the fuck out of here now. I no longer had FBI protection, and I had no desire to test my morals on whether I'd be willing to kill a firefighter to save my skin. My brothers wouldn't lose a second's sleep over killing an innocent, but I had enough fucked-up shit on my conscience.

Aaron's bullets continued to fly behind me from the rear passenger window, protecting Lauchlan while I continued to shoot at Mical's vehicle, which still had three men defending it. I shot the hand of the goon who was firing and the blood spatter ruined the pristine white paint job as he fell to the ground in agony.

"We must leave, *compañero!*" Aaron's normally stoic voice had risen two octaves. Was he hurt? I couldn't pull my attention from the battleground in front of us long enough to see. My stomach curdled at the thought of him surviving Carmen's attack, only to be killed by my brothers instead in a cruel twist of fate. I would not let him die.

Another hail of bullets embedded in the glass. It wouldn't hold for much longer.

Lauchlan's head bobbed between the Jaguar again, his voice muffled but urgent as our enemies reloaded their weapons.

"Alright, fuckers, when I say three, I need yeh to trust me. You're going to move out on this side of the vehicle, stay low, and get into that Benz over there." He dipped his head toward the silver Mercedes GLS, which had a few errant holes, but was still intact. "Get in the backseat. I'll take it from there."

Another stream of bullets came our way, this time into the Jaguar in an attempt to take out Lauchlan.

Mother-fucking *cunt*. Who the fuck did he think he was, risking his life—our lives—for this stupid little show? I channeled my compounding fear into unbridled rage and turned to return rapid fire through the open window. My raw anger at him, this situation, my brothers, and my father spilled out into a blood-blistering ball of fury. I shouted at him over the din of the gunfire.

"I'm going to fucking kill you with my bare hands, Lauch—"

A trail of blinding fire interrupted my tirade and lit up the garage as a glowing orange snake moved toward the vehicles of our attackers at a rapid pace. Shock registered on their faces through the splintered glass of the windshield, the men retreating into the vehicles as the fire burned closer and closer.

What in the fuck—

"NOW!" Lauchlan shouted, racing toward the escape vehicle himself. Aaron let out a curse—of pain or of exasperation—as he pushed open his door and crouched low, weaving through the vehicles after him.

There weren't enough expletives in the world to filter my rage, but I said every word I knew and forced my large body over the center console and into the passenger seat, crouching low as Aaron had and tucking myself behind the destroyed Jaguar before following the two men in front of me. Surprisingly, no sound followed me, the symphony of gunfire deadened by the sizzling of dangerous flames.

Lauchlan gunned the engine as I climbed into the backseat next to Aaron, the two of us crammed like sardines in a space designed for small women. Aaron's grimace told me all I needed to know about his pain, and I swore again. If we made it out of here alive, I was going to deliver a lesson Lauchlan would never forget. He wouldn't be able to sit down for a month without shedding tears, and I would make the marks so deep, he'd have the scars of my palm forever imprinted on his cheeks.

Screeching the tires, our crazed Irishman drove straight through the blaze he'd created, veering through the tight space to the right of the SUV blockade my truck would have never fit between.

Panicked shouts in Spanish followed, but the flames had already caught up to one of the vehicles. My brothers were too preoccupied with their own mortality to follow us. We left the brilliant colors of well-fed fire behind in the rearview mirror, as the flashing red and yellow lights from emergency vehicles greeted us on the other side.

Lauchlan didn't stop, maneuvering the sleek car through the newly erected barrier and down the sidewalk of the condo building, evading the firetrucks and the many condo residents who watched in confusion. Without a word, he tore out of the parking lot and sped into the night, pulling off an escape I'd never have accomplished. He smoothly switched lanes and took side roads often. The three of us remained on full alert for followers. Finally, he pulled into the chain-linked lot of a small mechanic's garage on the other side of town.

Sliding out of the cramped seat, I slammed the door shut and stalked around to Lauchlan's driver side, yanked him out of his seat by his shoulders, and shoved him against the metal door.

"You fucking cunt," I growled, unable to see anything but his widened eyes through the now soaked cotton of his mask. Blinded by my ire, a dark crimson colored my view, the relentless rage taking over my body as its own demon. "You fucking cunt!"

Lauchlan shuddered within my hold, a tight grimace entering his eyes as he uttered a sharp breath of pain. Releasing him, I let his body fall to the ground, where he landed on the cracked pavement in a heap. My palms felt sticky and wet. I squinted in the muted light of the street lamp at the blood coating my fingers.

"Kellan." Aaron's stern tone broke through my examination. "*Rojo* was shot, and saved us from a very unpleasant situation." He gingerly bent down to guide the man back to standing, his own pain flickering through his eyes. "Perhaps you should thank him for his quick thinking instead of adding insult to his injuries."

My fists clenched at my sides, mimicking the fierce pump of blood through my limbs. Aaron was right. This man, this infuriating, irritating man, had saved us tonight with his particular brand of crazy. He was not the source of my anger, not the dominant source. Antonio was.

My resources were tapped, my relationships dissolved, and I could no longer keep the people I cared about safe. Where I was once the protector, I was now the biggest liability. A fallen king.

"Are you all right?" The words burned on my tongue, but I pressed on, moving toward Lauchlan and examining the bloodied tissue of his upper arm, the darkened blood blending in with the black fabric of his sweatshirt.

Tired, bloodshot eyes peered back at me. "A graze, mate. Barely felt a thing." By the shudders wracking his body with the fading adrenaline, it was a lie. Judging by the wound's location, he would be fine, but he was going to be sore for a while.

"I'm driving. Let's get home," I announced instead of pressing it further. I opened the passenger door for my two injured companions to get back in. "And let's hope tonight was worth it."

If tonight's events protected Hillary from further incrimination, I'd consider it a win. As it was, a documented shootout in the private garage of her condo building was going to raise a hell of a lot of questions. With our masks, unregistered vehicle and guns, and undocumented connection to this case, we were unlikely to be tied into the evidence, but it would up their scrutiny of Hillary, and they'd put her under more surveillance. We wouldn't be able to keep the warehouse a secret much longer.

Exhaustion leached through my bones and into my bloodstream as we pulled into the private bay of the warehouse, the light of dawn following close behind. I'd make a call to get the vehicle destroyed later today. We needed to patch Lauchlan up, recount the shitshow of a night to Killer, and shower.

I'd scrub away my failures in the hot water. Then, once my body had a moment's rest, I'd plan my exit. My time had come.

We were all showered, seated in the common space, with the gloomy haze of dawn on the horizon. Hillary had waited for us to get cleaned up before demanding the answers she was owed.

We'd rolled the hospital bed out of the bedroom and into the main area so Aaron could rest lying down. Lauchlan and Hillary sat on the couch, his arm clean and bandaged in a light sling, and I had spread out in the oversized chair at the edge of the fireplace.

I grew more heated with each explanation, exhaustion warring with the cold fury flooding through my veins, so icy it blistered hot. The lack of missions for the FBI and Antonio, and no real gym on site was messing with my need to physically release all of this pent-up frustration. The calm collectedness I dug into when adrenaline was high and my mind was clear was absent, replaced by a horde of warring emotions I didn't have a name for.

I shouldn't have hit Lauchlan. It was a poor reaction. The rage inside me begged to discharge, but unleashing it on my team wasn't the way. Just another reason I was a danger to them. I was losing the grasp on my control, and I didn't like the man I was becoming.

More so than usual.

The prickling sensation of being observed crept up my neck besides the blistering heat. My gaze rose from the floor to seek the source. Aaron. As Lauchlan regaled Hillary with how he set off the firebomb, Aaron had fixed his attention on me.

His amber eyes were neutral, as usual, but ringed with an unsettling intensity usually reserved for Killer. I stared into them, unable to maintain my neutrality. The defeat and immutable frustration bloomed to the surface and his steady presence absorbed every one without comment.

When I was about to break the silent staring contest, he opened his mouth to speak, his stare growing more penetrating instead of retreating.

"Kellan is wound very tight by tonight's events," he said simply, the rich tone and crisp cadence interrupting Lauchlan's story. "As am I. It would be to all our benefit to relieve some of this pressure before we rest, yes?"

The gold in his eyes darkened to pitch. "Perhaps a punishment is in order. I believe I am still in your debt, *compañero*. Is tonight the time to honor it?" He uttered the words softly, smoothly, but he might as well have screamed through a megaphone with the way my adrenaline spiked and blood flowed to the crown of my cock.

I couldn't break the hold he had on me. I heard Lauchlan's intake of breath, and felt Hillary's stare trained on the two of us, but they were observers of this challenge between the Colombian heir and me.

Yes, sex was a safe way to unleash the demons inside of me tonight. But I had to control the tableau of bodies—they all had to submit to me in order to complete the exorcism. For their safety, and my own.

Drawing a deep breath, I tore my gaze away from him and finally recognized the two others in the room—the two others I was deeply attracted to. I knew the landscape of their bodies, the feel of their greedy holes wrapped around me, how they surrendered themselves to satisfy my soul, and my dick swelled even more.

Instead of confusion, I saw only interest. Intrigue. Lust.

I welcomed the gift this man had just presented to me, and I would not look a gift horse in the mouth. Resolutely, I nodded my head and issued my first order.

"*Caperucita Roja*," I commanded calmly, waving a palm in Lauchlan's direction. "You're going to deliver Rodriguez's punishment. Come here."

The Irishman's cheeks blushed as red as his hair. "Erm —what's that, mate?"

My Killer cocked her head at me, delicate brows curving into a confused frown. "I think he's handled enough tonight, Viking, let's just—"

"No." I barked the single word out with an angry bite. "This guy went off script tonight, and even though it saved our lives, it just as well could have killed us all. *Caperucita Roja* is getting his punishment too."

I glared at the man's handsome face through narrowed eyes, letting my true feelings of fear, wrath, and resentment for my family's decisions rise to the surface for a flicker of a moment before I swallowed them into the pit of my stomach.

I knew what it was like to want to save the people in my care. It was the silk thread I walked on every day, but I'd learned years ago the unfairness of life was not my problem. We worked with the hand we were dealt and had to let anything else go along the way. These two men had risked their lives, but I couldn't let them risk something like this again. It would destroy Killer, and what destroyed Killer would destroy me.

Understanding bloomed in the soft brown of Aaron's irises, and a calm smile stretched the sexy pout of his lips. He acknowledged what he was agreeing to and was submitting to my needs.

A frisson of hope hit the surface of my heart at his trust. My Killer loved Aaron, and it would have broken her to lose him, but a part of me might have fractured too.

We lived a lonely life, where few men could relate to the stress and pressures of being the groomed heir of an evil man's son. I understood that part of Aaron's psyche in a way Hillary could only ever have a taste of. The numb casual way we viewed the depraved parts of society as a means of survival. The constant pull between two worlds eventually destroyed your ability to care about much at all.

He was an equal. If I believed in spiritual crap, I'd call him a kindred spirit. If we had more time, I wanted to learn more about that side of him.

But we didn't have more time. We had tonight.

Resolve skimmed across his features before he dipped his head in a solemn nod. "I accept, *compañero.*"

My chest swelled with pride and anticipation, but I tamped down my feelings. I turned to the pain-in-the-ass Irishman instead, head cocked and eyebrows lifted in curiosity. Another man who had no business taking up my thoughts, and yet, the green-eyed taunting fucker continued to live there rent free.

He was the perfect puppet to carry out Aaron's "punishment."

"You have a hell of a lot of proving yourself to do. But you proved enough to me today to trust you beyond your cock."

Pouty lips pursed in response, and a slight blush crept over his cheekbones. He nodded his head in recognition before breaking out into the signature smug grin that made me want to kiss him and spank his ass raw.

"Aye, Conan. As long as you keep trusting my cock too, yeh?"

Fucking brat. I'd use that against him here in a second. He needed a little lesson in submission too.

Through this exchange, Hill remained silent, watching the three of us with tired eyes and a brittle expression. Like us, she'd walked through the ten circles this past week, and the toll it took on her body and mind was visible.

I'd see if I could distract her from her pain for a little while. She could watch, but she wasn't allowed to touch.

"Adjust the bed, so he's lying down." I commanded Lauchlan, who still stood next to Aaron's bedside. Without hesitation, he fiddled with the buttons with his good hand on the side of the hospital bed to slowly level it down to a flat position.

"Take off his boxers."

Questioning brows lifted on both men, and I met a side-eye from Hill, but Lauchlan did as I commanded, slowly rolling the black fabric down Aaron's thick thighs, exposing his swelling dick as he went.

Aaron's skin was free from blood and sweat, and the thick gauze across half of his stomach had been removed, exposing a vicious line of violent, angry stitches. I clenched my fist in anger, and tore my gaze from the evidence of his pain. Instead, I focused on the stiff cock in front of me.

I'd felt that cock in Hill's pussy, the thick mushroom head kissing the top of mine inside her channel, the ridges rubbing over mine every time I thrust against him. My own cock thickened in my pajama pants, painfully pressing against the cotton.

I'd seen all of Aaron's body in the shower after our threesome—each sculpted plane of muscle lean and honed for lethal use, unlike my body sculpted for brute strength and violence. He held a raw masculinity while remaining subtly soft. His thick dark lashes and pillowy lips made him seem more like a model than a trained killer.

Fucking hot.

Lauchlan looked expectantly at me, awaiting his next instruction. I leaned back against the wall, crossed my ankles, and folded my arms in a poor attempt to look casual. With Aaron splayed naked and vulnerable before us, I was anything but.

I dipped my head toward the gym bag by the door. "Grab the resistance bands in my bag. Four of them."

Curiosity sparked in Killer's blue eyes. She could see where this was going—and her lack of protest meant she was allowing it to continue. Not that I would let her stop me at this point. We were seeing this through regardless of how she felt about it. It was my punishment to deliver.

Lauchlan did as I asked, accepting he was now my gofer. He pulled out the varying colors of thick elastic and held them up in his hands questioningly.

"Spread his limbs and tie them to each corner of the bed," I directed, pressing my back harder against the wall to relieve some of the compression in my pants. It wasn't working.

"Are we participating in another torture porn, Kell-Bell?" He grinned and proceeded with his task. Hillary watched his awkward one-handed attempt for the first band and then stepped in to assist, tenderly securing the elastic fabric around Aaron's wrists and ankles, spreading him open for me before standing back to become an observer once again.

Aaron didn't resist, accepting his fate without objection, his cock visibly harder with each tie. He winced when Hillary and Lauchlan moved his right leg into place, but his expression remained stoic otherwise. Completely neutral, except for the steel shaft jutting up with a slight curve toward his belly button.

Aaron was attractive fully clothed, but naked, he could take a man's breath away. Jagged. Solid. Strong. Masculine with the most subtle touch of softness. I wouldn't get to touch him tonight, but it was a denial of self, my punishment for failing to act. Lauchlan had gotten us out tonight—not me. Shame threatened to smother my lust, but

I buried it for now. I had plenty of time to dissolve in its acid later.

Untying my pants, I pulled out my cock, pre-cum weeping at the tip, and stroked down my length with a lazy pull. I wished I had a camera to film him, to capture the eroticism of the moment to relive again.

When I wasn't around anymore to share it with them.

"Look at me," I commanded, drawing Aaron's gaze to my own. His stare fell to my exposed erection, watching it with unveiled interest as I continued to relieve some of the growing pressure.

"Eyes on me, *Guapo.*"

Heat flared to life in his eyes, transforming his neutrality to unfiltered lust.

"Kiss him," I ordered Lauchlan, not breaking my eye contact with Aaron. "Mouth first."

Surprise entered Aaron's expression, but that was it. Just acceptance of what was to come. Submitting to me. Trusting me. Warmth spread through my chest. The man I'd been coveting was surrendering his will, a gift he only ever gave to Hillary. And now, he was giving it to me.

Desperate need roiled at the base of my spine, and I tugged on my cock even harder.

The red-haired pawn hesitated. "Er-might want to confirm that one with him first, mate. I love some good foreplay, but I'm a consent kind of guy."

The Colombian kept his eyes on me, locked in an erotic staring contest while I palmed my erection and his remained untouched. His reflected lust shot icy tingles through my spine, piercing my cock with both pain and pleasure.

"Kiss me again, *Rojo,*" he commanded, the words catching in his throat.

Again? Interesting. I'd fucked many men in my lifetime, and I'd enjoyed most—but these two men touching each other could become my greatest weakness. The building desire at the tableau in front of me was unbearable, blisteringly hot against my skin.

My pawn moved into place, stopping on the other side of Aaron's head, not blocking my view.

"Hey, Roboto." Lauchlan leaned over just inches from Aaron's lips. Eyes dark, his own pajama pants had swelled with need. He enjoyed taking direction, my little subbie. "You like it gentle or rough, Daddy? Conan aims to torture yeh, but I'll make it good for you."

Fuck.

I'd watched this man's interest in the sexy mafia heir since we'd all been thrown together. He was doing it on my command, but he was as into Aaron as I was.

My student didn't answer, choosing instead to lift his head to meet Lauchlan's lips. The searing kiss set my insides on fire as if I was the one on the receiving end. Despite Lauchlan being my torture agent, Aaron took complete control of the kiss, pressing hard into his lips and forcing his mouth open, exploring it with his tongue.

It was just a kiss, yet it was one of the hottest things I'd ever seen.

Hillary settled into a chair in my periphery, and I tore away for a split second to glimpse her. She wasn't watching me at all. Her breath had caught as she fixated on the scene before us with wide eyes.

Good. We could all offer her an escape from her pain and worry tonight. It might be the last gift in the world I could give her.

I turned my attention back to the men before us kissing like their lives depended on it. Lauchlan cupped Aaron's cheek as they sucked each other's tongues in a way I'd imagined them both sucking my cock.

"Stop."

I shifted my weight from the wall to standing, and walked toward the bed as they heeded my order. Their attention remained locked on each other though, heavy breaths and flushed cheeks. Judging by the lust in their expressions, even without my intervention, it was only a matter of time before they fucked.

My chest twinged at the thought of the three of them together without me. How I felt about that didn't matter right now. Aaron's lesson was just beginning, and Lauchlan was still the one to deliver it, regardless if he was enjoying himself.

"Use that mouth on his body. Slowly."

Lauchlan immediately complied, pressing his lips to the column of Aaron's throat, laving a trail down to where Aaron's shoulder met the base of his neck. He nipped the skin there, and a visible tremor spread through Aaron's body.

"You like biting, Daddy? Good to know," Lauchlan cooed, continuing his kisses down Aaron's chest.

I'd enjoyed these bodies separately for different reasons. Watching the two of them share pleasure like this was on another level altogether—and it locked something in place inside me. I needed to protect Hillary, but I needed to protect them too.

We were my Queen's men, and I couldn't risk them getting caught in my crossfire.

"Suck his nipples," I ordered, and Lauchlan latched his lips over the right one, sucking it into a hard peak before giving the other the same treatment.

Aaron groaned deep in his throat at the contact, and his body shuddered as pre-cum dripped from the tip of his cock in response.

My cock was sticky and hot, the arousing scene setting my blood ablaze. I moved toward Hillary and lifted her off the chair, spinning her around, her back to my front, and tugged at the waistband of her silk shorts. She allowed me to undo the tie and shrug them off her hips as we both watched Lauchlan's ministrations and Aaron's tempting dick twitch with every movement.

"Hips," I commanded Lauchlan, and he moved past the stitches across Aaron's abdomen to kiss the jutting hip bones beside the corded V of his Adonis belt.

I clasped my hands around my Killer's waist and tugged us backward, collapsing into the chair behind me. Pushing the fabric triangle of her silk panties aside, I pulled her down on top of my cock in one rough tug, thrusting into her soaked channel and letting out a rough groan at the contact.

The resulting moan caught all of our attention. Three pairs of wide eyes locked on her closed ones as she whimpered in pleasure.

The vise grip of her hot pussy shot electricity up my spine and stars burst behind my eyes. For the briefest moment, I allowed myself to get lost in the lust of her body and their performance, every muscle aching for release.

Tonight was the only guarantee I had in my life. I was a dead man walking—this could be the last time I felt her around me, and the last time I had to experience genuine pleasure without it being tainted.

Did she know I loved her? Could she feel it in the way I cupped her breasts, the way I kissed the back of her neck like she was my most cherished possession? Maybe I'd be better at showing it in another life.

"Bounce on me," I urged her, the roughness of my voice betraying my need. I brought my fingers to her clit, providing the friction she was so desperate for, and felt her gush around me even more. "Ride me until you come, Killer."

Without a word, she complied, slamming down on my cock as I teased her clit with hard circles. The room was now saturated with the smell of sweat and sex.

Turning back to the two men, I gave Lauchlan the direction he'd been waiting for. "Put him in your mouth, and suck."

Pouty lips closed over the thick shaft, and Aaron's growl of pleasure shot through my limbs like an explosion.

"Don't let him come," I ordered between pants. Hillary had ramped up her writhing, causing the inevitable tingle of an intense orgasm at the base of my spine.

Lauchlan didn't stop sucking, but he changed his pace, slowly licking up the underside of Aaron's shaft and lapping each ball into his mouth with an audible slurp.

Whether it was minutes or seconds, I couldn't keep track with Killer bouncing on top of me, and my calves and glutes cramping hard with all of my efforts not to come.

When she tipped over the final edge, her scream of release combined with the tightening of her walls around my cock. I finally allowed my release, flooding her with every drop of cum, and my body melted into the chair as she collapsed back against my chest.

Lauchlan abruptly pulled off Aaron's cock, and his body convulsed as jets of white cum spurted like an erupting volcano.

"Lauchlan!" I barked, too sated to be truly angry. "The whole point was to edge him, you idiot."

"Sorry, boss," Lauchlan panted, grasping the edge of the hospital bed in a tight grip. "I've never had a hand's free fuck before. Bloody hell."

He stood and faced us, revealing the front of his pants wet with his own cum. "Guess that brings new meaning to a circle jerk, huh?"

I stared at him through lowered eyes, my gaze drifting to the relaxed and satisfied man on the hospital bed, and the woman curled against my chest.

What a ludicrous life of lust and lies we were all living.

Despite the well of disgust still deep within my belly and the permanent stress still stitched into the fabric of my skin, I laughed.

Fuck this man. He was the only one in the world who could get me to laugh so freely. My body shook from the chuckles, the deep booming resonance filling the room, hard enough to bring tears to my eyes. Hillary giggled into my pecs, Lauchlan smirked with mischievous mirth dancing in his eyes, and Aaron snickered as he stared at the ceiling in a sated stupor.

The laughter was a temporary balm on the shit to come, but we had all needed that fuck to release the demons of the day. Despite the impromptu release goaded on by a man who knew me too well, I could admit I liked the shared sex.

I kissed Hillary's temple and held her tighter to my chest, unwilling to let her go. I needed one more night with her in my arms before I was forced to walk away forever.

CHAPTER 12

Hillary

"Hillary Lane, the wealthiest woman in Sequoia and number 33 on the Forbes 'Wealthiest Women of the World,' was seen exiting Carlisle's 78th Precinct, her lawyer Weston Williams, of Tracy Williams Law, in tow. Now, why would Hillary Lane need a lawyer to visit the police station? This Carlisle columnist has heard a delicious rumor she's the primary suspect in the FBI's Mutilation Mistress case, and sources have confirmed there is a warrant out for the seizure of her digital property. Does this have anything to do with the condo fire reported in her building last night? Stay tuned, Carlisle Corrupted, for we have our very own scandal on our hands. Details to come!"

Lucky did his best to lighten the tone of the gossip column in the Carlisle Tribune as he read it aloud in a sunny, feminine Irish brogue over breakfast. He was in decent spirits despite his injury, but the attempt fell flat as the four of us lapsed into complete silence over toast and coffee.

The shared sex last night had been incredible—unexpected and uninhibited. Had we all come together under different circumstances, it would have been a beautiful reckoning, an awakening. I'd been blissfully satisfied by the time I'd fallen asleep between Aaron and Lucky, but my heart was poisoned with a deep-seated melancholy this morning. Our private love nest was just a distraction. It didn't matter if the chemistry and the feelings behind it were real and raw, we had no time to explore what we could be.

Aaron and I had helped Lauchlan strip bare so Kellan could clean out his wound and replace his bandages. After an exhausted shower, we'd all collapsed into bed.

It was now late morning, and my phone had been pinging with texts since dawn. From Gabby at Aaron's— well, mine now—company, and from Marty at my own. Apparently, reporters had camped out in front of both offices overnight, hoping they'd catch me for a comment in the morning. When news broke of the fire, another set of reporters arrived in the parking lot, shoving cameras into the fire crews' faces while they were still putting out the pockets Lucky had created.

As far as I knew, the arson had been effective. My penthouse condo was burnt to a crisp, even the glass windows were scorched on the top floor. To my relief, there'd been no reported casualties, which was the only positive outcome of the evening.

When the men had arrived back here, smelling of gunpowder and Lucky dripping with blood, I'd immediately called Sammy to arrange for a security detail for our group whenever we traveled, and for both office locations, knowing this was just the beginning of the media fallout.

Reporters—most of them—were carnivorous vultures, circling above and snacking on the fear and hesitation of anyone they could catch in their claws. I was a target on a good day, let alone when I'd been painted as an alleged villain.

Now, I was officially a mark of Antonio and the demon twins, in an effort to get to Kellan. An unexpected development, yet completely predictable. Kellan's punishment would maximize pain before Antonio killed him. And, to Antonio's knowledge, I was the only other person he cared about. Our Viking had done everything within his power to keep Cam and Travis a secret from his father, but if they were discovered, he'd kill them all without a second thought just to torture Kellan.

I scrolled through my phone, barely tasting my coffee, when the barrage of text messages from Winter sent my stomach plummeting through the floor.

9:07 am: Winter: Hill! I just saw the news! What is going on!?

10:43 am: Winter: You know you can tell me anything, right?

11:31 am: Winter: Seriously, Hillary, I need to know you're okay. Call me ASAP.

My gaze rose to Kellan seated on the other side of the table. Skin sallow, his knuckles were bruised and bloody from his training on the single punching bag installed in one of the empty rooms. The sunken eyes of a haunted man rose to meet mine. He hadn't come to bed with us, and he was already brooding at the kitchen table when we woke. He was so close to the edge of despair. Losing his hidden family—the only one he had—would destroy him entirely.

My heart physically hurt with the hoard of secrets I'd kept from my best friend. She'd be sick with worry, but I wouldn't risk her life, no matter what the cost to me.

Hillary: I'm fine. I mean, I'm going to be fine. But you need to keep your distance right now. Kellan's compromised, and we can't risk Antonio learning a thing about your family. Promise me you'll lie low for a little while, at least until this blows over?

Her response pinged through immediately, as if she'd been waiting by her phone for my text. She probably had. Like me, Winter was fiercely protective of her people.

Winter: You're kidding, right? They're accusing you of torture! WTF is going on?

A burst of air escaped my lips; Winter wouldn't let this slide. I planned to tell her everything, but what I needed most was time.

Hillary: I will tell you *everything.* Promise. But right now, let me keep you safe, okay?

Winter: As long as he's keeping *you* safe. I'll kill him myself if he doesn't.

My snort interrupted Kellan's forlorn staring into space, but I just shook my head when he cocked a questioning eyebrow. Winter was feisty, but sweet. Her version of murder would be to poison his casserole. If I didn't love the man in front of me, I'd encourage it.

Hillary: Noted. Love you, Sweets.

Winter: Love you. Tell Kellan we love him too.

I wouldn't. Not now, at least. Kellan didn't need another group of people to become a martyr for. He was already trying so hard to sacrifice himself for us. Of the four criminals around this table and our current shitshow state of affairs, I was most worried about him.

This man's tattoos were his protective shield, glue that kept the myriad of spider-webbed cracks from breaking him apart. The glue was failing. The defining words inscribed on his knuckles were too marred with scars and blood to protect him any longer.

Overcome by the jagged lump forming in my throat, I reached out to clasp the hand of "hope" and brushed my thumb across the ragged skin. He gently removed his hand from mine, then leaned over, placing a chaste kiss on my temple before standing and leaving the table.

My frowning gaze followed him to the dishwasher, where he silently placed the plate inside, then returned down the hallway to the bedroom, closing the door behind him.

The burner phone vibrated in my hand, tearing my attention away from Kellan's retreating form. Agent Smith's name popped up on the screen. Of course. We'd been waiting for her call.

"This is Hillary," I answered coolly. Lucky and Aaron's heads popped up from their morning paper sections in unison.

"Hillary, Agent Smith," the woman announced. "Where are you right now?"

I turned in my chair and faced the wide-open room between the kitchenette and the makeshift living space, the sound of my voice carrying through the echo chamber. "Well, as I'm sure you're aware, Agent Smith, vandals destroyed my home last night. Luckily, I was visiting a friend. I've been informed that my entire floor is a crime scene?"

I posed it as a question, maintaining my innocence until proven otherwise.

"You are correct, Ms. Lane. Your condo is, in fact, a crime scene. And thanks to whoever set your place on fire, we'll have full access to whatever evidence is in there without the need of that pesky warrant."

A deep grimace set into the lines of my forehead. The thought of complete strangers trolling through my private quarters and documents set me on edge. Lucky's plan and execution had a ninety percent chance of working, so I could only hope the digital files—the crucial, incriminating ones— were completely disintegrated. My grimace morphed into a devious smirk at the image of Agent Smith discovering my well-stocked toy chest.

Weston's advice floated in the air. *The best defense is a good offense.* We'd be rolling out that offense soon, but not today, and certainly not to Agent Smith.

"Agent, for whatever reason, you continue to treat me as if I'm a criminal. Change your tone, or change the agent on this case, because I only have so much patience. I'm the victim here, and currently homeless. Might I suggest spending your time chasing *actual* criminals, and come to me when you find something useful."

Her derisive snort resounded through the line. "I'd hardly call the richest woman in the state 'homeless.' Might *I* suggest a nice motel in the area, so you can get a taste of how us peasants live? We'll be talking, Ms. Lane."

Miserable cow. Perhaps she would find some joy from the Excalibur 3000, or the Purrfect Pussy Licker. I'd let her keep them to take the edge off.

I turned in my chair to three men standing in a makeshift row, their piercing gazes penetrating my layers of thinned patience. Kellan must have come back in while I was on the call. The storm in his eyes looked more precarious than usual.

"Agent Smith, threatening me again," I explained casually, though my pulse betrayed me. "We're going to need to move forward with our plan as soon as we can."

Standing, I walked over to Aaron and gently wrapped my arms around his sides, careful with the stitches still healing. "I don't want to rush you, but how soon will you be able to be in the spotlight?"

"Within a week," he answered succinctly, cupping my cheek. I closed my eyes and leaned into its warmth for the briefest second before peering into the amber of his eyes.

"You're sure?" I searched the liquid honey for signs of weakness, trepidation—any sign he wasn't ready or able to handle what came next.

"I'm sure, *Mi Reina. Rojo* will remove my stitches in four days. I will have pain, but pain we can use to support our story. Please arrange the press conference for a few days afterward."

Lucky placed a palm against my shoulder blade, pulling my attention to him. "I've been thinking, love," he mused, the focused regard in his eyes telling me just how serious he was. "The hacked files are sitting in FBI evidence right now, enough dirt on Alvarez to bury a miner, right? Him being guilty is as obvious as Kellan's erection every time Daddy Roboto here bends over."

He jabbed a finger in the Viking's direction, but didn't crack a smile. "We need someone to speak about how much he hates you—or someone who might tell us why. He partnered with Aaron's parents and threatened their son, but for some reason he really hates the likes of you. A man like him? Not a chance he'd be able to keep his mouth shut about it, and I think I know who he'd share some of those secrets with."

He exchanged knowing glances with Aaron before continuing.

"Gertie Baker—his assistant. Hard to believe that she'd be some criminal sidekick, but I betcha she's heard a thing or two about how nasty you are."

I blinked, my mind buffering two seconds behind the conversation. Gertrude Baker was a sweet, mild-mannered woman—the farthest thing from a criminal accomplice.

"She's already been interviewed, Luck. She had nothing to do with any of the sex-trafficking, just the above-board workings of Alvarez International. She's squeaky clean."

"Aye," he said agreeably, "but she was interviewed about sex trafficking and all the baddie stuff. Unlikely how he felt about *you* ever came into the conversation." He moved around me to face me front on, placed two wide palms on my hips, and stared down at me with steely determination in his eyes.

"She likes me. Let me take her out for coffee and give her just enough to test the waters. We need corroborating witnesses to help make this stick."

The calming green swirled with apprehension, but the irises were clear of doubt. He was serious about this and wanted me—needed me—to be on board. I leaned up and brushed my lips against his, a light reminder of my trust in him.

Since we'd placed our cards—and the priceless painting —on the coffee table, we'd built a bridge between us, and it was becoming more fortified with each action. He was a walking oxymoron, every move unorthodox and unexpected. I couldn't understand his methods, but I could comprehend his rationale. Lucky's insight into people and their motivations was a carefully honed weapon. His soft words and slippery smile ensnared his victims long before they knew they'd been captured. It would be a waste not to leverage that skill set against Alvarez to save ourselves too.

"Do it," I murmured against his lips, tasting the light trace of strawberry jam on my tongue. "But take Kellan with you."

A wide grin overtook Lucky's handsome face. The light in his eyes had the power to brighten the entire building. He pulled me tight to his chest with his good arm and buried his nose in my hair, smattering kisses over the crown of my head.

"No time like the present, Kell-Bell." He released his hold and strode past Kellan, reaching for his jacket resting on the back of the kitchen chair. "Let's go."

The Viking in question raised two bushy eyebrows in irritation, but he shook his head instead of voicing any scathing commentary. He lumbered toward me, cupped my cheek, and leaned in to kiss my forehead. The coarse bristles of his beard left a mark along with the scalding brand of his lips.

He shifted back, but instead of following Lucky, he moved beside me to Aaron and cupped his head in the same manner. I blinked back my surprise as he pressed their foreheads together in the most intimate gesture I'd ever witnessed between them.

"Keep her safe, *Guapo*," he muttered before pressing his lips against Aaron's in a quick peck. Though relatively innocent, it was enough to set my panties on fire. Apparently, I was very out of the loop with the development of their relationship since our threesome several weeks ago.

"It is done," Aaron agreed solemnly, grasping the hand at my side and interlacing our fingers. "Be safe, *compañero*."

Then they were gone, in search of the last piece of evidence we needed to nail Alvarez inside his coffin.

CHAPTER 13

Lauchlan

"I'm sorry."

He muttered those two tricky little words into the cab of the car like they were the secret nuclear codes or something. I smothered my grin with a—who was I kidding? I wasn't smothering shyte. I'd been waiting for the meathead to apologize for manhandling me, and here it was. It was a dud as far as apologies went, but I'd allow it. Such a nice guy I was.

Kellan needed time to process his emotions, like an oversized grumbly toddler bear. The big oaf—*my* big oaf—was channeling his sullen teenager, and he'd aced the role with his dark eyes, broody stare, and cloudy disposition.

He'd taken the wheel and was driving us out to a diner on the other side of Kensington, a small town two towns over, where Gertie had agreed to meet. It took only a quick phone call and a small amount of charm to persuade her to join me for lunch, promising her something more appealing—and cheaper—than our last dinner of seventy-dollar tacos.

I shifted my weight in the passenger seat, wincing as I leaned my head and shoulders flat against the window to question him. Blondie had wanted me to wear a sling, but I refused—too noticeable in a crowd, and the last thing we wanted today was to be noticeable. My upper arm burned with every movement, but the luck of the Irish had been with me last night, and I wasn't uttering one word of complaint. I could slag my gloomy companion a bit, though.

"What's that, mate? Couldn't hear yeh over the sound of my disbelief."

He snorted, the burst of breath blowing a rogue little thread of blond into his eyes. He wore a man bun today— the sexy kind, with all the little tufts of hair coming out of it like he'd just felled a tree like Paul Bunyan. Stone-cold blue eyes turned quickly in my direction, and then conducted a casual sweep of the mirrors and returned to the road ahead.

I had to hand it to him—this man was fecking *vigilant*. Even with our additional security detail trailing several cars behind, he hadn't let his gaze falter once. And with the shitshow of last night, I wouldn't complain about that either.

"I let my anger get the best of me," he explained sounding begrudging, not bringing those eyeballs back to mine, choosing instead to stare at a whole lot of asphalt. "I shouldn't have pushed you."

This man would stare a barging bull right in the face and not drop eye contact, but he was a twitchy little git when it came to saying sorry to little old me. *Too cute, Kell-Bell.*

"Conan, I know you're a big, bad, rage-y machine and all, but you can talk to us, you know." Carefully, I reached for his right hand rested on the stick shift and covered it. He didn't flinch or push me away, so I left it there, tracing the lines of his tattoos with my fingertips.

"Trish fucked you over. Your dad fucked you over. Lots of justified rage swirling around in there, mate. It's okay to unleash it all on the feckers who did this to you. Just maybe keep it for them, yeh, and not the people who are ready to die for you."

Those dark eyes finally snapped to mine. "Bold words for a conman, *Lauchlan*." He raised a bushy brow in challenge. "You're saying you'd die for me now?"

I doodled the shape of a penis on the back of his hand as I mulled that over.

"Don't want to die for anyone or anything, really," I admitted, unashamed to say so. Moral qualms were more of a selective choice than a way of life for the likes of me. "Not really a poster child for integrity, am I? But if I had to choose a cause to fight for, it'd be this one. With you three." I shrugged as if it was a simple declaration, but really, the only other thing I'd risked my neck for was my sister, and that battle had been won.

Sure, Alvarez was playing the part of master puppeteer, even as a criminal, but he'd been caught—thanks to me and Blackbird—with enough evidence to put him away for a long time. That was what I'd wanted, wasn't it? Revenge for her, justice for sadistic men who made their livelihood off of innocent women's bodies. That mission was over. I could hop on a plane, resume a new identity to hide from The Six, and live off of my nest egg on a Caribbean beach until I died of typhoid from drinking the wrong ice cubes, or something equally depressing.

I'd wanted closure for the fucks who'd stolen my sister's life, and here I was, on the cusp of drowning this arsehole in even more of his dirt, and I felt ... nothing. No grand sense of peace or satisfaction. Didn't even get to enjoy the cocky arrogance of winning. There was still a whopper of a hole in my heart where her smile used to be. Maybe I was a foolish fuck, but if I stayed with this lot, I might have a hope of feeling that accomplishment one day.

So—I was here because I wanted to be. I could have died last night, really, if I hadn't *MacGyver'd* the shit out of that garage, or if I'd been a foot to the left when that bullet struck me. What was the difference?

I liked Hillary. Might even be more than that if I really stopped to consider what that woman did to my head, my balls, and my heart. She was a one-of-a-kind catch who'd somehow put up with the likes of me. And, I liked the two sinfully scary trunks of baggage she came with. On the outside, they had the personalities of dull pencils—but on the inside, they were messy, complicated, dangerous men who held a conman captive with curiosity and enough sexual tension to corrupt a monk.

But instead of baring my heart to Kellan on my way to burgers, I just left that statement in the air until he finally remembered he knew how to speak.

"I'm not..." He made an uncomfortable face, like the words tasted funny in his mouth. "I'm not used to having anyone to talk to."

"Now you have three," I said simply, squeezing his hand and then removing mine to tap out a tune on the window glass. I had enough sense to back off for now. The diner was in sight and the next conversation with Gertie was important. But maybe he could get out of his head and release some of that pent-up tension without tossing me into another piece of furniture.

We'd talk like two normal blokes with the emotional intelligence of something more than a pickle, and then, like last time, he could fuck it out of me. Or—better thought—I could fuck it out of him. Kellan Carlos was going to bottom for me one day, and he would fucking love it.

Yummy thoughts of me spreading Kell-Bell's arse cheeks vanished at the sight of neon orange flashing signs in broad daylight. Kellan pulled into the parking lot of the retro spot and turned off the engine. We were twenty minutes early.

"I'll watch through the windows. Choose one of the booths and keep the blinds open, so I can see you at all times, got it?"

This man's intensity was so fecking cute. I liked it when he was being an overbearing ogre *for* me, rather than against me.

"Aye, aye, captain." I grinned and saluted with my good arm before slipping out the passenger door and into the diner, adopting the casual gait of a man in need of a good, greasy, American lunch.

I took a green vinyl-lined booth with a view of the front door and the bathroom hallway and settled in, accepting the disgusting cup of dirty water from the server with a beaming grin. I immediately added six sugar packets to the ceramic cup and drew a cautious sip. Better.

I hadn't decided how I wanted to play this yet, not really. Gertie was a sweetheart, and I was convinced she was a patsy, not a key player in Alvarez' sick operations. The fact she was still out in the land of the living and not locked up somewhere supported that, but a conman learned quickly everyone has secrets. And it was always the quiet ones that surprised you most.

She was a sight for sore eyes when she walked in though, all cherub cheeks and dark hair, her eyes nervously scanning the booths in search of me.

"Oy, Gert!" I called out in a friendly singsong, waving her over to my chosen spot. I leaped out of the booth and wrapped her in my arms for a bear hug when she was close enough, so I could whisper in her ear.

"We may have an audience today, Gert. Not taking any chances with the FBI investigation. Let's just be two colleagues catching up over lunch, yeh?"

She nodded into my shoulder and clutched me tighter than I thought her wee frame was capable of before letting go and sliding into the booth, removing her scarf and hat as she went.

"It's so nice to see you, Lauchlan." She smiled sunnily, playing into the bit nicely. "We have quite a bit of catching up to do!"

"We sure do." I smiled brightly and stopped talking as the server left a pot on the table. Sobering once the woman headed back to the kitchen, I leaned in and lowered my voice. "How're you holding up, Gert? What a roller coaster this has been, eh?"

The light in her brown eyes went out like a snuffed candle. "It's terrible." She stared at the rim of her coffee mug instead of at me. "I can't believe he would do those awful things. So many terrible things." Her eyes flashed up to meet mine, now bloodshot and red-rimmed. "Did you know?"

I couldn't be sure—no one is truly ever sure about another person—but my gut was telling me Gertie was clean. Innocent.

I had also packed a little device in my pocket that could detect wireless transmitters and it wasn't going off, so I was confident she wasn't recording this conversation, as far as being confident in technology went.

Blowing out a slow breath, I did a quick assessment as she waited for my answer. Open posture, slight lean in, even breathing—all signs of a person with nothing to hide. Her hands fidgeted around the coffee mug, but I'd chalk that up to the nerves of the situation rather than her being a double agent. Gertie was many things, but she was no Kellan Carlos.

The truth then. That's what we'd start with.

"I knew." I dipped my head, acknowledging that secret for the first time to anyone but our motley crew. This was a serious risk, but a calculated one. To imply Alvarez had a motive to target Hillary in this mess, we needed Gertie, and I'd bet my left testicle she had what we needed to link the two. I just had to hope in all our interactions I'd read her right and my gamble would pay off.

Imploring her with my eyes, I continued. "My sister was one of his victims, Gert. I was working with some people to take him down because of it—and I'm happy to say it worked."

The hand gripping her coffee mug went slack, dropping the cup and shattering it to smithereens against the Formica table edge. Hot liquid splashed down her blouse and into her lap, and she jumped up with a scream.

Well, so much for staying inconspicuous.

I jumped up too, dabbing carefully at her chest with the napkins on the table. "Let's go to the restroom," I suggested calmly, shooting a tight smile to the server watching us. "Get you cleaned up."

Steering her toward the rear hallway, I scanned the other diners as we passed and noticed nothing out of place. No doubt Kell-Bell would be pissed at the change of plans, but it was a conman's job to improvise. We'd be out in a jiff, anyway.

When we were safely behind the women's restroom door, I locked it behind us, then spun around, my palms facing outward. "Not going to hurt you, Gert, just want to make sure you're okay."

Despite the coffee-soaked blouse and flustered face, she raised her eyebrows as if I were the crazy one. "I'm not worried about you raping me, Lauchlan. But I need to know what you meant."

Right. I scrubbed the back of my neck with my good palm, trying to get the words out in a way that didn't incriminate me, in case I was wrong about the wire.

"Okay, here's the deal." I searched her face with an open earnestness reserved only for occasions like this—where charm and false words wouldn't get me anywhere with a woman, but a healthy dose of honesty might. "I may or may not know how the feds received a bunch of incriminating evidence on Alvarez, and I may or may not have had my own agenda for knowing such information."

Speaking in riddles wasn't exactly *honest*, I supposed, but it wasn't dishonest.

"And, even though Alvarez is going to pay some very hard time for his crimes, *eventually*"—I emphasized that word, since the rich in America had a tendency to get away with just about anything—"he's come after someone I care about, and I'm looking for information that'll help prove it."

Gertie screwed up her delicate face in thought, little lacy wrinkles scrunching everywhere. "And you think I have this information? Lauchlan, I didn't even know about the sex stuff—do you know how stupid I feel? Working with him every day for years, and I didn't have a clue!" She visibly shuddered. "I puked when I heard the news, and then puked more every time a new update came out. I *helped* that monster. I was *paid* by him."

She practically turned green at the gills as she said those words, reaching for the cheap vanity countertop for support. I gave her a moment to find her composure, keeping my mouth shut for once. Finally, her eyes met mine again, shiny and determined. "Who else has he targeted, and how can I help?"

"Hillary Lane." I drew closer as she turned on the hot water faucet, presumably to take out the stain. "Ugly threats, some vicious stuff. She has no idea what she did for him to hate her this much—it seems much more personal than a bit of business rivalry. Any thoughts?"

She stared through the mirror at me for a long time. Finally, her lips moved, with what I was hoping was incriminating evidence.

"Marco and Xander Analo—they both lost out on a major contract years ago when Ms. Lane was just getting her business off the ground."

Xander Analo—the git Marco hired me out to for several weeks to test their security systems. The man had seriously rubbed me the wrong way—another stuffy man in a stuffy suit who'd insisted I call him "sir." What a turd. Was no one not an arsehole in this fecking town?

Gertie must have mistaken my expression for disbelief of her story instead of disbelief of the sheer number of sorry sacks of shyte around here, because she hurried to continue.

"I only remember because I was in the meeting taking notes, and Mr. Analo went on a tangent about blond bimbos taking work away from competent men, or something equally dumb. Mr. Alvarez agreed, and they'd casually made death threat jokes about her, which I didn't find funny at all. The next time they met, I wasn't invited, but I'd accidentally left my Dictaphone inside his office, and it recorded the entire conversation."

My heart pounded in my ears as the rush of adrenaline spiked my blood like a smashing hit of a party drug. "What did the recording say?"

"They discussed tanking her company by illegally buying up stock to drive the value up and then dumping them back into the market. They wanted to ruin her financially. As far as I know, it didn't happen, but I'll admit, I'm not really knowledgeable about that kind of thing."

Okay, so white-collar crime wasn't the best ticket, but a recording of that sort would prove his motives—especially for what we had planned in a few days' time. I watched her carefully through the mirror, but she wasn't showing a single sign of dishonest body language. Just my pure, sweet friend.

She gave me a weak smile through the reflection, still fiddling with the ruined silk of her blouse. "They also said a bunch of sexist, hateful comments about women that made me look for another job the next day. But the pay was really good and my student loans are through the roof, so... I ended up staying and turned a blind eye. Chauvinistic men are par for the course in this kind of work, you know? I should have listened to my intuition. If I had known..."

Her voice broke with a cracked sob, covering her face with her palms. I rushed to her, wrapping my good arm around her shoulder to bring her in for a soothing hug.

"It's okay, Gert. You didn't know. He fooled everyone." I smoothed a hand over her hair and pressed a gentle kiss to the top of her head. "You can help us make this right though, Gert. Hillary Lane is as innocent in this as those girls he was messing with." Okay—just a wee lie on my part. "Please tell me you still have the tape. Some record somewhere. I need hard evidence that he's after her, whatever the reason. You can help us make this right," I repeated, squeezing her just a bit tighter to my chest before letting her go.

She gulped a few lungfuls of air and wiped at her watery eyes before looking up at me again. Steel entered her stare, and the Gertie with a backbone rose to the surface like Jaws ready to get revenge on that teeny tiny fishing boat.

"I have it," she declared, her hands balling into tight little fists at her sides. "And it's yours."

An abrupt pounding at the door stole my attention. "Lauchlan, open this door before I—"

Gertie transformed from a hungry shark to a terrified mouse in a matter of seconds, high-pitched squeak and all. I tossed her a cheeky wink and nuzzled her to the rear of the sinks. "It's alright, love. Nothing to be afraid of. I've just made a very grumpy bear a little angry."

I unlatched the deadbolt and did as he asked, yanking open the steel door before he could break a fist through it. I knew it—I'd left my position, and he was pissed. Before he could tear my head off, I interrupted him.

"Conan, I say this with all the love in my heart—calm the feck down before you drop dead of a fucking heart attack." I broke out into a toothy smile, waving my hand at the woman who'd just given us a lifeline behind me.

"Besides, Gertie here is going to give us her Golden Ticket. Get ready, Kell-Bell, we're going to Wonka's!"

CHAPTER 14

Hillary

After another long day of planning, I made a light supper of salads and grilled chicken, much to Lucky's chagrin, but the place setting we'd put out for our fourth partner went untouched as we waited for him to show up.

Kellan still quietly refused to sleep with us, despite the room in the Alaskan king-sized bed. I'd thought we'd put his demons to rest when he'd claimed me the other night, but if anything, it had turned the distance between us into the size of a small city instead of the 40,000-square foot warehouse where we kept ourselves hidden.

Several emotions warred across his handsome features this morning before I left for the office. He'd wanted to be my bodyguard, but couldn't—his brothers had effectively put a target on both of our backs, and the opportunity to take both of us out at once would be far too tempting.

Nervous energy crackled through me as the night drew closer to midnight. Kellan still hadn't come home. So much of our path forward was riding on tomorrow, and Kellan not communicating with any of us had given me an additional variable to worry about. I'd coddled his delicate disposition long enough—we were going to have to talk about this ridiculous distance and what it was doing to our family.

Our family. The word was foreign on my tongue. I didn't have a healthy relationship with the concept, but I couldn't think of a group of people in this world I'd grown closer to. We would succeed or fail together; the only way through was side by side. Kellan's absence had only shown how much I wanted a group of people to call mine in every sense of the word.

I didn't want to be Hillary Lane, billionaire heiress, alone and embittered. I'd demanded their loyalty from day one, but I could now recognize I craved their love—their devotion—far more.

I was brushing my teeth when footsteps echoed heavily along the wooden floorboards of the hallway. A wave of relief washed over me as I spit out my toothpaste and spun on my heel. I returned to the bedroom, where Lucky and Aaron had their heads bowed in quiet discussion while we all waited for our fourth before we went to sleep.

Kellan deserved to be free of the curse that plagued his family. He held my heart in his hands, and each step away from me tugged its strings taut. He was too noble to allow himself the pleasure of his own happiness. As long as his family was a threat to me, he'd never give me his heart. I needed him—his protection, his fierceness, the warrior housed within his skin. I would burn the world down around the four of us to keep him as mine.

As if summoned by my thoughts, his shadowy form appeared in the doorway, and the conversation in the room instantly dimmed. He'd pulled his thick blond hair back into a tight bun. The tendrils of frizz framed his forehead and hung into his haunted eyes. He wore loose black sweatpants and a blue hoodie, and a mostly empty duffle bag hung from his shoulder. Anxiety radiated off of him—the frenetic energy hit me like a ball of heat in the face, instantly curdling my stomach.

He rubbed a large palm over the short stubble of his beard and stared through the room, like he wasn't really seeing us at all.

"Good, you're all here." The terse pronouncement was hesitant, drawn out, as if the words were painful to say. My curdling stomach revolted, pushing bile into the back of my throat. I wasn't going to like what was coming.

"Aye," Lucky agreed slowly, elongating the word with his Irish lilt. The cock of his head and slitted eyes told me I wasn't the only one picking up on Kellan's melancholy aura. Aaron's stare remained passive, mildly expectant at best, his gaze never leaving the man's large form.

"Right." Our Viking's Adam's apple bobbed in his throat on a hard swallow. "Right," he repeated, before heaving himself out of the doorway and stalking toward the small dresser on the other side of the bed. He opened the top drawer and removed a roll of cash, a few of the documents from the box of fake identities Aaron had secured for all of us, and a white opaque container. Then, he opened the bottom drawer, and emptied the contents—mostly clothing —into the bag.

"What are you doing?" I fought to keep my voice stable while I buried my panic into the barrel of bile. Under no circumstances could I look weak in his presence right now. He needed a calm, direct presence, not a shrieking, angry woman. I couldn't make any promises.

He stood tall and still, keeping his back to us. In the dim light of the corner lamp, his shoulders rose and fell several times. The room remained silent as a tomb as we waited for him to explain. Turning on his heel, he faced us in stoic solitude, the stiffness in his jaw and clenching of fists by his side betraying the emotions warring inside his head.

"I'm leaving," he announced. The two words hung in the air like a freshly tightened noose. "You need the best chance at safety, and I'm not it. Antonio's going to kill me any day, and I'm not sticking around only to have you killed in the crossfire."

He's... leaving. My greatest fear, far more than Alvarez's revenge or Antonio's retaliation, was I'd lose the lifeline of these three men. The men who'd saved my sanity and protected my peace against their own gain. I was on a rollercoaster, sitting at the precipice with an unbuckled seat and a triple loop in front of me, untethered, and staring down the steep drop with the certainty I was about to die.

"*Compañero.*" Aaron's words broke through the haze first. "This is unwise. It is best we stay together, no? We are all marked for death—you are not an exception here."

"Right." Lucky's unusually grave tone belied the seriousness of the situation. "Three Musketeers, Kell-Bell. The most wanted men in Sequoia. Don't leave out of fear for us, mate." His voice dropped an octave, the next words coming out in a whisper. "We need you."

I was mute, if only for a moment, as I gathered my thoughts while fighting the urge to vomit.

Kellan thought of himself as Atlas, holding the criminal world of Sequoia on his shoulders, and the pressure cracks were taking their toll on the beautiful stonework. We'd witnessed every sign of him breaking. Yet, I'd held on to hope he'd silently get over it and heal on his own. My choice to remain silent hadn't given him breathing room at all. He was crumbling under the weight of it all, and determined to save us from the destruction's aftermath.

But who would save him? Visceral fear flooded my hindbrain, tasting like battery acid on my tongue. If Kellan left tonight, where would he go? Who would protect *him*?

What did I have to say to keep him? My instinct was to pick a fight—goad him into anger and challenge him to stay out of spite. The icy determination in his stiff stare told me that was the wrong move on the board—pushing him farther would achieve just that. It would justify his actions, as if he had to be the adult in the room to protect the spoiled billionaire princess. I was no princess, but Kellan continued to think I needed coddling like a delicate paper doll.

After years of relentless push and pull with this brute of a man, I was tired of playing coy. Our gigantic egos and pervasive pride were going to be the death of something that had the potential to be beautiful between us. I didn't want to fight him. I wanted to—*needed* to—love him, *finally* love him. To shield him as he shielded me. We would face the music beside him, whatever notes the band played.

With resolve, I strode over to the hulking man and knelt at his feet, bowing my head in a pose of submission, a language he understood.

"I don't want you to leave, Viking." My gaze rose from the floor to the wild seas of his stare, finding hesitation and confusion rife within them. Earnestly, I tried to convey every emotion I couldn't say through our locked eyes: passion, tenderness, understanding, devotion. Love.

"I need you here with me. I am more protected with you at my back, the sword and shield you've always been." The words gathered in my throat and stuck there, the purity of emotion behind them so raw, they choked me. "I love you, Kellan Carlos. Please don't leave us when we need you most."

A single tear slid down the plane of my cheek at the admission. I refused to wipe it away, displaying my pain so he could see the war he was waging on my heart. Hillary

Lane didn't cry, but tonight, I'd make an exception. Kellan Carlos was *mine*, and it was time he knew what that meant.

The conviction in his stare wavered, a shimmer of sheen glazed his eyes and softened the severity of his resolve. His rough palm came down to cup my cheek, his thick thumb gently brushing away the teardrop as he cradled my head.

His lips closed over mine in the gentlest kiss I'd ever received. The pious press of puffy skin stuttered my heart and softened the edges of the spiraling thoughts in my mind. He pulled back quickly, fixated on my face. His own was a mirror, the purity of his dedication on his gruff features clearer than a flawless diamond.

"I've always loved you, Killer. From the day I first saw you." Pouty lips quirked slightly at their corners, the quiet admission louder than any shout from a rooftop. They remained suspended for the briefest time before thinning into a straight line and shattering the beauty of the moment with their harsh edges.

"But it's not enough to keep you safe." He removed his hand from my chin and stepped back, the forced distance causing a deep shiver to permeate my bones. Vicious nausea rocketed through my stomach, like my body had been tipped upside down on a thrill ride. A fitting response, since he was throwing the world he held on his shoulders into the abyss, while I desperately held on with clawed hands.

"There's nothing I can say to change your mind." It wasn't a question, but a numb statement. I knew that look too well. It was the look of a cartel king, trained to take over the world and bear all of its burdens.

"Nothing." Pulling the bag tighter over his shoulder, he turned back to the doorway. He spoke to it, rather than to us, and his last words hit the tiled wall of the hallway like shot bullets.

"I can't be with you as long as he is alive. He'll destroy you to get to me, and I'll never risk you, Killer. I'd rather live a life alone than ever risk losing you."

"Take care of her," he gritted out with halted intonation. "Take care of each other." Then he strode out of the room without a moment's pause, as if looking back was too tempting to risk.

"Mate!" Lauchlan protested, while Aaron steadily followed him down the hall with a hand pressed to the wall. I remained a heap on the thick rug. Numbness transformed into bitter anger like an alchemist spinning straw into gold. I bolted from my place on the ground and stalked down the hallway on quick feet.

He'd just confessed to loving me just to leave me? Coward! His reasoning didn't matter. Families didn't abandon each other in the name of protection. Family negotiated the terms. They didn't dictate next steps because they were the largest, strongest person in the group.

Family didn't leave.

"You COWARD!" I screamed, rage building to such a crescendo in my body it blinded me with its strength. "You fucking COWARD!"

Tears streamed down my face in tiny rivers, but he completely ignored me and slammed the door behind him. Aaron stared at the steel, a rare expression of shock molding into gentle care once he turned his attention to me.

"*Mi Reina,*" he cooed, wrapping his arms around my shaking form. "I am sorry, *Mi Reina.*"

I barely felt his embrace as I stared at the hole Kellan had just left in my heart. The finality of his leaving hit me harder than his fists ever could. For years I'd been caught in his orbit. The brute of a man who could never give himself over to me, but refused to release his hold on me all the same.

He loved me. Words I knew he'd never say unless he meant them, and yet his version of love meant abandonment; disassociation, panic under the guise of protection. He'd rather leave me to rot, safe and alive without him, than risk failing to shield me so we could die together.

Scalding, bitter tears continued to fall. I collapsed into a messy pile of human pain on the floor, vibrating anger finally consuming me through chattering teeth and shaking shoulders.

Somewhere in the mix of melancholy and maelstrom, I screamed, the curdling sound foreign to my own ears.

Large arms wrapped around me, the tight hold lifting me from the ground to settle into the planes of a hard chest.

"I know it hurts, lass." Lucky's hushed words brushed against the tiny hairs across my cheeks. "It hurts." Gentle fingers wove through my hair, the soft pads delicately tracing circles across my scalp as he murmured more soothing words against my skin.

"He knows he's in the wrong, love. I promise you he'll be back. Needs a little break to see what a gobshyte he's being."

Instead of giving him an answer, I buried my head in the firm muscles and soft cotton of his sleep shirt. I shook in his protective cage. Each shock of my bones hitting his released a torrent of grief, cleansing and cathartic.

"Let's get you to bed, *Mi Reina*." Aaron's deep voice was steady, but a light tremor of trepidation tinged its edges.

Commanding. Concerned. Careful.

Momentum jolted me in Lucky's arms as he carried me to the rear bedroom, returning us to the once-peaceful den. Lowering me onto the soft cushions, he pressed a tender kiss to the throbbing skin of my forehead.

A hot, shirtless chest welcomed me into his embrace. I leaned into the comfort only Aaron could offer, nestled within the haven of his arms. He pulled the duvet over us as another body slid in behind mine, thick fingers tracing light outlines along my spine.

Cocooned between two of the hearts I called my home, I closed my eyes and sunk into their warmth. Closing my eyes, I focused on the rise and fall of their chests against me to calm my sobs. The steady thrum of their heartbeats brought mine back to earth.

A light kiss pressed against my neck at the same time another nuzzled into the tender skin below my ear. They were soothing touches, not sexual or suggestive, but the turn in my belly shifted the energy housed beneath my skin.

My puffy eyes and swollen cheeks were tomorrow's problem. Makeup could mask their effects well enough. I needed a balm for the pain in my heart, a salve to stifle the burn. These men—*my* men—could offer that escape.

I reached my hands down to grasp each of theirs—Lucky's resting on my hip and Aaron's gently cupping the underside of my ribs. I interlaced our fingers and squeezed with little vigor, just enough to get their attention.

"Distract me," I begged, too tired to demand, and too needy to care. "Please."

The words remained suspended above our heads until my dark knight broke the spell.

"As you wish, *Mi Reina*."

Aaron's honeyed eyes stared through mine as his fingers released their grip, sliding down the crest of my hip where my sleep shorts sat on my skin. He dipped into the seam, dragging them down my thighs at an agonizingly slow pace, the depth of his gaze leaving me tingly and wanting.

Lucky helped him pull down the other side as his lips latched onto the sensitive spot between my neck and shoulder. He sucked the muscle between his teeth and nipped the nerve, shooting zings of current straight down my spine and deep into my belly.

Aaron's hands traced the line back up my legs as he completely removed my shorts, bypassing my pussy to skim the skin of my abdomen. Landing on the swollen undersides of my breasts, he palmed them with a soft squeeze, rubbing his thumbs in concentric circles over my nipples.

I writhed between them, moisture seeping from my pussy onto the front of Lucky's PJ pants. When I ground against the head of his stiffening cock behind me, his curses broke the silence and he thrust up into me in response, the cloth-covered head barely giving me any of the friction I needed.

"Mo—" I tried to moan, but the heat of Aaron's mouth completely cut off my plea, the taste of fresh toothpaste and mafia man deliciously invading and holding me prisoner. He attacked my mouth like he attacked my nipples, thoroughly and demanding, each pass of his tongue and thumb inciting a riot of pleasure through every facet of my body.

Lucky massaged down my hips, thick fingers stroking along my seam. His shudder of excitement vibrated through me as he delved a little deeper, coating the tip of his index finger in my wetness.

"You're so fucking wet for us, love." He cooed the praise into my hair, pushing the finger entirely inside me. I welcomed him greedily, thrusting against his hand as he curled one digit up, stroking my walls with delicate precision. "I can't wait to sink my cock into you and fill you with my cum."

When Lucky turned off the charm and turned on the dominant dirty-talker, my brain re-wired, like it was adjusting to the phrasing of a new language. I relished it, eager to forget the burning sensation in my chest by embracing the sensations in my core.

Another body-wracking shudder bolted through me when he added a second, then third finger, scissoring them inside my channel, deliciously alerting so many nerves at once.

Aaron's erection pressed hard into my thigh, but it grew impossibly stiffer at Lucky's words. Apparently, his dirty talk had the same effect on both of us.

My hands found the seam of Aaron's boxers under the confines of the covers. I reached in, to pull out the steel rod seeping pre-cum, and brought it to my pussy, teasing the tip against my clit with languid strokes of the shaft.

He let out a rough gasp at the contact, but an even rougher gasp came when Lucky removed his fingers from my pussy and gripped Aaron's cock instead, jerking him off with a firm hand over mine as we both brought his tip to my entrance.

"Ever tandem fuck before, Daddy?"

Aaron looked over my shoulder, locking eyes with Lucky with a manic gleam of lust. "No, *Rojo*. But I will tandem fuck with you."

Oh God. Oh... God. Yes. This was a good distraction. My two men, enjoying pleasure with me, with each other. Yes, yes, yes.

Lucky pulled down his sleep pants with his free hand as he continued to grip Aaron's cock in the other. His heavy erection slapped my ass cheek, skin-to-skin, the sticky residue of his own pre-cum leaving its mark.

"Blondie," he whispered into the nape of my neck, "we're going to take turns with you, alright? A thrust for a thrust. You just need to be a good girl and take it, okay, love? Be our good girl, and take our cocks like you own them."

Tremors of anticipation wracked every nerve ending as he lined up behind me. Aaron's lips latched back onto mine, capturing my sigh as Lucky's thick cock entered me from behind. He wasn't gentle. His thrust was wild and aggressive, wedged in as deeply as he could get at this angle. Just as abruptly, he pulled out, leaving me empty and wanting.

"Your turn, Daddy." The directive came out on a strangled gasp, desperation and lust carrying through every syllable. My Dark Knight shifted his weight, gripped his shaft, and plunged into my heat. My body convulsed with pleasure at the intrusion.

"Fuck, *Mi Reina*." Aaron's praise was also uttered through gritted teeth. "You will milk us both with that pretty pussy. I will be undone in minutes."

"Just wait your turn, Daddy," Lucky teased, nudging him with a hand on his hip, urging him to pull out. "That'll help you last."

Aaron's acquiescing grunt accompanied him leaving my body, but no sooner than I had time to experience the pain of longing Lucky entered me from behind again, flooding my body with salacious sensation.

I floated between them as they sunk into a rhythm, each taking their turn with quiet, almost-practiced movements, showering me with kisses between their thrusts. I let them consume me entirely, allowing them to use my body for their pleasure, savoring each grunt and groan as they wrung me dry.

Their lips left my body to explore each other. Their mash of tongue and teeth hovered right above my head with each drive of their dicks inside me. Lucky's lips left Aaron's for mine, his tongue leaving the taste of my mafia man in my mouth before the mafia man himself claimed me, the three of us locked in a messy three-way kiss.

Fingers—I didn't know whose at this point—rubbed my clit through the kiss, the padded thumb bowing my spine and pressing my breasts up into Aaron. The thrusts got faster, more frantic. Then a forceful rut and the pinch of my clit shot me into blissful oblivion. The intensity of my orgasm blacked out my vision and melted every bone in my body to jelly.

Lucky hissed against my lips as I held him inside me with a vise grip as I convulsed around him in aftershocks. He squeezed both my hips and rutted into me with two hard pumps. flooding my insides with his hot cum and a vibrating growl through his chest.

When he pulled out, a trail of sticky fluid seeped out onto the mattress between us. He gripped Aaron's cock and guided him back to my full pussy, notching the head between my lips before letting go.

"Fuck her, Daddy. Fuck your dick into my cum and feel both of us cover your cock."

Even in my sated state, my body electrified at those words. I felt the grin of the taunting man's lips against my shoulder before he continued. "The next time you feel my cum, it'll be inside you."

Fuck. Oh fuck. My pussy clenched against the phantom of Aaron's cock not yet inside me, despite my release. Imagining these two men—fucking—while I watched... I needed Aaron to finish me. Now.

He finally shoved himself inside my slick channel, but he halted, a fierce stare fixated on Lucky's face.

"The next time I feel your cum, *Rojo*, it will be all over my chest. But you will be filled with me."

Oh fuck, oh fuck, oh...

I screamed when Aaron picked up his pace, pistoning his hips to pierce me so deeply I buckled beneath him. His pubic bone ground hard on my clit, and his deep rutting forced more of our combined cum to leak out, making the moment impossibly hotter. Another orgasm tore through me, every atom in my body experiencing euphoric release as my childhood friend came inside me and claimed me as his.

We lay there for a time, completely spent in a tangle of limbs and bodily fluids, sharing chaste kisses and gentle touches in our aftermath.

Eventually, Aaron pulled out of me, and Lucky jumped out of our cocoon to grab cloths to clean us up.

When he returned, the mischievous gleam I'd come to love cast a glow across his skin. He held the cloth to my swollen pussy and gently wiped away our combined mess, but when he turned to Aaron to do the same, he dipped his head to his crotch instead, lapping his tongue along the softening shaft coated in us.

Aaron's careful eyes cataloged his movements, his expression stoic as another man's mouth cleaned his cock with care. But when Lucky rose, Aaron gripped his jaw between two fingers and brought his lips to his in a tongue-sucking kiss.

When he released his hold, Lucky drew back in muted surprise, his eyebrows reaching his hairline as he stared into Aaron's neutral gaze.

"You have tasted my cum twice, *Rojo*. It was time I experienced the same." The rare, sexy grin—a shy, smirky smile—spread across our scary mafia man's face, causing a giggle to erupt from my throat, and an incredulous laugh from Lucky.

I rose out of the bed without help, quickly peed, and pulled my shorts back on to catch any errant cum leaks overnight. We were far too tired to shower. But if I left the safety of our cozy den for too long, I knew I wouldn't save myself from falling apart.

"Thank you," I whispered into the dark as I settled back into my place between them. Lucky pulled the covers back over us once again, and the two men pulled me into their arms in a loose, but protective hold.

"Always, love." Lucky's muscular arms squeezed me between them, and then softly released.

"Forever, *Mi Reina*." Aaron's breath rustled my hair before he placed a light kiss to the crown of my head.

I drifted off to sleep with the soft dream in my mind of a woman who loved three men and got to walk away from this life with each of them by her side.

A pleasant dream to numb the pain—and soften the nightmare of tomorrow.

CHAPTER 15

Hillary

"So, are we not going to talk about the scary goons at the front of the building?" Marty angled one perfectly manicured eyebrow at me, his silver eyes filled with concerned curiosity.

Of course, he'd heard the rumors. There wasn't a person in the state who hadn't heard every talk show blather on about my fallen status, even though not a single arrest had been made or any actual evidence brought to the public. It was very telling that the world would just as easily worship you on a pedestal as try to clobber you with it, depending on what the media moguls wanted them to do.

Painting me as the villain was selling far more newspapers than the mayor's current escort scandal, or the crack addiction of a high-profile evangelical pastor. Both men fit the current acceptable narrative. Better to turn their attention to the *Billionaire Barbie of Brutality* as one paper so eloquently put it.

I would have scoffed at their jibes months ago, when the risk of being caught was minimal. That confidence had waned, replaced instead with anxious dreams in Lucky's arms and layers of planning that had a sixty percent chance of working.

Alec had transferred the ownership of the nightmarish collar that held my dreams hostage to Antonio. When Joey offered to pick up my sedatives, I'd declined. They were a symbol of the man's hold on me, and I wasn't willing to relinquish my power to him anymore. I wasn't sleeping well, but I was sleeping, thanks to the two men who kept my body warm and my mind protected beneath a layer of silk sheets.

The pain of Kellan leaving had hung over me like a thick storm cloud for the last three days, but I had more than enough to keep me busy with the announcement tomorrow. I'd disassociated enough to grin and bear it, but the cavernous ache in my chest returned every time his shadowy form entered my thoughts. He could have been with me today as my sword and shield. But he was well and truly gone. No sign of life, just a series of unanswered texts, and a hole where my heart used to be.

So, instead of having the man who I'd entrusted with my safety for several years, I had one of Sammy's heavily vetted teams: four guards stationed outside of my already heavily fortified office building. Aside from my condo, it was likely one of the most secure buildings in the state. But after Blackbird's appearance on my coffee table shattered my security, I couldn't take the chance. Not when I had good, innocent people like Marty who could get caught in the crossfire. Slicing off the penis of a pedophile or predator and watching the blood stain their expensive shoes was an enjoyable pastime of mine, but I didn't want any of these people, *my* people, getting so much as a paper cut under my care.

"What's to talk about?" I quipped as we sat side by side on the supple cream leather sofa in my office, reviewing the briefs of the day. My private life had been scattered into the wind during a dust storm, but it was business as usual at Lane Enterprises. Capitalism stopped for no one. "Surely, you've heard what people are saying about me?"

My tone was light, mocking even, in the way Marty and I communicated best, but even to my own ears, the joke felt forced. Still, he indulged me, keeping the conversation light and distracting. Marty always knew what I needed, when I needed it. I hoped wherever he ended up, they took good care of him.

"Oh, right. Thaaaaaaaat." He stretched the word with an exaggerated eye roll. "Is my cock safe?" He joked, placing the notepad over his crotch in jest. "Or do I not qualify for castration by the alleged *Mutilation Mistress*?"

"Dear God, it's terrible, isn't it?" I grimaced and slid deeper into the soft seat of the couch. "It's hard to run a company when I'm so busy finding new men to mutilate." I rubbed two fingers at each temple, the throbbing thrum of my permanent headache back with a vengeance. "They won't be here long, Marty. My intention is to get this ridiculous investigation wrapped up as soon as possible. Weston's great at what he does. I'm glad he's on my team."

A warm smile crept across my assistant's face at the mention of his husband. "Yes, he is. Promise, Laney, he'll make them pay for all this bullshit." The smile curved down into a disgusted curl.

"Speaking of men you might *want* to mutilate..." Marty's lips pressed into a firm line before popping obnoxiously, as if to emphasize his next point. "Your father's been calling."

Of course, he had. He'd heard the rumors and was panicked his cash cow was about to be put out to pasture. More importantly, he'd want to make sure he had access to my wealth in some form if my assets were frozen, which, if they came up with more evidence before Aaron could hold his press conference, was the next likely step.

Weston had helped reach the right contacts for what we'd planned at the end of the week. Private contractors and reporters who had been sworn to secrecy—which naturally meant it would be leaked to one source or another, and we could expect a huge turnout. No one knew it was Aaron Rodriguez speaking. Instead, we'd used me as the bait, stating I would speak publicly about the allegations for the first time. At the time of the press conference, all supporting evidence of Alvarez's ties to Aaron and me would be presented to the FBI, local police, and the Securities and Exchange Commission. Gertie Baker had come through, so we had everything we needed to prove Alvarez had been after me from the start. I only wished we could pin Blackbird's murder on him, to give my friend the peace she deserved beyond the grave.

Kellan had been most worried about security, and I couldn't blame him. We'd gone to great lengths for several months to keep Aaron safe from Antonio. To have it all come crashing down now to put Alvarez is his metaphorical grave...

Well, I couldn't think about it without a golf ball-sized lump in my throat. Losing Aaron was *not* an option. Not after I had lost Kellan.

We had contingency plans and the maximum amount of security Sammy could offer, and it would have to be good enough. Burying Alvarez, clearing my name, giving Aaron the opportunity to have a real life again. We needed every piece to move on the board in the right sequence, so we could knock Antonio out of the game completely. It would take white-collar castling and bloody attacks, but we'd end the game with a checkmate. There was no other way.

"Laney?" Marty prompted, breaking through my thought spiral. "Would you like me to call him back, or..."

"No, that's fine. I'll do it." I shuffled the paperwork we'd been reviewing on the coffee table and offered him a faint smile. "I'll call him now and get it over with to save you more voicemails."

Marty stood and stretched his lanky limbs before heading through the glass door into the hallway. "I'll grab you another coffee for mental strength."

That garnered a laugh. "Always taking care of me," I teased and walked over to the cleared glass desk overlooking the landscape of crisp blue sky and buildings below. The mountains loomed so close, it felt like I could touch them just beyond the pane.

"Laney?" I turned to face Marty hovering in the doorway, dark-eyed and tense. "I'll always take care of you. But make sure you're taking care of yourself, okay? You're only human."

He didn't wait for my response—striding down the hallway without a backward glance, on a mission to keep me caffeinated and sane with the inevitable exasperation that came with being Camden Lane's daughter.

You're only human. Since college, I hadn't felt human. I was an enforcer, a juror of justice, a purveyor of pain. I built my empire in the daylight and stalked shadows in the twilight, each issued punishment another plate in my armor. These last few months had stripped each molded shield off my body, exposing my naked vulnerabilities and the deepest desires of my heart. I had been learning just how human I was in these last several weeks, and I loathed its uncertainty.

Warily, I picked up the phone and dialed my father's number.

"Hillary," he barked into the phone. His irritation filtered through the line like I was a disappointing teenager instead of the adult daughter who'd saved him from rotting in a jail cell.

"Daddy," I replied coolly, the pulse between my brows reminding me to make this call short and salty—it would be anything but sweet. "To what do I owe the pleasure?"

"To what do you—have you seen the news?" he sputtered angrily. "Can you tell me why you're letting the Lane name be dragged through the mud like we're impoverished riff-raff? I raised you better than this."

Visceral, spine-shaking anger tore through me, its power potent and surprising. No "How are you?" Not "How can I help you through this?" Though I never would have expected it. My tolerance of this behavior had evaporated as quickly as my sense of security. My crumbling walls had made a significant dent in my self-assurance and, along with it, my patience for my father.

"Let me stop you right there, oh, sperm donor of mine."

Daddy was no longer applicable. Daddy implied a man of trust, of protection. Someone to count on, to nurture and provide. Camden Lane was none of those things, and he would no longer get the privilege of the title.

"*Your* name has nothing to do with this. *Your* scandal has already been highly publicized—or have you forgotten? This is my name on the line. *My* empire. And frankly, none of your business." I switched gears before I said something I'd truly regret. "What do you want?"

Harsh breaths echoed through the speaker, and I pictured my red-faced father huffing at his desk in his precious study—the desk and study I had generously paid for. The soft tones of a woman filled in the background, along with the clink of a crystal tumbler and splashing liquid.

When he finally spoke, his words had softened, if only slightly.

"I want assurances you will fix this. I don't care if you did it. I don't care if you continue to do what they're saying, just *fix it*. Lanes don't quit, we don't concede, and we don't get *caught*."

Laughter erupted from the pit of my belly. The waves of chuckles cramped my abdomen and brought tears to my eyes as my body shook with the audacity of it all.

"Lanes don't get caught," I repeated, the words tasting like ash on my tongue. "But they do, don't they? Shame on me, sperm donor, because you didn't learn your lesson. I bailed you out, hoping you'd have something in your heart worth redeeming. Maybe I did it because I was hoping to feel closer to the mother you never let me ask about. I guess I've had to learn my lessons the hard way too."

"You ungrateful bitch," the man at the other end of the phone spat out through gritted teeth. "I'll have you..."

I tuned out his tirade and stared out the window again, using the light of day and the bitterness bubbling in my chest to strengthen my resolve. The mountains gleamed in the afternoon sunlight, the crisp reflection off the snow-capped peaks so beautiful in the glow of inevitable spring. Yet here I was, in my office, speaking to a man who had treated me so poorly I had developed a desperation to take care of him, even at a distance, to subtly seek the approval I'd never received.

My unresolved Daddy issues had finally risen to the surface of my skin. The embarrassing burn crept across my cheeks and singed the baby hairs as I allowed myself a single moment to steep in my shame, before scrubbing it off my soul altogether.

"I'm done," I announced, cutting off his tirade. "All access to my money, done. I'll be speaking with your handlers, and you'll be moving locations because, as of today, I'm putting the house on the market. The cushy life you've grown accustomed to? Done. This relationship? Done."

I stood from the desk and grabbed a file from my corner cabinet, the one holding all of his information—copies of the evidence that put him away, the contacts on his file. Everything I needed to wipe the slate clean forever.

The line was suddenly deathly quiet, though I heard the barest muffle of a feminine tone. My father wouldn't grovel —I don't think he even knew how. Instead of ending the call, I waited, curiosity winning out at his next response. It didn't disappoint.

"I don't need you anymore. A Lane always has a Plan B." It was a triumphant proclamation, not the haughty threats I expected. "Good luck with your life, Hillary. But with the way things are, I'd say you're nice and fucked."

The line clicked abruptly in my ear, but the grating sound was far more welcome on my pounding head than the noise of the indignance of a privileged man. I released a body-cleansing breath through gritted teeth as I considered his final parting words. I was certain I'd never speak to him again without my lawyer present.

Plan B. Knowing my father, he *would* have a Plan B. A Plan B that involved selling off my assets for...

The jackhammer of pain against my skull continued, but it didn't stop the connections forming between synapses inside my brain. A knot of thread was untethering, and I needed to get back to the warehouse to confirm its origin.

The security detail was following me everywhere I went, but Joey was still my driver. I sent her a quick message and quickly packed up my things.

It was time for answers.

I found the man in question seated at the kitchen table, playing a game with Aaron, using Froot Loops as the play pieces.

"As much as I want to know what this is"—I waved at the table between them—"I need to ask you a question, Lucky."

"Shoot, Blondie." The Irishman peered up at me with sultry sea-glass eyes and a languid grin, his lean and muscular form sprawled out in the metal chair with a casual grace only Lucky possessed. The stress and pressure may have added a few more wrinkles around his eyes, but his body language was as relaxed as the day I met him.

Aaron looked much better himself—not quite the man who'd stood menacing and tall before being stabbed eleven times, but close. He was seated far more upright, legs crossed at the ankles in front of him as he leaned back in the chair. He offered me a warm smile—the smiles he reserved only for me—and I smiled back, so grateful the man I loved so deeply was here on this side of the earth, playing a game, no less. Lucky was bringing out little moments of joy in him, and their pairing—as unexpected as it could be—brought joy to my heart too.

I turned back to Lucky, determined to get answers before I distracted myself with the two gorgeous men in front of me.

"I assume when someone hires The Six, they pay a deposit to secure the contract, right? How much do you think the deposit was on me?"

He whistled through his teeth, the high-pitched tone ringing through the cavernous space. "For something as valuable as your painting? A hundred K, minimum. Then installments on top of that." He leaned forward, eyes alight with interest. "What's going on in that beautiful brain, love?"

One hundred thousand dollars. The paintings missing from my father's—*my* house—could easily fetch $25,000 per, if not more, with the right buyer. "I've been wracking my brain for weeks about who would have hired you—for a *painting*. It's so specific. I have so many assets, and hundreds of millions in stock options, but that painting, sold on the black market, would be untraceable. And, the most profitable. Few people even knew I had it in my possession, and unless the person was a true art connoisseur, they'd go for something far easier to steal."

"So, you think you know this person, *Mi Reina*?" Aaron cocked his head quizzically, and I could see his own mind mulling the possibilities through the landscape of his amber eyes.

"Oh, I know them all right. My father. I would bet my entire fortune that Camden Lane hired The Six to fuck me over. I just have to prove it."

Lauchlan's eyebrows kissed his hairline, the green irises pinpricks within the whites of his eyes. "Er, that explains a bit, actually." He cleared his throat awkwardly and stood, leaning his frame against the island counter.

"Spoke to Ma the other day, and she was pressing me for the painting again. Remember that dud of a deal she offered me, to split the profits on a black-market sale by swindling The Six?" He swallowed hard, his Adam's apple bobbing in his throat. "She had a right hard-on to get the money and run with her boyfriend. Called him 'Cammie.' What are the chances your Da got with my Ma, Blondie?"

My eyelids blinked so rapidly they peeled a layer of film off my eyeballs. "Marcie? Marcie Davidson is your *mother*?"

"Wait." Lucky's brows furrowed into a confused frown. "You knew she was dating your Da?"

"I didn't know she was your *mother*?!" The words came out on a low shriek. How in the world had I missed *that* detail, of everything else Blackbird had dug up on Lauchlan O'Donnell? All this time, these two scheming, lying, opportunistic bastards had been plotting against me and using Lucky as their bait. It was a brutally simplistic plan, and I had missed it entirely.

"Might I make a suggestion, *Mi Reina*?" Aaron's soothing tenor wrapped around me like a blanket amid my minor meltdown. "*Rojo* has requested the use of my forger contact to replicate the painting to satisfy his contract with The Six. Are you willing to ship this to her and pay the fee? I will take responsibility for its safety—but I can assure you —not even the most scrutinizing critic will find fault in its authenticity."

Forge the painting, give it back to The Six, who would give it back to my sperm donor—and then we'd report the painting stolen and lead them back to the source. It required time and patience, but it would land Camden back in a jail cell where he belonged.

"I want them to serve time for this." My words were directed to Lucky. Just because I wanted Camden to rot in prison didn't mean he wanted the same for his mother.

Lucky strode over to me, wrapped his good arm around my waist and softly squeezed. "Pretty sure she set me up on this one, love. Can't argue with her paying the price for it." He kissed the top of my head as if to accentuate his point. I reached down for his hand and interlocked our fingers, squeezing in response.

"I'll pay for it. Can you set this up before tomorrow?"

Before tomorrow. Before the world opened up to us, or crashed and burned. There would be no in between.

"It is done," my beautiful Colombian said succinctly, turning his attention back to the game in front of him. Waving a large palm, he beckoned me forward. "Come, *Mi Reina*. I will teach you *Trique* before dinner."

They were trying to distract me. We'd all been buried in our own pain after Kellan had left, but were equally committed to putting on a good face. Our lives would change tomorrow, for better or worse, and we wouldn't waste our precious time wallowing. Outwardly, at least.

Lucky released his grip and pulled up another chair between them, counting out another color of Froot Loops on the tabletop. I leaned in to learn, enveloping myself in the family I had built for myself, and sent a brief prayer to the stars tomorrow wouldn't take them away from me.

CHAPTER 16

Kellan

The sound of the hot-wired engine coming to life was music to my ears, drowning out the voices of doubt pounding violently inside my head.

I pulled out of the tiny fast food parking lot, long since closed, and hoped whoever I'd screwed over had insurance on the junker I'd stolen. Exacting justice on the sacks of scum in our society was one of my favorite pastimes, but harming innocents—especially the working poor—was a line I hated to cross. They had enough battles to fight without my adding to them.

I'd driven aimlessly for a few hours northward before driving east, deeper into mountain territory. It was the second car I'd stolen that night, but it was that, or risk my brothers following me. Tonight, I had chosen me. With the warehouse out of the question and my bungalow—the closest thing I had to a home in this state—no doubt under my father's surveillance, I didn't have anywhere else to go.

And whose fault is that, idiot?

My thoughts hadn't given me a moment's peace since I'd left the woman I loved sobbing on the floor. I'd been a true asshole delinquent. It nearly broke me to see her beautiful body collected in a heap, the tears as bitter as poison. I did that to her. As long as I was around her, I'd keep doing it to her. My birthright made me the worst person to fall in love with, and, as hard as I'd tried, she'd fallen for me, anyway. Just as I'd tried to stop myself from falling for her.

Fucking impossible. Hillary Lane was everything I could ever want in a woman—in a partner. Fierce loyalty, a calculating brain that rivaled her beauty, and a body that could kick my ass when needed. She was too damn perfect, and didn't deserve the life I would give her.

Hell, thanks to my father, I couldn't guarantee a life on this side of the dirt whatsoever. She deserved more than that. She deserved better than me.

Lauchlan and Aaron would take care of her. I took comfort in that fact. Two men with the skills to protect her and the will to watch over her. Aaron would lay down his own life before he'd ever let her get hurt, and Lauchlan— the man might not have said the words, but he was just as in love with her as we were.

My heart twinged at the thought of leaving both of them behind too. Men I cared about in ways I never could have imagined. Pretending we could have had a life together as one big fucked-up family was only going to make the hurt worse. I needed to focus on the future or I'd never make it through the night, let alone alive.

I'd spent the last few nights in a seedy motel on the other side of Sheldonville trying to figure out the rest of my life. I was at a loss. No actual plan, other than marching up to my father's door and stabbing him through the chest with the blade Aaron loved so much. One of Antonio's goons would shoot me on sight. An easy death, and someone would rush in to fill my father's place—likely one, or both, of my idiot brothers.

Or, I could slow-play—get into my father's good graces and wait for the right time to pounce. This was the stupidest version of a plan yet—once Antonio stopped trusting you, you were fucked. I would have to murder every single person he had a vendetta against in cold blood for him to ever reconsider my status in the family.

The devil himself already owned the deed to my soul. I wasn't going to accelerate the process of my demon-hood by acting as Antonio's personal assassin, just for another five minutes to possibly drive a stake through his heart. The man would kill everyone I loved to make a point, and then dangle me on a cross to serve as a warning to others.

It really didn't matter what plan I chose—my death was the inevitable end. Trish wouldn't protect me, and no one else could. Unbidden thoughts of my mother rose to the surface. The tepid smile of the woman who'd been broken by my father. She had been stunning. Hair of spun-gold, blue eyes like mine—one of my father's favorite possessions to play with. Until she was too fragmented for him to get any joy out of any more. He'd driven her to insanity with his head games, and she'd eventually chosen suicide as the way out.

She'd left me, a twelve-year-old boy, in Antonio's eager hands to manipulate and mold in his image. Venomous bile pooled at the back of my throat, and rage blistered the inside of my mouth. Ingrid Lindberg left her only son to a monster. She had escaped his cage, only to put me in her place.

Did she think she was protecting me? Did she think of me at all? Long-buried emotions sat like stones in my stomach, immune to the biting acid. When doubt made its way through my mental shields, thoughts of my mother plagued me like an incurable disease.

I couldn't curb the nagging sensation of uncertainty balling up over and over in my gut. I needed to detach the cancerous tumor, but it was a relentless beast on my conscience.

My brain knew leaving was the right decision. My heart was being a fucking nuisance.

While my mind was caught up in the middle of a painful memory lane, my subconscious controlled my wayward driving, bringing me to the outskirts of Brenton.

Brenton. My half-brother, my nephew, and their family lived here. And at two in the morning, in a stolen car, with not a single other vehicle in sight for over an hour, it was likely the safest time to see them.

Decision made, I drove directly to their home nestled in a private mountain suburb. I punched in my personal code to enter the gate, and security lights followed me as I drove up the concrete driveway into the private portico.

I opened the door of the crappy car and let the crisp, cold air fill my lungs, unsure of what to do now. A sleepy female voice laden with consternation echoed against the stone building.

"Kellan Carlos, you better have a damn good reason you're here and not with Hillary right now."

A slow smile twitched across my lips at my sister-in-law's tone. I'd shared a night with Winter almost a decade ago. Since then, she'd fallen for my nephew, my brother, and three other men. After we'd worked together to take out Georgio, my oldest brother, we'd stayed in touch. Over the years, she'd become a close friend—as close as anyone could get to me. And she had no issues reaming me out when the night called for it.

Like now, apparently.

I climbed out of the vehicle, my large body unfurling from its cramped quarters. "Nice to see you too, little bird."

She strode over to me, decked out in pajamas covered in cartoon bunnies, and wrapped her arms around my waist in a firm hug. I pulled her to me to share the embrace, noticing Cam, my youngest half-brother, standing quietly in the doorway.

"You lost, brother?" He locked eyes with mine as his deep Southern drawl carried across the large driveway, his accent as strong as it was when we'd met six years ago. "Haven't heard from you in a while."

Cam was the largest and strongest of their group. Years ago, he'd been a prized fighter for the brother I'd killed. I liked and respected him. He'd been handed a raw deal when his adoptive parents passed away, and he'd worked hard to build a life he was proud of. My nephew, Travis, had come from nothing after my brother abandoned him and his sick mother for the whims of our great Cartel leader. He'd built a home with five other people—and now, he had a son.

I'd protected them all from the devastation that was my father as best I could over the years. So much so, Antonio had no idea Cam or Travis existed. It was why I rarely made an appearance up here. I wasn't willing to risk their lives for my own whims. That, and the fact these men had everything I'd ever wanted and would never get. Even now, in their quiet home with their loved ones safely tucked upstairs in bed, I couldn't stifle the electric daggers of jealousy that zinged through my spine.

"It's good to see you, brother," I replied with a wan smile. "It's hard to show up regularly when I work for the Devil." I tucked Winter under my arm and guided her toward her husband, each footfall lighter with every step forward. These people felt the closest to home I'd ever had, other than the people I'd just left behind.

"Could you make some tea, Big Guy?"

Winter's request halted the burgeoning hole of emotion forming in my belly as she led me through the foyer into the kitchen. She loosened from beneath my hold and pointed to the metal island stool to my right.

"Sit," she directed, and took her own seat across from mine. "You have some explaining to do."

Hesitation filled my bones like lead. This woman wouldn't let me leave until I'd presented every sin and folly to her on a platter. Many of the secrets I held weren't mine to tell, and Hillary would kill me if I betrayed her trust, even if it was to her best friend. Navigating this conversation could be worse than a live minefield. At least in that, I'd have a greater chance of making it out unscathed.

"Spill, Viking."

Her blue-green eyes pierced me deeper than a stake to the heart, her tone brooking no arguments or bullshit. Cam handed me a mug filled with minty-smelling tea, then sat down beside her, the icy blue in his gaze equally penetrating. The two of them refused to blink as they eroded my will with their stares, a mix of curiosity and concern.

I drew in a long sip of burning liquid, a stall to gather my thoughts. They knew the tightrope I balanced on, but they didn't know either side had untethered its line, leaving me to fall to my death on the rocks below. So... I'd start there.

"Several months ago, Antonio wanted me to take over the sex-trafficking side of the business," I said, unraveling the spool of knotted thread that was my life. "At the same time, Hillary was having trouble with a business partner..."

I left several details out—anything to do with Alvarez specifically, but kept the spotlight on me. *My* fucked-up choices, *my* deal with the Devil. How Trish ousted me when I was no longer useful, and how the twins were now determined to kill me—which had put Hill in danger. I laid myself bare on the table like the emperor who wore no clothes. Nakedness was far easier to handle than the baring of my soul. I told them Aaron and Lauchlan—who I guess they'd already met—had become a part of our lives, and how we'd been working to clear Hillary's name, which was going to happen tomorrow.

"So, I left a few days ago," I summarized, my jaw hurting with the many words I'd uttered in such a short time. "I'm not willing to risk their lives along with mine when Antonio gets too close."

Winter's withering stare could have disintegrated an ant in its path.

"You're an idiot." She folded her arms across her chest, the cartoon bunnies mocking me with their own blank stares. "What do you think, Cam? Idiot?"

"A straight fool," Cam agreed, his baritone sweeping across the granite and hitting me with its soft lilt. "Sharp as a marble." Cam was like me, a man of few words, and that was all he needed to get off his chest, because he just let the words sit in the air like dense fog.

Prickly hairs stood on end at the back of my neck, my defenses rising with every blink that followed my movements. I swallowed the rising anger and checked myself with tight, shallow breaths. I'd shown up on their doorstep—I had to at least hear them out, even if their advice was shit.

"Thanks for your input," I tossed back sarcastically. "Very helpful."

"You want helpful?" Winter rose on her haunches, holding her slight frame slightly above mine on the island stools, a rare hostility blazing cold in her eyes. "What is the point in 'saving her' with your distance, if she won't want anything to do with you when she's actually saved? Hill values loyalty above *everything*. Do you think you're being very loyal right now, leaving just when they need you the most? Do you think she'll ever trust you again? What's the point of killing Antonio so you can eventually have a life with her, if she's just going to hate you in the end?"

"She's not going to—" I stopped because I'd seen it, the betrayal across her beautiful face when I turned away and walked out the door. It was an expression reserved for the lowest of the low, the scum at the bottom of a milk barrel.

She *was* going to hate me in the end.

"Brother." Cam's warm tone broke through the frigid noise. "If you love her, be with her. Whatever comes of that. Your 'protection' won't mean shit, if she can't count on you when it matters most. I almost lost Winter because I was too fearful once. Don't throw away the only thing you've ever wanted for a man you despise."

He saw through me like clear plastic wrap. The rawness of this vulnerability chafed my insides like sandpaper to the groin. Fuck.

Fuck, fuck, fuck.

Why did it take a four-hour drive and a basic discussion over peppermint tea to have the most obvious answer hit me over the fucking head like a wrecking ball?

"I'm an idiot," I admitted on a remorseful grunt. "I'm a fucking idiot."

"You sure are," Winter sing-songed cheerfully, before slurping the last dregs from her cup. "I'll make up your bed for the night, but you'd better haul ass in the morning to get to her in time."

She rose from her seat and wrapped dainty arms around my torso, planting a kiss in my hair. "The Viking prince gets the girl, haven't you heard? He just had to slay a dragon first."

I clamped large palms around her waist and returned the hug with a gentle squeeze. "Antonio is the biggest dragon I've ever known."

"And once upon a time, Georgio was mine." I looked up to see a sweet, sad smile trace her lips, the memory of those days still haunting shadows for us all. "But once a slayer, always a slayer, Viking. I know you'll win."

She turned on her heel to walk down the hallway leading to the main floor guest suite. I followed, my body finally succumbing to the heaviness of pure exhaustion. She brought me extra pillows, a towel, and a packaged toothbrush, and leaned against the doorway with a sardonic grin.

"And you'd better win, Viking, or Cam's going to kick your ass."

She left me alone with a strengthened resolve and a renewed sense of purpose. I'd make everything right. With Hillary, with Aaron, and with Lauchlan.

Tomorrow.

CHAPTER 17

Aaron

"Y̲ou're very handsome, *mi caballero oscuro.*"

My Queen's voice softly drifted over me as I straightened the Windsor knot at my throat, its familiar grip a protective comfort to baring my neck to the vultures in the next room.

I was dressed in a suit again; a fitted, Vicuna-wool dark gray ensemble. The generous gift from my lover to "bring out my best self" on the day I was to rise from the dead. Indeed, the feel of the soft fabric against my skin and the cut of the cloth against my broad form brought forth a feeling of power and dominance. For but a moment, I was the Rodriguez heir once again, standing at the helm of the battlefield, ready to reclaim my throne on the other side.

My love stood behind me in the small space set aside for prepping news anchors, her reflection adding radiance to an otherwise dull surface. She wore a cream silk power suit jacket and skirt elegantly draped across her slim body, her hair styled in gentle waves against her shoulders. She had several daggers strapped to her body, but no guns. We couldn't hide the weapon in her clothing, so she would rely on our sets of guards and her wits, should she need to. Like me, she was more comfortable with blades than with bullets. I took as much comfort in her skills as I did in my own.

She stood powerfully by my side in my hour of absolution. I drew from her strength to fill my bones as I drew in her visage to fill my heart.

I offered a small smile as I stared through the mirror and into her soul. "As you are beautiful, *Mi Reina*."

Small fingers wrapped around my suit-clad biceps, the light touch of the squeeze barely felt through the quality material. Steel rimmed the roiling blue sea of her eyes, the puffiness absent from the night before. Kellan's absence was a hollow chasm we would not speak of anymore, repressing the taboo topic under the weight of today's burdens. Shifting my position, I pulled her body forward and wrapped my arms around her waist. Burying my face in the crook of her shoulder, I breathed in the sweet scent of jasmine and rose.

Rojo was not with us—we'd opted to have him wait in a vehicle on the outskirts of the atrium, with watchful eyes and a police scanner to warn us should we have unwanted visitors. I missed him, knowing he could relieve the somber aura of our energy with a simple quip. It was his greatest gift, one I was starting to cherish.

The sex this week had been to provide an escape for our distraught queen, but I had also found comfort in

Lauchlan's embrace, and pleasure from his body against mine. My promise of filling his holes with my seed was a vow I intended to keep, when we finally had time to explore each other properly.

Hillary clasped her hands over mine, delicate skin cradling my rough knuckles, and burrowed into the shell of my body. We stood still in the silent moment, mourning the loss of the man who should have shared it with us.

My *compañero* was a stubborn, tormented man, choosing to drown in the depths of his misery under the falsehood his sacrifice would save his friends. I did not wish my friend to sink under the heaviness of his misconceptions. I wished for him to remain and join our life raft so we might find safety together.

My wishes were no match for his demons. His decision had harmed us all, even if *Mi Reina*'s was the most visible pain. I swallowed the discomfort forming in my throat at the resurgence of emotion. I was not angry, as Hillary was, or patiently waiting for a change of heart, as *Rojo* was. Disappointment was my primary sentiment. The man I admired, a man I desired to call my own, had chosen abandonment over risk, under the untrue belief of protection. He did not trust us to protect him as we had entrusted him with our lives. He'd succumbed to his darkest doubts—that he was not worthy of us, a convincing lie.

I longed to shake him as much as hold him, to remove all uncertainty from his mind. He belonged with us. To us. Kellan Carlos could be our active sword, but he was now ours to shield.

A rap on the steel door broke me out of my thoughts. "Ms. Lane, five minutes."

I slowly unraveled my frame from Hillary's, sweeping an errant hair from her brow as she drew away from me to grab her phone on the small counter. Her security detail stood as silent as sentries outside of the small room we'd been allotted. Four media channels awaited our arrival on the stage, all secured through Jediah's underground network of bandits and thieves, and Weston's above-ground contacts.

We'd ensured the messaging was cryptic but enticing. Hillary Lane was defending her honor against several allegations, and bringing proof to substantiate her claims. My part had been purposely removed from the narrative until such time my account would be revealed. A shell game of stories.

"I love you, *Mi Reina*." I sought to rid the shadows that had taken up her stare, but my love was not enough to barricade the demons completely. A temporary balm was all I could offer.

"I love you, Aaron," she repeated with a whisper. "We've got this."

Her tremulous smile was rife with nerves, but as soon as she turned to open the door, the nerves faded into grim determination with practiced ease. I too molded my mask into the self-assured shield of a leader without qualms. Today was Alvarez's final crucifixion, one step forward to putting my parents into the coffins I'd promised them.

Sammy's team of four mercenaries escorted us through the long hallway down to the atrium floor. I would have advocated for an outdoor venue, but March in the mountains was a poor time to plan such an event. Lauchlan lay in wait, and we had an additional two security teams in plain clothes roaming the room. It was the best we could acquire when we lived as shadows in the night.

I waited in the wings while Hillary took to the stage. Brilliant white light flooded the wooden platform, but from the darkness of the sidelines I could make out several reporters—at least forty in the crowd, along with a television crew with cameras focused on the podium. The camera crew was an important addition—should Alvarez attempt to assassinate either of us, it would be caught on live television, providing further proof of our story.

A violent hush fell over the small atrium as Hillary took her position at the podium. Her shoulders straightened under the crowd's attention.

"Hello, Carlisle," she began, her gaze moving around the room despite the blinding lights. "Thank you for joining me today on such short notice."

The crowd tittered in response, but did not interrupt her. *Mi Reina* commanded any space with her presence, pulling the oxygen from the room like a mesmerizing fire. I watched her crackle in the flames, my veins humming with the madness of uncertainty, my heart thrumming with love for the woman who was the very heart of my existence.

"There are quite a few rumors circulating about me these days." A devious smirk that could have been stolen from Lauchlan's lips took over her face. "I've been called a shark in the boardroom and a queen in the bedroom, but this has to be a first. Mutilation Mistress." She said the words slowly, as if feeling them glide across her tongue. "It's a pretty title, but not one I've earned or can claim to own."

Her lies were flawless fables, spoken with such authority I was inclined to believe them myself.

"I've remained silent these last few weeks as I've gathered my thoughts. You see, there is a story here, but it's not the one you've been told. But in order for you to know the truth, I had to ask a dear friend of mine to take a risk. one, I am thankful, he was willing to make."

Her gaze briefly landed on mine in the eaves, the subtle dip of her chin preparing me to enter. As swiftly as it had come, her attention returned to the captive audience of perfectly procured puppets.

"You've been lied to, Carlisle. I am not the Mutilation Mistress you are looking for. But before I reveal the real culprit, I'd like to reintroduce you to... Aaron Rodriguez."

A collective intake of breath rippled through the crowd as I walked through the red velvet curtains and across the stage to stand by her side. The people were less veiled at this angle—a grainy, gray landscape of scavengers in professional clothing, eager to profit off our ailments.

I kissed her cheek decorously, then turned to face them. As my eyes readjusted to the light, I watched a hulking shadow shift at the rear of the horde, the gait as familiar as my own. Even in the darkness, I would recognize Kellan's form anywhere.

Had his guilt compelled him to show up? Perhaps he had received a tip-off about his family and had come to offer additional protection. A surprising sense of relief trickled through my limbs at his appearance. His reasoning was irrelevant in this moment. I was grateful he was here, if only as a shadow of solidarity.

"Good afternoon." My address was solemn, as was needed for the rest of the tale. I stood at my full height in my expensive suit and shining shoes, feeling the most like myself in many months. Standing on this side of the podium, no longer hiding in sweatpants, filled me with a jolt of the power I was used to holding within my grasp. I owned it, infusing every vein with its intensity as I offered a tiny morsel of it to the throng before me.

"Several months ago, I was reported missing, suspected of passing in a car crash over Cascade Falls. This is correct. What was unknown before now is that I was intentionally run off the road by Marco Alvarez's men."

Another gasp, this one less awestruck and more trepidation at the accusation.

"Back in the fall, it came to my attention that Marco Alvarez was running an adjacent operation to his tech companies. Human trafficking, but proof was elusive. As a long-term business partner on the microchip project, I took it upon myself to investigate. In that time, I was threatened directly by Marco himself. It was fuel to continue. I eventually discovered an underground network of depravity and reported it to an FBI agent known to me, who agreed to investigate further."

The man I suspected to be Kellan retreated further into the darkened corner. Leveraging his credentials had been a critical element of this plan, though we hadn't explored a new version of the story with the change in his status. He had not been around to discuss it this morning, so the executive decision had been mine to make. Should he have an issue with it, he could come back to us and address it as our equal. My tolerance for bowing to the leadership of retreating men had considerably diminished.

"Through our work, we discovered an interstate network of trafficking that involved women and children. This is already on record, and Alvarez's trial is pending. Sandra Orton, the reported missing woman of late, had also known about Marco's underground network through her work rehabilitating children, and had taken it upon herself to pursue her own version of justice. She is the Mutilation Mistress you are so desperate to claim."

The vigilant neutrality in my tone had veered to distaste. I captured the sneer making its way across my face and pocketed it before it could sabotage my contribution.

"When she was caught and questioned, she confessed she'd tapped into her husband's ex-military contacts to work for her, extorting money from the highest profile offenders to pay for their salaries. We foolishly did not report her, and she went missing the next day."

I did not like this spin on the story. Sandra Orton's memory deserved to be tarnished as ancient copper, but Lauchlan insisted we needed another woman who would fit the profile to be our substitute. "Make it easy for them," he'd argued. "They need a scapegoat to wrap this up with a bow." *Mi Reina* agreed. Still, the words were sour on my tongue. The only solace I could muster in the moment was knowing her carcass still lay in the mountains, torn apart by birds and beasts.

"I am unaware of her whereabouts." I stared stoically into the mute crowd. Their silence was deafening, as they hung on every word of the carefully woven fabrication. They would draw their own conclusions, which would protect *Mi Reina* even further.

"Marco knew I was going to bury him in his own evidence. I was driving to Cascade Falls for a weekend away with my lover, whom you know as my business partner"—I reached for Hillary's hand and interlaced our fingers in demonstration, the baseness of the word not nearly enough to describe what she meant to me—"and when I failed to show up, she used the breadth of her resources to find me. How fortunate for my life, as I was barely alive at the bottom of the falls, my car buried under several tons of rushing water."

The communal inhale of the crowd this time was indignant, laced with ire and disbelief. I was a dead man walking, yet here I was, accusing my false perpetrator with proof of my life.

"It took time to heal, and I remained in hiding to protect my company and Hillary Lane. We continued to gather evidence, which contributed to Marco's current charges. I am now speaking out against this man, as it is clear he has no intention of stopping his crimes, even now that he is caught."

It was time to wrap our present for the FBI, and discharge the final blow to Alvarez's empire.

"Marco had a personal vendetta against Hillary Lane." I nodded to the woman at my side, who maintained her silence as my hand remained in her grasp. "We have recordings admitting attempted stock tampering, defamation, and veiled threats, all of which have been forwarded on to the FBI. It is our belief that Marco intentionally framed Hillary for Sandra Orton's actions, to once again devalue her shares and destroy her companies. It is our belief that Marco hired the criminals who fire-bombed her condo last week, leaving her homeless."

I stared into the camera, channeling the man my father molded me into—the callous, calculating mafia leader with the ruthless energy of an untouchable king. "This man's obsession will not stop until he has ruined her, and it ends now."

All oxygen vacated the room as my captive audience held onto their breath, awaiting their next directives as pawns on our chessboard.

My queen stepped back into the light, gently nudging me outside of the microphone's range. I let go of her hand, resuming my post as the dark knight at her back. My gaze landed on the spot I'd last seen my *compañero*, but his shadowed form was absent.

I was not used to the uneasy prickles of melancholy in my heart. Few in my life meant much to me to be sad for, yet I could not find a more appropriate word. Would he choose to make himself known, or had he appeared in a moment of weakness, only to vanish again? I could not bear Hillary's tears if he continued to tease us with his presence, only to pull away like a vagrant. We would not be game pieces for his guilty conscience to play with. I would not allow it.

"I have taken care of this city, and its people," *Mi Reina* declared, not wasting words. "My companies pay more taxes than my counterparts, and I employ more people in this state than the government. This is my town. You are my neighbors. I won't accept these false accusations any longer."

A shimmer of blond hair fell down her back as she turned to look directly into the camera, exuding the power and grace of a royal empress. Pride swelled in my chest, and love filled my heart at the sight of her on her throne, commanding my respect and demanding my devotion.

"To the FBI, shame on you. Agent Smith, I expect a personal apology for your gross misconduct. Marco Alvarez, your terrorization of me and my family ends now. Our people will not stand for another rich man buying his way out of the consequences he so rightfully deserves."

The room erupted into a din of excited chatter, two of the community's wealthiest adversaries now locked in a public battle. Before questions could explode like errant landmines, Hillary spoke her last words.

"I will not be answering questions, as the FBI is waiting for my official statement. You can direct your questions to Agent Agatha Smith, currently taking residence at the 78th Precinct. Thank you."

Adrenaline washed through my veins like a cleansing tide. This moment had taken the last several weeks to get right. Our single opportunity to salvage our names and our companies—fifteen minutes of fame to freedom. I breathed the first real sigh of relief in days as the crowd clamored to get a response from my woman.

"Ms. Lane—Ms. Lane—Ms.—"

Ignoring the cacophony of attempted questions, we left the stage, each surrounded by our own security detail and escorted down different hallways—her, returning to the room we'd just vacated, to meet with Agent Smith's superiors, whereas I would be escorted to the rear exit doors, where we would convene at Lauchlan's vehicle.

I too would be required to make a statement, but we'd agreed to meet elsewhere for the task, not wanting to remain so exposed for too long. The risk to our safety had always come into consideration, and this was the best compromise we could offer.

A bitter tang coated my tongue when I lost sight of *Mi Reina*. I swallowed the acrid saliva and focused on the next task ahead—returning to our makeshift home alive to focus on the remaining phase of our plan.

A door opened to my right as we passed it. Before I could register the motion, solid hands pulled me through the alcove. Darkness fell on the room as the door shut behind me. I whirled in place to face my attacker, reaching for my favorite dagger tucked at my thigh to pierce the foe bold enough to trap me.

"I requested a favor from Sammy's men. They'll stay outside. You won't be needing that."

The graveled butter of Kellan's voice echoed like bullets in a metal canister in the tight closet. War waged within my frame, the compulsion to kiss him and stab him fighting in opposition, though in equal measure. I stepped forward. Less than six inches of air separated our bodies, and I held the lethal weapon to his crotch.

"I believe I do, *compañero*. An apology is in order, no? Perhaps not to me, although you have disappointed me as well. You have brought *Mi Reina* much anguish. Surely, one testicle is enough to live your life? Or do you need both to fuck the three of us when you come to your senses?"

It was difficult to see his eyes in the closet's dimness, but not impossible. They remained the stalwart sheen of an unapologetic man determined to destroy his own joy for the sake of martyrdom. He was a fool.

"What is the word you say to her? Submit? Surrender? I believe it is time for these orders to leave your lips and be commanded by my tongue instead."

I drew closer and the dallying scents of bergamot and amber filled my lungs as I burrowed my nose into the cradle of his neck. I brought the knife up to caress his throat, resting it gently against the stubbled skin. His thick blond hair was tied into a bun on the crown of his head, leaving him dangerously exposed to my teeth.

I hadn't forgotten the fight we'd been forced to endure only a few months ago. This man was larger, broader, more classically trained. Yet he would not harm me, no more than I would harm him.

His silence stood tall like a brick wall between us, yet he did not move. I pressed into him further, with my body and my burdens, pushing for the answers he refused to release.

"Why have you come here, *compañero*? Shame? Guilt? Tell me what makes you disappear and reappear as a magician?"

His large Adam's apple bobbed against the steel of my blade. The depth of his navy stare pierced through me sharper than the dagger ever could.

"I came back for her." The admission left a shallow cut at the base of his throat, the single drip of blood decorating my silver with beautiful crimson. "I came back for you. And... Lauchlan."

My cock swelled as much as my chest at the words I longed to hear. Despite his stubborn façade of failing to care, he had returned to us. To her. To me.

"You have come back to save us? To join us? To..." I prompted, the push of the dagger causing another pinprick of red.

A guttural sigh resounded through the base of his throat, vibrating the knife in my hand. "A very smart person reminded me that if I actually live through my father's bullshit, I'm going to have no one to share it with because of my bullshit." His nostrils flared, the admission one of rueful sorrow.

Chagrin looked good on my *compañero*. It softened his rigid edges into velvet lines, devolving his dangerous veneer into a mere human man.

I liked it.

Removing the dagger from his throat, I sheathed it back in its home and clamped firm fingers over his jaw instead, holding him in place to press my lips on his.

His soft skin scalded mine, and the prick of coarse hair scraped along my jaw; both sensations pumped my cock with blood, thickening it against Kellan's thigh. My tongue traced the outline of his mouth, demanding entrance without mercy, desperate for the full taste of him.

His groan vibrated through my chest, masculine and aroused. I pressed my erection deeper into his own growing cock, relishing the brief friction as he allowed me access to his body. Our tongues and teeth battled in ways our words would not achieve. I savored his flavor, a taste I barely knew, yet it was quickly becoming one of my most prominent cravings. We rubbed against each other, seeking more friction to relieve the frantic itch of desire, our frames vibrating the wooden door on its hinges.

"I need to take you, but there is no time," I whispered against his lips when we paused for a gasping draw of air. "Show me your willingness to be a part of this family, with no need to control it. With no need to own it. You can only return if you are a piece of our puzzle, not the box that we come in. She will not allow it, nor will I."

His thrusting, confined cock stilled at my words, and the tension in his jaw became impossible to ignore. The room grew heavy with silence.

"I want to be part of this family," he declared, the sincerity in his tone a pitch that couldn't be faked with false promises. "I want you—all of you—to be mine."

His cheeks reddened to a dark pink with the confession, but his eyes—they sparkled the brightest blue I'd ever seen on this man, honesty lifting the veil he used to cover himself.

"Stay with us, and you may keep us." It was a challenge to his nature of running away, but stated as an earnest vow, unbreakable and true. He cupped my cheeks and pulled me in for a kiss—chaste and sweet—before pressing our foreheads together.

"Thank you, *Guapo*. I am yours." A solemn promise spoken between the battered souls of two men bred for battle.

My lips crested into an honest smile. "As I am yours, *compañero*. Perhaps we should go tell Hillary that you are also hers to keep, no?"

The wavering sigh informed me his confession to me was far easier than he expected *that* conversation to go, which was likely true. Still, we'd been gone far too long, and her FBI interview was due to be over. The only reason I'd felt comfortable enough to partake in this indulgence was the four men stationed outside the hallway and the FBI agents present in the building.

"Come," I beckoned, interlacing our hands as I pulled the door handle open. "You will join us at home, and we can figure out the rest later. You remain with us."

Yellowing light flooded into the closet, but the warning came far too late when the heavy body propped against the door dropped to the floor at our feet. Empty eyes stared up at us, burgundy blood trickling from the guard's mouth.

I immediately brandished my dagger and Kellan withdrew a gun from a concealed shoulder holster, but it was too late. All four men lay silently frozen in death in the tight hallway, their bodies splayed in awkward angles, their weapons removed.

"I will say, this is most surprising."

The familiar feminine timbre drifted down the corridor, its cool tone belying its heated edge. Carmen Delgado—the assassin that should have been dead—stared back at us with unfeeling chocolate eyes, a small pistol in each hand trained on both of our chests.

"I was only after one target today, Kellan, but the smell of lust in the air tells me I'll be taking two." She cocked her head, long brunette hair swishing across her back with the movement. "Is this why you didn't kill him, *culicagado*? He is your lover?"

So, Alvarez's men would not get to us today, but Kellan's greatest fear of leading us to his family had become our reality. A cutting irony. I held the dagger lightly in my fist, awaiting the right time to strike. My vow was absolute. Kellan was mine to protect just as I was his. I would not let her tear this man from his rightful place as King. She was a pawn in Queen's clothing.

"Are you a zombie or a witch, Carmen?" My companion's response was carefully measured, not a single emotion conveyed in its tone. "I thought you were dead."

The vile woman clicked her tongue in annoyance, unamused. "I am very much alive, *traidor*. But the same will not be said of you." She released the safety of her weapons for emphasis. The abrupt click of metal shut out the sound of my heart.

"There are FBI agents in the building," I cautioned, fingering the hilt as Kellan tightened his grip on the gun. "You won't get very far."

"Your brothers are assigned to the princess." Carmen's beauty morphed into a vicious sneer. "They will only touch her if you cause me trouble."

My eyes latched onto Kellan's, the previous shine of ecstasy now dulled to dark wax. The barest hint of fear flickered through them before titanium-fortified resolve replaced the wayward emotion. I didn't need to hear the words to know with certainty what he would choose.

He tucked his gun back into the holster and raised his hands in surrender, sealing our fates, but providing the lifeline for *Mi Reina* to leave unharmed. She would be furious, but she would be safe.

It was a choice I too would make, without thought or question. I sheathed my dagger and raised my palms to match his.

"Take us where we must go."

CHAPTER 18

Hillary

Sequoia FBI agents were arrogant, rude, and determined to piss me off today. I was in the power seat, and they knew it, but still they had to take up triple the time we'd agreed to in a pathetic attempt at exerting authority.

I stalked down the hall with a whole team of Sammy's super soldiers at my back, my body vibrating with the manic energy of the moment. Cautious satisfaction and tremulous relief continued to spike my adrenaline, and I was dead on my feet with the constant crash. Just a few more steps and I'd be out the exit doors, with Lauchlan and Aaron waiting for me.

No Kellan. I'd boxed every feeling I'd had about him leaving, wrapped it in thick packing tape, and tucked it in a recessed corner in the closet of my mind. I didn't have the time or the energy to unpack the cataclysmic hurt, and I couldn't afford the distraction. He'd left. It was done. I refused to think about where he was, or what he was doing, or who he was doing it with. I even stopped myself from checking his tracker this morning, unwilling to test my resolve.

Focus on the mission. The mission hadn't changed despite the ogre Viking's inability to feel his feelings like a Neanderthal child.

The first step was removing Alvarez from the board entirely. After today's press release, and by providing all the required evidence to the FBI, Alvarez was going to be incarcerated much sooner, and it was there he'd get a little visit from a prisoner who owed me a favor. With the quick incision of a sharpened toothbrush, Alvarez would kindly offer his blood as paint for the concrete floor of the tidy little jail cell he called home.

The next step was scrubbing the filth that was Antonio Carlos from Carlisle, from Sequoia—from the entire country, and bringing down his entire deplorable empire of sex and sin. Kellan's petulant actions be damned. I would follow through on my commitment to bring down the bastard.

I'd kill him myself if it meant freeing this state from his scourge and releasing Kellan from the poison that was his family. The man's head up his ass notwithstanding.

Our cohort stopped short at the end of the hallway that led to the next set of doors to the outside, causing me to stumble forward in my heels from the abrupt halt. The four large male bodies bracketing me stiffened, their back muscles rigid through the Kevlar lining of their vests, hands gripping the many weapons strapped into holsters at their sides.

I peered through the hole between two guards' arms, only to see the visages of two surly men blocking our path, their guns aimed at two of my guards' heads with the casual stance of trained killers.

Shit. Mical and Jonah Carlos, the psychopathic demon twins, stared at us with empty smiles and dead eyes, their souls long stolen by the devil that was their father. The brother they were hoping to take home for a "family reunion" wasn't here—which meant they were here for me.

The FBI still had to be on the premises. Did I want to make enough noise to have them run to my rescue? Would I even have enough time? If we had an open gunfight in this narrow corridor, not a single one of us would make it out alive—the space was too tight and the firearms everyone carried were far too powerful.

So, hand-to-hand was the only option to get out of here in one, hopefully, hole-less piece. Tough, soulless men only had one way into their hearts—their ego. And from what I knew of the twins, they had more than enough to play with. I swallowed every ounce of emotion trying to punch through my thoughts and drew in a breath to fortify my mental defenses before making my move.

I pushed on the flank of the soldier in front of me to nudge him out of my sight line. He reluctantly shifted, giving me a full view of my new opponents.

"Gentlemen," I greeted in a light tone, as if this were just an introductory business meeting. "How nice to see you again. Judging by your weapons, I assume this isn't a friendly call?"

Mical sneered. An ugly scar divided the side of his cheek and pulled the skin too tight. "Not here for chit-chat, *puta.*" He calmly waved his gun in the air, as if the weapon were an extension of his arm. "We're here as a little warning. Stay the fuck away from Kellan and Carlos' business. He's not your concern."

Despite containing my emotions in a tidy box, violent anger erupted across my skin. Kellan had handed his brothers their entire world six years ago, and they hadn't so much as blinked when their daddy told them to kill him. They didn't know loyalty, didn't understand what it meant to risk life and limb for someone you loved. I would *never* stay away from Kellan, even if he needed to stay away from me. Lane loyalty never died.

Another swallow, the furious rage burning the back of my throat as it slid into my belly. Still, I kept my tone even, level. A hostage negotiator between testosterone-fueled idiots with shit for brains and bullets for brawn.

"I have no intention of leaving Kellan alone." Standing my ground between four chiseled chests, I crossed my arms behind my silk suit and stared down the barrel of his gun. "So, thank you for the warning, but his business is my business. Kellan is *mine*."

"He is a dead man." Jonah's scoff raised the errant hairs on the back of my neck, but I didn't retreat from his penetrating stare. "You are smarter than to side with a dead man."

I wasn't smarter. Empty words might get me out of this corridor alive, but they wouldn't stop their witch hunt. I had a chance to end them today if I played the game a few moves ahead. I lightly fingered the two daggers tucked in the small of my back, slowly easing them out of the sheath with the tips of my index fingers. The knives cleanly fell into the palms of my hands, and I clenched them in my fists, small beads of my blood collecting against the blades.

"I'll make you a deal, *el tonto*." I stared into the hazel eyes of Jonah, the more intelligent of the two, making my challenge clear. "I'll fight you for it. No guns. Hand-to-hand combat. Me and one of you."

I was taking an enormous risk, but I couldn't see a way out of this without serious blood being shed. I'd just agree to leave Kellan alone, and they'd let me pass? Not a chance.

Antonio's messages didn't come with a warning beforehand. The man was efficient. The verbal threat would accompany physical enforcement.

One, or all, of us were getting shot today. Call me an idealist, but I'd do what I could to save these men's lives, even when their job was to save me. I drew my hands out by my sides, keeping the blades hidden within the bell sleeves of my suit jacket. I prayed the drops of blood wouldn't be noticeable against the cream color of my outfit.

"Hah!" Mical barked, vehemently shaking his head at my offer. "Tempting, *puta*. Unlike our brother, we do not fall for the tricks of pretty women." He shifted his gun to point it at my head, the stretch of his scar menacing and cold. "I will simply kill you for refusing a kind offer, how about that?"

Jonah lowered his weapon and placed a halting hand on Mical's shoulder. "We are not killing her, brother." He turned to grin at me, the predatory gleam in his eyes dancing icy fingers of fear up my spine. "But I like this hand-to-hand idea. We like to play with our food before we eat, don't we?"

Disgusting, the lot of them. Antonio and his spawn needed a deep grave to contain the deplorable filth that was this bloodline. The only person who would ever be worth saving was in a place I couldn't name, but I would do him this favor all the same.

"So do I," I responded before I whipped one dagger straight at Mical's open throat. The blade landed exactly where I needed, and I didn't spare a second to throw the other one in Jonah's direction. He moved in the nick of time, but instead of impaling his jugular as I had planned, it ripped through his eye socket, the nauseating squelch of metal in jelly.

Mical's gun clattered to the floor as he brought both hands to his neck to stop the outpouring of blood, but it was too late. That move was my most practiced maneuver, and I rarely missed my target. Thankfully, today wasn't the day I lost my edge, but the eye stabbing wasn't ideal. Jonah's scream of agony echoed down the hallway, but worse was the shattering sound of errant gunfire as he unloaded the magazine blindly toward the five of us before falling to the floor, gripping his face.

Sammy's best guard, a quiet man named Benjamin, forcefully shoved me behind him, putting his thick frame between me and the raging hellfire. When the violent symphony of shots faded into a ringing din, he fell to his feet beside me, thick rivulets of blood spurting from the bullet wound through the fleshy part of his cheek. I didn't need to be a doctor to know he wouldn't make it.

I hadn't made it through unscathed. My thigh took a bullet, the fiery sting unlike any other pain I'd ever felt.

My blood boiled like lava at the injustice of it all. Ben had sacrificed his life for me... for what? Emotionally stunted men with small dicks needing to exert their dominance through other's pain? They'd deserved their deaths, and I would make their end a disgusting indignity for the pain they'd caused my people and this city.

Adrenaline coursed through my bloodstream to replace the blood loss as my body leaped into survival mode, embracing the surrounding chaos. I shifted my weight around the fallen guard and rolled on the ground toward Mical's gun, kicking it far down the hallway before gripping the hilt of my dagger still embedded in his neck and twisting it harder, cutting through his trachea altogether. A gut-wrenching gurgle deadened by the resonance of my remaining protectors returning gunfire was the last sound Mical would ever make.

Jonah dropped on his haunches, wildly trying to reload without his sight, the dagger still stuck in the hazel eyeball I'd just stared down. One guard shot him right through the forehead. He flopped to the floor with all the elegance of a fish on a dry dock.

It was a disappointment not to pull the dagger out and stab his other eye, but we were running out of time even if I wasn't nearly empty of petty.

Shit, shit, shit. The hallway was littered with bodies and smothered in the spray of at least three blood types. The explosion of gunfire through the building was the last bit of attention we needed. No time to hide the evidence, no need to claim them as our kills. We needed to move *now*, and give explanations later.

"We need to move!" I shouted behind me as I rose to my feet, the blistering burn at my thigh forcing my teeth to grind my molars into my sockets, but I pressed on.

I didn't even make time to assess the guards at my back; instead, I stumbled on my heels toward the rear doors and into the bright March sunshine, a stark contrast to the hellfire we'd just escaped. The sunlight briefly blinded me with its strength before my gaze could seek Lucky's position in the mostly empty parking lot.

The vehicle we'd arrived in was nowhere to be seen. Instead, my eyes landed on two familiar bodies lying limp on the wet pavement, their hands and feet bound by zip ties. A pretty Latina woman and a large, surly bald man were hefting the bodies up into the back of a cargo van, moving as quickly as possible, slamming a blond head into the rear metal door as they struggled under his weight.

The evil twins were a distraction, I should have known. The timing was too convenient, too controlled. Now, I knew why.

"Kellan!" I screamed, my fear outweighing practicality as I limped toward the van as quickly as my Louboutin heels and a scorching leg wound would allow, the clack against the asphalt not nearly as loud as the pounding of my heart. Aaron's suited form was still splayed on the ground when the two criminals turned their attention to me.

Our worst-case scenario was playing out before my very eyes. Somehow, Antonio's people had captured and incapacitated Kellan—what the *hell* was he doing here, anyway?—and Aaron, the two men who should have been most equipped to fight back. Their brashness surprised me —if they were here, they would know the FBI had been on site just moments ago. Antonio must have felt very secure in his position to risk capturing Kellan this way. We had to be missing something.

A vicious smile lit up the woman's face as she took me in, racing toward her with my enduring bodyguards in tow. She quickly shoved the remaining limbs of Kellan's body into the cab and turned swiftly on her feet, drawing a small pistol from her back and aiming it directly at the guard to my left. Without a single second of hesitation, she fired, and the man—Luis, I think his name was—dropped immediately to his knees, the kill shot through his forehead barely shedding a drop of blood.

Another crack whistled through the air as the guard on my right took a shot through the neck, the Kevlar vest he was wearing not high enough to protect his throat. Hot blood sprayed from his jugular in an arc. The sticky liquid coated the side of my face as he fell to the ground with a resounding gurgle.

Terror crackled through me as I crouched to the ground, with no shelter, no gun, and two guards down. The remaining man behind me must have done the same, because the metallic pop of a silencer broke through the din beside my right ear, my eyes only able to follow the bullet's path in my periphery.

When nobody shrieked in pain or dropped in the distance, another shot went off, this one embedding into the side metal panel of the vehicle. I didn't need to see her responding shot to know it had killed the last guard when the resounding thud of heavy weight crashing onto pavement echoed behind me.

I lowered my torso slowly to the ground with my palms over my head to gain time while my brain calculated my odds of survival. My racing pulse thrummed in my ears as I drew in shallow breaths in a pathetic effort to remain calm. The blood of three men spread across the asphalt in search of a burial ground. It seeped into the fabric of my skirt instead, the weight of their sacrifice pulling down the already sodden material from my throbbing thigh wound.

I hadn't just survived the demon twins to die in a puddle of my blood in a parking lot. I needed to stay alive to get my men out of here. Otherwise, we were all dead. With two remaining daggers strapped to my thighs beneath my skirt, I had weapons, but I'd be shot through the heart before I could grab them. If only I could get closer—

"The Queen graces us with her presence," the woman purred with only a slight Spanish accent, the sneer evident in her tone. When my eyes finally rose to take in the carnage in front of me, Aaron was no longer on the ground, presumably shoved into the cab by the bald man while this woman unleashed her bullets. "I see I shouldn't have sent men to do a woman's job."

The woman held herself confidently, her brutal stare empty and cold. Instead of pointing the pistol directly at my head, she let the gun hang loosely by her side, grinning the toothy smile of a predator who had cornered its prey.

Come on, Hill. You're trained for this. Decide you're not a victim. Step One: Stop the threat.

Krav Maga. It might be my only possibility of survival. I stared back at her with lazy eyes, tapping into a deep well of endurance. My thigh burned with the heat of a thousand suns, and I was out-manned and outmatched, but I was *not* a victim. Not now, not ever.

I slowed my breathing and took in my surroundings as best I could while maintaining eye contact with evil-incarnate in front of me. The dead guard to my left was only a foot away, a gun loosely tucked into his belt just another six inches from my hand. If I could just reach it...

"You are quite pretty. I can see what he sees in you." She cocked her head as if I were a curious creature in a cage and continued to smile at me with razor teeth.

The comment took me off-guard, but I refused to show it, fixing my stare on hers so long my eyeballs felt like they'd dried out like raisins in the sun. If I could stay a curiosity, I might get enough leeway to move and grab the gun. At least bide enough time before the FBI came around the corner—surely, they'd heard the shots?

Ironically, I'd been running from their discovery moments ago, and now I hoped with every fiber in my being they would show up in the nick of time. What was taking them so long?

Every girl who'd survived high school knew how to be a mean girl without saying anything directly mean. It was in the tone, the presence. I dug into the barbaric teenager I once was and channeled her, tightening my smile with a pout of my own.

"I'm afraid I know nothing about you," I volleyed, keeping my voice even and level. "You are?"

"Forgive me, Princess." The smirk that consumed her face showed she was indulging me. Good. The longer she could underestimate me, the better. "Yes, allow me to introduce myself. Carmen Delgado. Longtime associate of your lover here." She dipped her head toward the rear doors of the cab, still open, the shadows of shoes the only thing visible from this angle. The bald man watched me with careful eyes, but made no move to interfere.

"Even after he tried to kill me," she added, amusement dancing in those cold, brittle eyes. "As you can see, I am still very much alive."

Was this the woman Lucky had supposedly killed? Hot rage infiltrated every blood cell in my body as I stared up at the person who'd dared to carve Aaron up like he was a meaningless piece of collateral instead of the *caballero oscuro* he was. I would slice through her skin like she had done to him and record her screams as sweet music for him to listen to when he needed a pick-me-up.

Carmen Delgado, whoever the fuck she was, was going to die. I just needed to reach—

The abrupt screech of car tires behind me nearly tore me out of my skin. The killer's attention whipped to the new presence and I used the distraction to tuck and roll, grabbing the gun tethered to the corpse's hip and releasing its safety as I landed on the other side of the body. A scream of agony ripped from my throat as the burned flesh of my thigh tore with the movement. My heel fell off, but I had no time to grab it and put it back on.

The crack of another bullet rocketed through the space above my head, but this time, it wasn't Carmen's gun doing the shooting.

"*Coño!*" she cursed as she raised her gun to fire back at our newest addition to the standoff. She projected her voice across the parking lot to greet them.

"You have come to finish the job, have you? I am unkillable, *culicagado.*"

A Gaelic curse flew back with another shot. *Lucky!* Lucky had arrived. Relief and fear coursed through me, a mixture of incompatible drugs. I needed to save my men, but I didn't want to risk losing Lucky too.

The gun in my hand was slippery, still warm from the coating of blood along its barrel, but I kept it still as I aimed and fired two shots in quick succession. One ricocheted off the dinged rear metal door at Carmen's back. The other grazed across her left shoulder, leaving a jagged hole at the edge of her flesh.

"Bitch!" Carmen screamed, ignoring the threat at my back to instead lunge across the twenty feet of pavement to get to me. The gun slid in my grasp, bounced off the asphalt and skittered to a stop well beyond my reach. I desperately clawed at the dagger sheathed beneath my clothing and crab-walked backward through the fallen bodies, unable to rise on my feet in the skirt and the now single heel. I'd barely moved five feet before she was on top of me, fingers wrenching the hair off my scalp in a tight hold.

"Blondie!" Lauchlan's terrified shout was only a muffle in the distance as I grappled with the killer in front of me, her sharp nails scraping into my scalp and drawing more blood.

She pulled me forward by my tresses. Instead of fighting against her motion, I leaned into it. She hadn't anticipated the dead weight falling into her and I used the element of surprise, shoving my dagger upward, aiming at whatever bit of bone I could pierce while she held me in a headlock. The blade cut through her muscle like butter, and the piercing howl of pain split my eardrum even as she refused to let me go.

Another set of hands gripped my shoulders and yanked me up, throwing my body over his shoulder as he raced toward the waiting van. White-hot pain rocketed through me like I'd been shot again as my thigh bounced against the tight bone of his shoulder, but my screams were muffled into the fabric at the small of his back.

I frantically tried to shift in his hold and gain purchase on *something*, but he held me too tightly for me to gain any leverage. The flash of a bald head came into my vision, the stale smell of sweat and strong astringent laundry detergent forcing bile into the back of my throat as I bounced off his torso with each jarring movement.

"Let's go, Carmen," he ordered, the gruff demand in his tone showing he was the one with the ultimate authority. "The boys will take care of the feds. Get moving!"

He was bringing me toward the van. Dread deadened my senses and honed in on basic hindbrain instincts. If I was put into that vehicle, I was never getting out. None of us would be.

I had two seconds to give our fourth the information he needed, provided he didn't leave here in the back of the van too.

"Lucky! They have Kellan and Aaron! Get backup!"

Fighting for my life and the chance for Aaron and Kellan to escape, I pressed my head into the small of my attacker's back, taking hold of a patch of fat and biting as hard as my incisors could penetrate. The man arched his spine in pain, digging his nails so deep into my calves tears stung my eyes, but he didn't miss a step. I squirmed every limb in his hold, my desperation to escape my only priority as he fumbled with something in his right hand, the crinkling of plastic barely audible over the din of gunfire.

"You'll die today, bitch." The vibration of his grunt reverberated through me as I hung against his tall frame, and the pain in my thigh and the prick of a needle were the last sensations I felt before my entire world went dark.

CHAPTER 19

Lauchlan

I had no idea what in the feck was happening.

Three minutes ago, tucked away in our getaway car, I'd debated if I should storm into the building and search the bloody place, since both Roboto and Blondie hadn't shown up on time. Two minutes ago, I heard shots inside the building, followed by shots fired on the other side of the parking lot and pushed my arse in gear. I hadn't anticipated the sight of a dead woman with a gun trained on the woman I loved, the whole damned army of bodyguards in a dead pile around her like a scene out of a bad action movie.

Seeing the killer I'd thought I'd shot dead through the heart was one thing, but my lass on the ground, about to die because I'd failed to do the job properly? Not on yer life.

I drove the jeep right to the edge of the makeshift shooting range, braking hard before hauling my gun up to sight and shoot the bitch dead out of the driver's side window. If I was as good with a gun as I was with my mouth, the woman would have been pushing up daisies, but I didn't much love weapons that could immediately kill me, and it was one area of my training I could have used a bit more gusto. I picked a hell of a time to have regrets.

The shot went wide and hit the side mirror of the Dexter killing van instead of tearing through her heart like I'd intended.

"*Trasna ort féin!*" I cursed in Gaelic as I took aim at her a second time. The shot just barely missed her this go around, redeeming my shyte shooting skills just a wee bit. My lass—the brilliant badass she was—had used the confusion to grab a gun from the ground, and one of the two shots tore through the flesh of evil-girl's arm.

"That's my girl!" I muttered, shifting my position in the front seat to take aim to get Carmen's chest this time, when my own heartbeats froze. Carmen grabbed Hillary in a headlock, and there was no way I was risking my shyte shots to take a piece out of my woman. The unkillable witch wrenched her forward, tufts of her beautiful blonde hair tearing out with each pull.

"Blondie!" I let out an embarrassingly schoolgirl shriek, but that was the least of my troubles. Did I try to run them over and hope Hillary didn't get the brunt of the impact? Did I shoot anyway and hope my goddess *Epona* would give me a little grace?

Think, Locke. THINK!

I scrambled out of the SUV and used the door as a shield to line up my next shot through the still-open window. I just needed to get a little closer to my mark—

Carmen screamed, pulling me out of my moment. Hillary had embedded one of her knives in Carmen's torso. Feck me, this woman was tough. My heart swelled with pride as I scrambled to leave the vehicle, but before I could train my gun on the witch's head to blow her brains out, a bald man came out of nowhere, hauled Hillary off her feet and threw her spent body over his shoulder, then turned on his heel, running toward the back of the van.

Feck me, the assassin was quick on the draw. She now had her gun trained on my head, and we both knew she was a far better shot. A deer in headlights, I debated my next move, while the mafia version of Dr. Evil got further and further away. Hillary's plea pierced the air as another punch to my already churning gut.

"Lucky! They have Kellan and Aaron! Get back-up!"

Fuck. I was not only responsible for saving Blondie's life, I now had the blood of my whole family on my hands. I drew in a deep breath as she retreated from my periphery, my helpless gaze fixed on Carmen's watchful eyes. If I made one wrong move right now, she'd kill me, and if she killed me, we were all dead. I had a lot of brutal things on my conscience over the years, but nothing nearly as rough as being the arse that got my whole family killed.

Over the pounding of blood in my ears, I heard the distant muffle of car doors slamming followed by the shuffle of many pairs of boots along the pavement. My blood ran deathly cold. This was it. Antonio sent another crew to finish us all off and—

"FBI! Guns on the ground with your hands up!"

Carmen's sneer could have curdled milk as she stared at the new arrivals behind me. She flipped her hair, then mad-dashed toward the van, evading the hailstorm of bullets that rained down on the parking spaces between us. I dropped to the ground, barely avoiding being pierced as they tore through the cab of our getaway car. The sharp ringing in my ears dulled all exterior sounds, except the vapid screech of tires on the other side of my temporary buffer.

Within seconds, some buffoon in a uniform wrenched my arms behind my back and clipped them into metal handcuffs at the base of my spine. A large pair of meaty hands raised my body forcefully.

"Lauchlan O'Donnell, you have the right to remain silent. Anything you say can and will be used against you in a court of law…"

I couldn't hear a word the officer said after that, focused as I was on the van tearing down the street and off into the sunset. My one last drop of hope drained into the sea of blood all over the ground.

CHAPTER 20

Hillary

It wasn't the icy pebbling of my skin that roused me from my drug-induced slumber, or the agony radiating through each of my limbs like a hot brand had been inserted between my ligaments and into my bones.

It was the smell, the nauseating stench of death in between the stages of decay and debris hanging pungent in the air like a thick blanket over my mouth and nose. A fierce gag overpowered my tired body, pushing burning bile up my throat and onto my chest. Scorching drops of the internal lava splashed my cheeks and dribbled on my chin, reducing me from triumphant Queen to the constrained hostage.

I was hanging by my wrists crossed behind my head and bound by cool metal. The position arched my shoulders forward in a painful bow. My feet, now shoeless, barely touched the ground. My pantyhose-clad toes could just touch the surface, unable to take any pressure off my spine. My thigh had gone numb, and the only comfort I could claim was they hadn't removed my clothing.

Even if my suit was soaked in the blood of at least five men and a good portion of my own.

Being drugged brought back the incapacitating muscle memory of terror. The last time I'd been dosed, I'd been forced to watch Alec steal my lover's life and body from her. The overwhelming sensation of shame forced trickles of tears to stain my cheeks, mingling with the remnants of my stomach.

Trickling water and the incessant buzz of what could be a beehive were the only sounds in the dank space. Trepidation kept my eyes closed for the briefest moment before I dared to open them and take in the surrounding landscape of hell.

My desperation to confirm proof of life for Aaron and Kellan gave me the strength I needed to peel my eyelids open and frantically search for them in the dim light of the space.

Suspended in a concrete cell, the only light came in from a sole opening in the top of the wall. It was impossible to tell what time of day it was from that tiny permeation, but I used the gray wash to scan the room around me as best I could with my constricted neck.

I couldn't contain an audible gasp when my eyes landed on Aaron, his face so beaten and bloodied he was almost unrecognizable in the dark, save for the remnants of the expensive wool suit he still wore. The garment was slashed in several places, but from this angle it didn't look like stab wounds—more like he was dragged behind a truck through rocky ground.

His arms were suspended over his head in the same way mine were, his head hanging against his chest in the quiet constraint of unconsciousness. My heart only resumed its own beats when his chest rose and fell in a continuous rhythm. Relieved tears replaced the fearful stream. My Dark Knight was alive.

Slowly, I swung my neck in the opposite direction. More tears fell at the sight of Kellan's hulking form dangling several feet from my left side. The side profile of his face reflected the brutality on Aaron's. Crimson crusted along the bristles of his beard, long having dried from a gash along the crown of his head. He too, was unconscious, with the tiniest rise of his chest against his chin. Both men hung from the ceiling at a higher height than I was, so their feet could barely kiss the concrete.

Dread settled in my gut why that was. What torture was waiting for us when Antonio or his goons returned? Several other questions raced through my mind as I took stock of our situation.

How long had we been here? Was Lucky still alive? Had he gotten help? Did my men have any internal injuries? It didn't feel like I did. I was sore, stiff, and woozy from whatever drug cocktail they'd injected me with, but I hadn't been stabbed, just the original bullet wound from my skirmish with Evil 1 and Evil 2. A small mercy.

And what was that smell? The air was moist and held onto the stench with a tight fist. Mountain air was not humid—had they taken us out of state?

I used my toes as leverage to twist my entire torso in the hold of the bindings, only to wish I had remained ignorant. A male corpse, dressed in a navy pullover and tan slacks, was spread out on the ground several feet from Aaron's position, its face barely recognizable with several patches of flesh missing. The bloated belly had been slashed open, loose intestines cascading down the torso and onto the earth like a waterfall. Flies buzzed around the body, hungrily feeding off the buffet.

Vomit rocketed up my esophagus and spewed from my mouth, only this time I had enough sense to project it forward to miss my body completely. The exorcised grunts of my retching echoed around me in a cacophony, disrupting the sadistic silence of what was to become our tomb.

Aaron stirred beside me first. A slow grunt escaped through swollen lips before an equally puffy eye cracked open to stare directly into mine.

"*Mi Reina*," he rasped, pain clear in the waver of his voice. "Are you hurt?"

Trust Aaron Rodriguez to think of me while grappling with his own agony. How I loved this man.

"I got shot in the thigh on my way here, but I'm okay. Just sore," I admitted, forcing a deep breath into my lungs to relieve the strain on my shoulders as I turned to look at him properly. "What did they do to you?"

He twisted his hands above his head, and a sharp grimace tugged at his cheekbones. "I believe my wrist is broken, and my face may have scarred, but I am alright."

"Ladies dig scars," I joked, my quip a poor attempt at levity. No longer the sole person conscious in the bowels of hell brought a wave of adrenaline-soaked relief, especially knowing that, temporarily, my knight was okay.

"As long as you 'dig' scars, I will be fine." The tiniest smile tugged at his lips. "Do you know where we are?" His gaze scanned the room, stalling on the body too close to his position for comfort. The muscles in his shoulders tensed as he stared a bit too long at our guest.

"I don't know where we are," I admitted, drawing his attention back to me. "Or how long we've been out. I—"

A sharp intake of breath on my other side interrupted me. I spun on my toes in Kellan's direction to see his head lolled to the side, the crazed glaze of a madman pervading his crisp blue eyes. He spat a large wad of bloody phlegm on the opposite flank of his hanging body before raising his gaze to meet mine.

"Killer. *Guapo.* Are you okay?" His nose wrinkled at the stench of the corpse and the unbridled aroma of the acidic puke just a few inches away from his feet.

When his eyes landed on the body on the floor, his eyes widened to saucers. "Maverick," he murmured, a familiar knowing embedded in his tone. "What the fuck did they do to you?"

Maverick. Kellan's number two for many years in the FBI. I hadn't recognized him without most of his cheeks and chin, but Kellan did. My insides clenched, knowing Antonio had done this to a well-known and high-up FBI agent. He had ordered hits on the men beside me, and it was unlikely he cared much about the connected billionaire hanging between them. If Lucky didn't come through, we didn't have a chance in hell of surviving this room.

"We're alright, *compañero.*" Aaron pulled Kellan's attention back to us, his tone somber but measured. "I am afraid we have limited options of escape, however."

"How'd they capture you?" Kellan's eyes looked rabid, a combination of fierce anger and despair.

"I ran late with the FBI interview," I admitted, knowing if I'd only been a few minutes earlier, none of this might have happened. "Your brothers were waiting for me. We fought, and I won. I'm afraid you don't have any brothers left—well, except Cam." I released a caustic laugh, so bitter it burned my throat. "When I finally got outside, I saw Carmen and a bald man loading your unconscious bodies into a van. I tried to stop them."

I couldn't shrug my shoulders with them behind my back, but I said the words as casually as I could.

"Seriously, Hillary? You took on the twins and lived, and decided going up against a trained assassin was a good idea?" Kellan's fiery anger turned to blistering ice. "You and what army?"

"Sammy's army," I shot back, my own ire blistering up my spine. "You think I would just let them take the two of you? Get your head out of your ass, Viking. What part of 'you're mine' don't you understand?"

I swallowed the wrath burgeoning in my belly. This situation, despite what Kellan was determined to believe, wasn't his fault. If we had any hope of getting out of this fun house of hell, we'd need to pool our skills and act as a unit. I loved these men with two-thirds of my heart, and I would do everything my body would allow to get them out of here safely.

More softly, I added, "They're all dead. But Lucky showed up at the end, and he knows they have the three of us. Hopefully, he can get help."

Before Kellan or Aaron could respond to that final nugget of truth, the creak of metal scraping on metal echoed in the room behind us, the ominous sound of a door opening on unoiled hinges. The three of us held our collective breaths as a presence came to stand at our backs though we had no ability to twist around to face it.

Time stood still as we waited the presence out, not daring to speak, shudder, or squirm, our bodies as taut as stone as we forced our opponent to make the next move.

Finally, two figures came into view, rounding the corner on Kellan's side to stand before us. Their matching smirks reflected their malicious intentions.

Carmen's slight frame managed to tower over us, the confidence in her stance one of a successful killer. Delicate but dangerous hands sat on her hips and her stare roved over us like a hungry tiger who'd found her next meal. A sadistic sense of satisfaction rippled through me despite my fear, at the wide bandage covering her right arm—a beautiful remnant of my dagger.

"Welcome, friends." Antonio waved his hands in over-exaggerated greeting, belying our deplorable surroundings. "I look forward to sharing this day with you."

I stared at the cartel king of the west through slitted eyes, refusing to indulge him with an ounce of shown fear. My insides weren't so stoic.

"I see you've met our friend." He nodded toward the rotting body, a cruel smile twitching on his lips. Eyes blacker than coal, he turned his attention to Kellan. "It would seem Patricia tried to fill your position with someone else. She is not as smart as she thinks she is."

He pushed the leg of the corpse with the toe of his leather loafer, "And he lacked the gift of subtlety. I will send both your bodies back to her when I'm finished with you."

Carmen's titter was haunting background noise to the declaration of our deaths. Of all the ways I had imagined my end, being tortured by Antonio Carlos was not one of them. I bit the insides of my lips to keep my panic at bay while father and son stared one another down.

"Is that your endgame, then?" Kellan's gruff voice held no inflection, his own emotions kept in check. "We all die no matter what?"

Shockingly white teeth flashed a truly gut-wrenching grin.

"Of course not, *hijo*. Great leaders must make hard choices. I have been too easy on you in your position." He licked his lips as if eagerly anticipating his next move. "But that is no longer a consideration. I will allow you one last opportunity to resume your birthright, but it will require a sacrifice."

He walked over to Carmen, who had pulled out a long, serrated knife from somewhere while I'd been so heavily focused on Antonio. He held it up to the dim light still streaming from the dingy window, as if scrutinizing it for streaks. Then he waved it in the air like a sword while walking toward our dangling forms.

Unconsciously, I shrunk back as he came closer, the jagged teeth of the knife practically shining with malicious intent.

"Choose, *traidor*. Who will get the knife? Your beloved princess, or the fallen son?"

Kellan stared at his father with burning revulsion in the depths of his blue eyes, his jaw clenched to quell his rage. Making this choice, even if Antonio allowed him to live, would weigh on his conscience for an eternity, and he'd hate himself for it.

Aaron's voice split through the dead air. "Choose me, *compañero*," he directed in a quiet plea, my knight once again choosing to protect me, even in our last moments. "I will not break."

I choked back the tears threatening to form. He might not break, but watching the attempt would break *me*. Kellan refused to respond, his jaw clenching so tense I was afraid his teeth might break under the strain. Antonio's grin widened impossibly.

"Choose, *traidor*. Or they will both die."

The tears I refused to shed burned the back of my throat as I swallowed them whole. Antonio was successfully holding our feet to the fire, and every one of us was about to be burned. I held my breath in agonizing anticipation, even though I knew his choice. Kellan would sacrifice his entire world to protect me. It was a love I hadn't appreciated nearly enough, and now, it would ruin the other man who held my heart.

"Thank you, *Guapo*." Kellan directed his response to Aaron, not to Antonio. "I won't forget this."

Aaron dipped his head in a shallow, solemn nod and turned his restrained gaze back to Antonio. "Do what you must."

Antonio's grin grew into a spiteful sneer. He held the knife behind him, beckoning Carmen with the action. She quickly darted forward and palmed the blade with a careful hand, and strode toward Aaron with the grace of a panther cornering prey.

"No." The true cartel king's bark was as fierce as a bite. His dark brown eyes landed on mine, the depraved portals holding a depth of evil I had never known. "This one."

"No!" Aaron and Kellan shouted at once, but I could barely hear their voices over the pounding of my heart. I drew shallow breaths as Carmen stood in front of me, the seconds impossibly long as she drew the knife up, resting it on the forearm above my head. The sickening scent of her patchouli perfume coated me in a nauseating fog.

"I must take the thing you're truly terrified to lose, *hijo*. It is the only way."

The hot slice into the soft skin below my wrist was the brand that sealed my fate. My eyes squeezed shut and my teeth held onto the insides of my cheeks with every strike, but I refused to utter a sound. This man would not get the satisfaction of my screams, even if it was my last action on earth.

Likely, it was.

CHAPTER 21

Lauchlan

It wasn't the first time I'd sat in a jail cell like a street kid, but it was the first time the stakes were more than a priceless heirloom and a bit of prison time. I'd been lying in the stagnant cell for a few hours, and each minute ticked by like a timed bomb was about to destroy every part of my life.

"Oy," I called to the guard at the end of the hall. "I want to speak to your boss. Please," I amended as an afterthought. Now wasn't the time to panic. I was a charming fellow and needed to use it, even if the agents in question were daft, brainless lumps of coal.

I'd been thrown into the cell with the American Miranda Rights sing-song, but only because I was the only living fuck at the scene of the crime. They had eyes—they could see Hillary Lane, super billionaire businesswoman who'd just done a press conference about people targeting her, had actually been kidnapped—and yet I was the one in jail, and no one had come to speak to me yet to get my side of the story.

"I have a right to counsel," I called out to the feckwit, who had ignored every single attempt at getting anywhere. "I want my phone call."

Crickets. Fucking crickets, while the biggest baddie on this side of the world held captive the most important people in the world to me. If I had access to my phone, I could at least track their whereabouts. I'd placed skin tracers on everyone before they'd left this morning as a failsafe. I couldn't track them if I didn't have my phone, because I'd expected the bad guys getting to us, not the most incompetent law enforcement agency in the country.

Not that they knew that. I could have gone the cell phone tracking route, but that had too many possibilities of failure. The trackers I'd gotten from a mate in Ireland would take two or three showers to come off, and I doubted the cartel was focused on cleanliness in the midst of a torture-fest.

That terrifying thought was enough for me to call the guard again. "If I don't get my phone call in the next hour, when I finally do, it'll be to the embassy." I gripped the bars of the cell and stared so hard at the lazy, leaning feck, he could feel me burn holes through his useless FBI jacket. "You want any information from me, you'd better get me a little ring-a-ding-ding."

The young guard rolled his eyes, but he moved his arse, disappearing around the corner to the desk where he could make a phone call.

I sat down on the bench and folded my arms, running through as many scenarios as my puny human brain could process. I didn't know Antonio, but he'd issued a kill order on Aaron, and Kellan betrayed him, so he was now kicking Kellan out of the family—which I assumed in cartel terms meant death by the most torture possible.

I had no idea why Kellan was even there after he'd thrown all our hearts in a blender the week before, or how Hillary had gotten caught up in a shootout with the apparently unkillable supermodel assassin from hell. I really knew fuck-all, other than Carmen worked for Antonio, so that was likely where she brought the three of them. It had been four hours since they'd thrown me into lock-up, which meant the people I loved could be out of state by now.

Feck, feck, feck.

"Lauchlan O'Donnell?"

I perked up from my perch to see a tall, bald, Black and beautiful man striding down the hall like he owned the place, stopping directly in front of my cell. The guard sluggishly trailed behind him, glaring eyes and pursed lips doing nothing to stop the interruption.

"Yeh?" I shot up from the hard seat to face the man I only knew from the photos in the paper—Weston Williams—criminal lawyer to the rich and famous.

"I'm your legal representation today." He turned his considerable form to the puny guard with a stare that could melt sand. "Open up, please. We're late for his interview."

Interview. Like I was here for a jolly little job title.

The guard reluctantly unlocked the metal door and slid it across the floor. I waved a snarky salute to him, then followed Weston's wide steps down the hall to another hall, and then up a set of stairs. He led us to a stereotypical interrogation room straight out of the nineties. Weston dipped his head toward the metal chair on one side of the rectangular table in the center of the space.

"Have a seat, please. I'd like to talk to you freely, and agents will be here any moment."

I promptly sat, my curiosity getting the better of me as I settled into the cold, brittle chair. "I'm glad to see you, mate, really I am, but why are you here?"

He sat down beside me, a bit of an intimidating presence, but I liked a confident man—obviously. Dark eyes scrutinized my relaxed form before speaking.

"Ms. Lane was convinced that her life was in danger from several sources, and I was left with instructions if she went missing. She never checked in after the announcement like we'd planned, and you were one name on her list to seek out. When I found out you were being held here, I came to represent you, as promised."

My Blondie, always thinking several steps ahead. I'd tracked them all with highly illegal, almost-immovable tracers, and she'd set up a lawyer in case one of us got caught. What a team we made.

"Great," I said cheerily. "Then let's do this as quickly as possible, because if these fuckers don't get a move on, Hillary Lane's gonna be dead. And I don't think any of yeh want that kind of headline when the American Billionaire Sweetheart shows up headless because the FBI is an incompetent bunch of peckerheads."

"I believe the word you're looking for is 'pussyheads'."

A silver-haired woman entered the room with impeccable timing, and I stared into the fierce eyes of Patricia Stanhope, Kellan's old boss. When I'd found out he was FBI, I'd looked into his entire team—and she was at the top of the top, at least on this side of the country. The woman who'd hung Kellan out to dry like a pair of old, holey socks. Cunt.

She took a seat opposite mine, along with another younger female agent with lips so pursed, she looked like she had a lemon permanently stuck to the roof of her mouth. I knew right away I wouldn't be able to traditionally charm these women, but I had other tricks up my sleeve.

"Pussyheads it is, then." Winking, I folded my arms across my chest and leaned back in my chair as nonchalantly as a guy brought in for a wee bit of card counting. Child's play.

I weighed my options as I stared at my opponents on the other side of the table. The junior agent was a pawn, no authority, no control. My mark was Patricia. I just needed to get a read on something or someone she cared about—and if that didn't work, I'd fall back on the old classic—blackmail.

"Mr. O'Donnell, I'm Agent Stanhope, and this is Agent Smith. I'm going to cut to the chase. What were you doing in the middle of a shootout on government property?"

"I would think that was obvious, Agent. Did you miss Hillary Lane being taken off in the ice-cream van by a band of cartel criminals? I was trying to save her life."

Two sets of beady, suspicious eyes grilled into me like I was a plump steak.

"With an unregistered weapon, as a foreigner on American soil? Not a good choice to make, Mr. O'Donnell."

Weston's hand grazed my arm. "You do not need to respond to that."

I smiled and shrugged my shoulders. "Wasn't my gun. I grabbed it from one of the hired security team after they were all murdered by the real criminals. 'Stand your ground,' and all that—isn't that what you Americans call it? My life was at risk, and my girlfriend was being carted off to who knows where for who knows what. Too bad I'm a shyte shot."

"So that is who Hillary Lane is to you? Your girlfriend?" Agent Smith's lip curled in disgust, as if being in love with the ballsiest woman in the world was some sort of crime in itself.

"Sure is." I shot another sunny smile at her sour face before turning to Agent Stanhope, my expression narrowing to deadly seriousness. "Kellan Carlos and Aaron Rodriguez were also kidnapped and in that van that took off. It's not Alvarez this time—it's Antonio. Do you think he's going to let any of them live?"

Well, they didn't call her "The Fish" for nothing. Not a twitch in a facial muscle, not even mute recognition in her eyes. I'd be thoroughly impressed if not for the fact my lovers were on the precipice of *dying*. Didn't she care about the man she'd mentored for most of his life?

"And why should that concern us? Aaron Rodriguez's family is known to the FBI, and Kellan is Antonio's son. Big deal." Agent Smith was one hell of a terrible poker player. Evidently, she didn't like billionaires, or men of any sort of criminal affiliation, even the ones they groomed for the FBI. What a fecking shrew.

"The big deal is that a recognized former FBI agent and a well-known billionaire have been kidnapped by a cartel organization that's been running unchecked in your country for over two decades. One you had a wee 'arrangement' with. A little odd that shots were fired in a building you lot were in, and it took you longer to show up than I did. Bit coincidental, innit? A hell of a story for *Time Magazine*, eh?"

Patricia's lips widened into a sardonic grin, her eyes squinting into little slits, like she had me pegged. "So *you* say, Mr. O'Donnell. Or should I call you Mr. Donovan? Liam Donovan, is that correct?"

Ah, so they knew who I was—and the only way they could know that was through The Six. Welp, it was a Band-Aid that had to be ripped off, eventually. There wasn't a chance they'd traced me back to the hacking, so they had nothing on me for crimes on American soil.

"Liam Lauchlan Donovan Jr." My shoulders rose and fell, as if hearing my real name aloud for the first time in years wasn't a jarring shout in my face. "I've turned over a new leaf in America. You'll see in my records I legally had my name changed once my Da died. I'm just a humble software engineer who picked the wrong employer and fell in love with the right woman."

Agent Smith couldn't hide her snort, but I was done with her. We were running out of time. Lives were on the line, and I wasn't interested in playing footsies with this farce of an organization.

"Here's the thing, ladies. Kellan Carlos is a dear friend of mine too. You know who signed a sworn affidavit with this man here?" I gestured a thumb toward Weston, who was surprisingly good at keeping a straight face, given everything I was saying was an outright lie. "Kellan Carlos did. The bloke confessed his involvement in all of Antonio's operations, his illegal recruitment, how you've effectively been allowing the cartel to kill Americans for years. Does the DEA know about this little arrangement? How about NSA? The American people sure don't. You cut your best fish loose, and he got himself some protection from you sharks."

I'd been speaking out of my arse about their timing tonight, but it *was* suspicious. Why hadn't they been shadowing Blondie the moment she left their sights—the evidence and the accusations were too strong. How'd it take them so long to show up and arrest me—the least likely criminal of the bunch?

I leveled my gaze at the two women with stones for hearts. This next bit was a gamble, but fuck it. Either I convinced them to move their arses, or everyone I loved died. It was a risk I had to take.

"You used Hillary Lane as bait tonight. Not a doubt in my mind. You let him die, and we'll release it all to every national news outlet. Don't care about some billionaire who's saved more kids and women in this state than you sorry lot ever have? Fine. But you're gonna care about the man who gave you his entire life, when you bent him over and fecked him without a single drop of lube."

Weston cleared his throat. The aggressive 'ahem' cut through my final statement like I hadn't just threatened two federal agents with bullshit blackmail.

"What my client is trying to say,"—he briefly met my eyes with a "shut up now," expression—"is that he has ample proof of wrongdoing within your organization, and to deny the pursuit of justice for a former federal agent and an American citizen who has done nothing wrong, would be the exact opposite of what the Federal Bureau of Investigation stands for, and potentially have catastrophic consequences for all sides."

He let that statement settle into all our bones, the four of us caught in a teensy staring contest standoff as the FBI considered their options.

"I am not Kellan's legal representation yet," Weston added, "but I'll warn you that whistle-blower protections are in place for a reason."

"I can tell you where they are if you give me my phone," I blurted, bravado now disintegrating into brain-melting anxiety. "I've got trackers on all of them—with their consent," I hastily added when I saw even Weston's eyebrow raise in question. "Can't blame them," I argued, sweeping my handcuffed hands upward as if to say, "Look around. Seems everyone and their dog wants a piece of this pie."

"I can't think of a more confusing mix of people." Patricia's penetrative stare held me glued to the hot seat. I simply stared back into the steel gray abyss, hoping like hell she had either a conscience, or feared for her own career. Otherwise, I—we—were fucked.

"I make friends easily," I quipped, praying to every god in the universe this worked. They'd answered me to save Aaron's life—I hoped the man was every bit of the black cat he was in personality, and had a few more lives in the hopper to save.

"You've made a compelling argument, Mr. Donovan." Two stares—one shrewd and one constipated—glared back at me from across the table, but in that moment, I knew I'd won.

Thank feck, I'd won.

"Agent Smith, please get this man his phone, so we can get a team mobilized for a hostage rescue mission."

I received a curt nod and a dismissive wave before both women stood and turned their backs to me, lowering the heads to speak in muffled tones before the never-been-fucked agent left the room.

Weston squeezed my shoulder and pulled, a gesture to stand. I rose to my feet a little awkwardly as Agent Stanhope—*hag*—cuffed my hands behind my back. I turned to face my fate sitting in her old, weathered palms.

"You won't be released until your information checks out," she informed me with her hand on the doorknob. "You are to remain here until Agent Smith brings you your phone, and we can discuss the major details of your 'innocence' in the shootout later. I suggest you get comfortable."

"I'm unable to stay," Weston interjected as he too walked toward the door. "But I expect to be present at that conversation. Agent Stanhope."

We received only a snarky lip curl before she exited the room, not even leaving the door open for Weston to follow behind her.

He walked back toward me when the heavy door closed shut, lowering his lips to my ear.

"That was one hell of a bluff," he murmured in a whisper. "You're lucky."

Lucky. I'd be damned if the cute little nickname Blondie had given me could be enough of a good omen to get us all out of the feckin' mess.

I watched him retreat through the door and turned my attention to my cuffed hands, clasping them above my head to say another universal prayer. We were going to need it.

CHAPTER 22

Kellan

"Again."

My father's order ripped through my heart worse than his bullets ever could. Fear, icy and relentless, sat on my spine as I watched the "hell" on my knuckles come to life before my eyes.

Carmen had the fucking audacity to grin as she drew the sharpened serrated blade back to the top of the sole of Hillary's foot and sliced a deep gash down to the tip of her heel, matching the other foot she'd maimed just a minute ago.

My Killer bit into her lips to stifle the scream in her throat, as tough as I'd ever seen her, but the flood of tears down her cheeks gave away her pain.

I stifled my own, the burning itch at the back of my eyelids fighting to be freed, but the relentless self-control beaten into me from birth forbade them from falling. Aaron watched with eyes as slitted as razors, but stayed silent, the stoic mask on his face as stony as mine.

She shouldn't have been here. Neither of them should have been here, hanging in this fucking dungeon, at the mercy of a psychotic woman and my psychopathic father. Rage and redemption equally consumed me as I realized the only reason these two people were sharing this burden with me was because they cared about me. Loved me. Despite my baggage, my history and my lack of a future, they'd chosen me.

I didn't know what to do with that level of dedication, and I didn't know how much longer I'd be able to maintain my composure while the woman we loved was brutally tortured.

Carmen had slit the delicate skin of her wrists, just enough to bleed her out slowly and take the last of her energy reserves, knowing exactly which parts of the vein to slice to keep her alive. Hillary hadn't uttered a word. She'd fixed her gaze on the small window above our heads with each cut. Then, Carmen had put her blade against her feet. Encrusted blood coated my Killer from head to toe, an almost lifeless warrior wrapped in silk rags.

My throat bobbed with another hard swallow at the disparaging sight, my mouth the texture of sandpaper from hours without water. Of all the horrors I'd witnessed in almost forty years, this was the worst.

"The foot is a wonderful receiver of pain," my father mused in the background, his voice carrying over the incessant buzzing of insects hovering above Maverick's corpse.

I spared a glimpse at my old colleague's body, still lying on the hard concrete about ten feet away, decaying into the ground as quickly as the blowflies could eat him. I'd always shielded my agents from anything to do with my "other" life. Was he the agent Trish had been trying to turn to take my place? Was his death on my head too?

"It hurts, doesn't it, *Princesa?*" Carmen cooed softly, the grin on her face at chilling odds with the grave air. Wrath swirled like a whirlpool in my gut, but still, my Killer didn't waver.

When Hillary didn't respond, Carmen dropped Hillary's foot to the ground, the bloody sole dripping all over the concrete, forming a small puddle under her toes. The soft skin of her heels was ragged, like Carmen had processed her skin through a paper shredder. My beautiful Killer might never walk in a pair of sneakers again, let alone her power heels. I felt the phantom of the serrated knife cut through my chest, the pain just a fraction of what hers must be, my formidable woman cut down by a soulless *perra*.

"The Germans perfected this technique," Antonio continued, as if talking about the weather. "But I particularly like Carmen's spin on it. *Eres peligrosa, mi belleza.*"

Mi Belleza. My beauty. Was Carmen my father's concubine *and* his killer? Disgust rivaled the queasiness boiling in my gut. This woman was nothing more than my father's rabid dog, desperate for his attention and his affection. She wouldn't have either for long.

"This is what happens to you when you defy me, *mi hijo.* So many secrets. So much lying." He circled our line of hanging bodies until he stood directly in front of me. The smell of his familiar sandalwood aftershave was more nauseating than the sickening scent of human flesh.

"Your secret world is a secret no longer, hmm? Two lovers mean two weaknesses. How unfortunate for them.

How unfortunate for you. Death will be my greatest mercy when we are done with you."

I refused to utter a single word—my silence a final defiance in the face of death. He winked a single brown eye at me, amused by my lack of acknowledgment, and then moved on to Hillary's hanging body beside me. Her head lolled to the side. Her pain, exhaustion, and the aftereffects of the drugs barely kept her conscious, but her eyes were open, tiny ocean-blue slits of desolation that broke my heart.

My spine stiffened, and I struggled in the cuffs over my head when he reached out, taking her cheek in his palm. She shuddered under his touch, but without the ability to shrug out of his hold, she hung there, gaze blazing cold despite her pain.

God, I loved her so fucking much. And I'd never get to touch her again. It was the cruelest consequence of this shitty fate.

"I think we are done with you for now, *bella*." Antonio removed his hand from her face and pressed it to her thigh against the torn flesh of her bullet wound. This time, she couldn't stifle the scream of agony, the sounds piercing every nerve ending in my body with unbearable pain.

The damn tears hovering on my eyelids escaped, leaking a trail down my cheeks as I willed her pain to come into me instead. I'd never felt so fucking helpless, but I wouldn't break down and beg for his pathetic excuse of mercy. The three of us had made an unspoken pact as the torture began: no begging, no pleading, no bartering.

My father's grin rivaled the Devil's as he closed his eyes to absorb her shrieks. When he opened them, they shone brighter, fueling the rage bubbling up within my chest. He took two steps back to stand next to Carmen's smirking form, and the two of them stared back at their handiwork with triumph.

Three damaged people, buried with baggage and laden with their own sins. We were marked for death in here. The only option was to die bravely.

Lauchlan was surprisingly resourceful, but there was nothing to say he wasn't already dead. The "hope" sitting on my knuckles was an illusion, one I no longer carried on my skin or in my heart. The last memory I would carry of him to my unmarked grave was of me stalking off in the night in a sorry attempt to run away from my demons. No kiss goodbye, no telling him what he actually meant to me. A missed opportunity in a light-year-long line of missed opportunities.

"It is hard to see those we love in pain," Antonio said sagely, like he had a fucking heart suddenly. "Sometimes, the greatest mercy is taking the pain from them. Can you do this, *traidor*?" He forced a solemn expression onto his face, because he'd never mourned a moment in his life. "I will take away your pain if you will take away theirs."

He nodded toward the beautiful woman, her body bleeding dry, and the man next to me, who was as miserable as I was. "Kill them, and I will accept you back. It is a simple trade of lives. Continue to resist, and I will kill them as painfully as possible, with you as the last to die."

His last words were the dangling carrot he thought he could tempt me with. "I've invested so much in you, Kellan. Your future. You are my prodigal son, and I will forgive your sins only once. But I will forgive them."

I stared down at this man who called himself my father. He was my prison ward, my dictator, and today, my executioner. A liar, a jailer, a shitty mentor and a terrible guide. Never a father. The moment I bent to his will, I'd be on his leash forever—just as I had been these last thirty-eight years. The cord was severed. The line was dead. I was no longer a Carlos son.

"He is your only son." Hillary found her voice, cracked and raw from holding in her screams. "I killed your idiot twins before your lackey shoved a needle into me. The Carlos line is almost extinct, Antonio," she taunted, a picture of battered strength and resilience even in the face of death. "Kill him, and your entire empire crumbles to the ground."

Savage rage flashed across Antonio's face in rivulets, but it was likely more at her audacity instead of genuine pain for the lives of his sons. Maybe he didn't believe her, or maybe he didn't care. I still didn't fully understand this man's obsession with power, other than it overruled every other emotion.

She was trying to save my life. I'd been trying to protect her for years—*had* protected her for years—and I finally realized the lengths she was willing to go to protect me. Even if it meant losing her own.

When I'd left Hillary with Lauchlan and Aaron, I'd intended to kill this man—not so they'd welcome me back, but so they'd actually find safety, and I, even alone, would have freedom from this life. When he'd ordered me to take over the human trafficking side of his business all those months ago, I knew in my gut how this all would end. Him or me.

It would tear strips off my soul, but I'd kill them if they asked me to. And then I'd take the knife myself and end the rest of this torrid legacy for good. If Lauchlan came through, they'd have an extra three bodies to deal with, but it would end Antonio's empire, and we could die knowing our deaths had a purpose other than being this psychopath's source of entertainment.

My legacy wouldn't be killing the people I loved to save my own skin. That generational curse ended with me.

I found my voice amid the bullshit I was swimming in. "I'll kill them when they ask me to. You're likely better off just killing me."

Hard eyes appraised me like I was a piece of butcher's meat on a hook rather than the man he raised and molded in his image. They narrowed into pinpricks of madness before he forced his mouth into a placating smile.

"Very well. It is *el muerto's* turn." Antonio's declaration and Carmen's beaming smile brought every hair on my neck to attention. "Perhaps you can use some of the tricks you learned at the club? Show us how well you know him."

No. No. *No.* This woman had played double agent in Aaron's club for months, at the direction of my father. She used her body to manipulate him, her weapons to mangle him, and now… In his final moments, she'd use what she'd learned about him sexually to strip away the last shreds of his dignity.

Horror set every nerve in my body on fire as I watched her brandish a new, bloodless knife and cut the suit pants off Aaron's body. He barely twitched as she removed his clothing, but his throat bobbed hard as each piece of cloth hit the ground. When he was naked from the waist down, he closed his eyes and hung his head, accepting what was to come.

I should have killed him rather than subjected him to this. I should have—

"Forgive me, *Mi Reina*," he mumbled under his breath, the only words to penetrate the dead air around us. My Killer's breath hitched as Carmen stroked the skin of Aaron's calves before sliding them along the lines of his thighs, caressing the jagged scar she'd left from her knife the last time she'd held Aaron under duress. She stuck out her tongue and dragged it across the severed skin before moving her hands to cup his balls.

His eyes remained closed, and he forced shallow breaths through his nose as he gritted his teeth with each tug of her hand, his body responding directly to her assault. "Forgive me, *Mi Reina*," my *Guapo* begged. A single droplet of pain leaked from his tight eyelids, followed by several more with each stroke of her fists. "Forgive me, *compañero*."

A deep, feminine, guttural sob came from Hillary's chest beside me. It took every ounce of energy I had left not to wrestle with the cuffs around my wrists, to escape and choke the life out of my father, to snap Carmen's dainty neck, and to comfort my lovers one last time.

It wasn't possible. I was too large of a man to try any sort of acrobatics with these cuffs. At best, any attempt would snap both of my wrists, leaving me useless to do anything at all. I would die with this as the last image in my brain, but I refused to let Antonio take everything else along with it. Our lives might end tonight, but he wouldn't destroy me.

"I love you, Killer." My voice was raspy and raw, and so were the words. Antonio couldn't remove the only good in my life, even now. I'd spent my life a lonely, miserable fuck, and if this was to be my end, I could say I had three people who knew who I really was, and had chosen me anyway. "I love you, *Guapo.*"

Hillary stifled her sobs, choking on mucus as the tears flowed freely down her chin. "I love you, Viking." She stuttered on a hiccup. "I love you, *Cabellero Oscuro.*" To the open air, she whispered, "I love you, Lucky O'Donnell."

Aaron's eyes opened with our declarations. I could only see one clearly from my position, but it brimmed with emotion, the last crack in the stoicism he was famous for.

"As I love you, *Mi Reina* and *Mi Rey.* It is an honor to die with you."

Carmen squeezed the now limp cock in her fist and stood, the threatening sneer vicious with hate. "There is no honor in death," she spat, dropping her fist and moving away from Aaron's hanging form. "Only weakness. You disgust me, *culicagado.*"

Before any of us could respond with replies on deaf ears, an ear-piercing alarm sounded from above our heads, the abrupt shrill tone enough to numb my senses. Antonio pulled out the phone in his pocket to check its screen and cursed.

"Leave them!" he barked, shooting us one last contemptuous glower before turning on his heel, fast-walking to what I presumed was a door or hallway behind us.

Carmen's head whirled around, body frozen in confusion. Before she could retreat, Aaron shifted his legs with whip-like movements, raising the naked limbs and wrapping them around her neck.

She struggled under the weight, grunting and wheezing as she clawed at the thighs crushing her cheekbones and stealing her air. I watched in fascination as the injured man's face wrenched into a vicious snarl, his raw hatred for this woman as pure as my hatred for my father.

He let out an animalistic roar and violently squeezed with the last remnants of his strength until she fell to the ground in an unconscious heap. Aaron's legs dropped, and his entire body limply dangled from the exertion. The alarm continued to blare above our heads, less ominous now we were alone.

"It's Lucky!" Hillary's voice was much weaker than mine, but it held onto shreds of hope. "It's Lucky," she repeated, before several navy-clad FBI agents flooded into our torture cell, weapons drawn and flashlights raised.

My whole body convulsed with the new emotion rising in my chest.

Hope had found its way into my heart again.

Maybe there was a little out there in the universe after all.

CHAPTER 23

Aaron

My body hung in the cell, violated and exposed. I did not see the FBI agents filling the room from behind, instead overtaken by a vision beneath my eyelids. The memory of the final time I'd shed tears in front of my father swam in front of me, as if I were an underwater observer, rippling and undulating as soft sea waves.

I sat in his office bent over the large cherry wood desk with my legs exposed to his mercy.

"Men do not cry." Vicente's stern admonishment hovered above my head as the strike of his switch brought a fiery ache to the backside of my calves. "Rodriguez men do not cry, especially. You are a man, Aaron. Show me you understand this, or I will hit you again."

I was six. Not a man. I had been unable to control my tears as little boys cannot, and he'd beaten me so badly I could not sit for weeks from the bruising.

I thought I'd never feel her lips on mine, or smell his skin, or hear the lilt of his accent ever again. The home I had found in our group of tattered souls was a loss I deeply mourned as I swallowed my pride and let her touch me, for the hope of one more moment in their presence.

That *Mi Reina* and our protector were still alive, and I still had all of my limbs, however sore, forced a fresh flood of tears to wash my dirty cheeks. I squeezed my eyes shut as I allowed them to cleanse me from the inside out, the dam of my walled emotions finally disintegrating under the true power of my love.

A few muttered curses broke through my haze, and I cracked open a wet eye. A shocked agent stared at my situation with an open mouth before moving to release the cuffs above my head.

"I need a little help here!" he called to his colleagues as he struggled to uncuff me and hold my dead weight at the same time. Several agents came forward—through a single eye alone ten were within our radius—and guided my spent body to the floor. Unimaginable burning pain rushed into my arms and shoulders as blood once again found the veins. I gritted my teeth at the pain and relished the feeling all the same. It meant I was still here.

The scraping pebbles dug into the tender flesh of my naked legs. The carcass of Kellan's agent was too close for comfort. The stench coated me in a thick layer of grime. But his was not the body that interested me. Carmen Delgado still lay on the floor within feet of my body, still unconscious, but alive.

The despicable woman would be put through the legal system and eventually sentenced for her crimes, but she would evade death, too kind a fate. Could I allow this to happen, after everything she'd done to cause harm to my family?

No, I could not.

If I had the luxury of time, I would torture this woman in ways she could not imagine with the techniques I had learned as a teenager, but I had no such gift. If I were to be saved today, I would grant this wish to those I loved.

I ignored the agony in my broken wrist and burning limbs and reached over the chasm of two feet, grasping the knife still housed within her pocket. Barely gripping it with numb fingers, I pulled it from the loose cloth of her linen pants and stabbed the dagger through her heart.

Warm blood rushed over my fingers as the knife connected with the tissue I'd aimed for. I twisted it deeper into her chest, wrenching it roughly until the hilt hit bone. She shuddered once beneath the blade while every drop of her poisoned essence drained from her under my hold.

Carmen Delgado was dead.

Shouts erupted all around me, the noise its own dagger inside my head. Several hands gripped my shoulders and waist, hauling me away from her fresh corpse. I had no energy to fight, and no need. My contribution was complete, the consequences be damned.

The laugh of a madman escaped my swollen lips while I was carried through a long corridor. Then my mind shut down to nothingness and I promptly passed out.

I was not a normal child. The sole heir of a mafia empire had many privileges but came with many poisons. My parents had trained me to endure torture. Vicente through his hewn weapons and toxins, Veronica through her barbarous words and acidic tongue.

Still, I was unprepared for its reality. My body could not move. The searing heat in my abdomen from overextending my healing wounds made me immobile in the hospital bed. I was a lump of flesh in the form of a battered man. A visceral ache overtook each individual limb, down to the pads of my fingertips and toes, and deep within the fabric of my bones where the binds had fractured one wrist and torn the ligaments within my shoulders.

We'd been airlifted to the closest major hospital in Sequoia, having been driven three hours outside of Carlisle to one of Antonio's private distribution sites to endure our torture session.

Hillary slept softly in the bed adjacent to mine, Kellan on her other side, our orientation identical to the way we hung in the cell. We'd been here for several hours, and would be here for several more while we healed our bodies and our hearts. We had nowhere else to be.

Mi Reina had been groggy from pain medication and almost incoherent in speech, yet she'd insisted on paying for a private wing when we'd arrived so the three of us could share a room, though she'd barely accompanied us in the last several hours. The doctors rushed her into emergency surgery to repair the broken bones and severe tissue damage on the soles of her feet, while removing the bullet deeply embedded within her thigh. *Mi Reina* was bruised and beaten, but not broken. My heart swelled in size as pride blended with my highly medicated blood.

Nothing would break my Queen. We would never allow it.

Rojo was still being held at the precinct. Weston had called the hospital to inform us he would have him out in a few hours. I was relieved to hear he was alright and more relieved he had escaped capture. The man had many odd and wonderful talents, but would have been scarred far deeper than Kellan or I if he'd endured Antonio's torture room. I wished to protect him as I would my two companions in the hospital room next to me.

A debt was in order if Hillary's assumptions were true. The Irishman with as many jokes as brains had come through to save us all. I would be sure to show him my thorough gratitude when we were finally free to our own devices.

Provided I would not be incarcerated. The decision to end Carmen's life had been an impulsive display of emotion. I did not regret her end, but I might come to regret the consequences. I had heard nothing from the FBI since our delivery to the hospital, but I could not deny the butterflies within my belly as I awaited the hammer. I could do nothing in the meantime but take care of my own.

I slowly angled my torso on the thin mattress to face Kellan. His stare was blank, yet focused, as if seeing a vision beyond this world that was only his to view.

"How are you feeling, *compañero*?"

The simple question was somewhat idiotic, but necessary. The brute man had just come up against his demon and won, but only through outside intervention, not his own hands. Were it me, I would feel relieved, yet cheated, the thirst for the blood of my own father unsatisfied.

Kellan grunted to the ceiling above, but eventually shifted his weight to face me, his expression losing its blankness and turning forlorn. He brought a large palm up to stroke through his beard, barely tinged with blood now since the nurse had given him a sponge bath. The ill-fitting hospital gown he wore barely covered the thickness of his thighs, and even in exhaustion, it stirred light arousal in me. The man was beautiful.

Perhaps he would remain mine.

"I don't know," he admitted, the crease in his brow far more prominent than just three days ago. "Relief. Terror. I don't want this life anymore. Any of it."

Any of it? I did not like the roiling in my belly at his statement. He had walked away once under the misguided assumption we did not need him. Would he do it again?

My face must have betrayed my thoughts as he quickly amended the declaration.

"I don't mean you, *Guapo*. Or her—Lauchlan. Us." He stumbled over his words as if this admission tasted funny on his tongue. "There's no place for me in Sequoia anymore. I'd just—I want a fresh start."

A fresh start. What a beautiful dream. I considered the idea as we fell into comfortable silence, staring at one another.

Would *Mi Reina* desire a fresh start as well? Where could that be? There were still several strings tethering us, and certainly her, to Sequoia. She had companies, assets—a designated mission that had inevitably led to this end.

My stomach twinged. A fresh start would not be possible for a man in prison.

"I would welcome a fresh start." I dared to say the words aloud. "I will go wherever she goes."

Kellan swallowed hard before dipping his head in attrition. "Me too."

An abrupt knock broke us out of thoughts of our future, and my head painfully whipped to the door, the faint hope of *Rojo* waltzing through with a quip and a smile painfully squeezing my chest.

It was not *Rojo*. The two guards standing beyond the door let in the severe form of Patricia Stanhope, the woman who'd abandoned Kellan and allowed our capture. A sinister snarl danced on my lips as the FBI director strode into our room. As if she deserved to share the air we breathed.

An unfamiliar and uncomfortable emotion rocked within the waves of acid: fear. Had Patricia come to take me? I could not leave *Mi Reina* without a fight, but I was in no condition to take on law enforcement.

She stared at us with tentative eyes, her gaze briefly appraising the sleeping billionaire wrapped in bandages between us, before fixing solely on Kellan.

"I'm glad to see you're okay, Kellan." Her voice was softer than I expected, a tinge of humility threaded into the command of authority.

The deep navy eyes of my partner hardened into glass marbles, his pouty lips molding into a scathing sneer that matched mine.

"The people you were supposed to protect almost died, Trish."

His tone was as hard as his stare, as sharp as my missing dagger. His hand swept outward, toward our two bodies lying on uncomfortable beds, damaged, but not broken.

"You point fingers at Antonio's empire and call him power-hungry, when you're no different. You played me from a little boy to now, so you could try to play puppet master to the biggest crime organization." He bared his teeth at her, the hatred exuding from every pore of his skin. "How many promotions did it get you? How many special titles? You pretended I was a kingpin, when all along, I was just your pawn."

Her steely stare would have faltered lesser men, but neither of us shrank from our positions, though she paid no attention to me. Perhaps I was of no consequence, and I would not be taken today. I allowed the tiny tendrils of optimism to seed themselves in my belly.

"I did what I had to do, Kellan. I've always had to follow orders too, no matter how I felt about you. The bigger picture will always be the top priority. You know that."

Kellan met her hollow explanation with pursed lips and awkward silence. He reached out to stroke a thick finger through our woman's matted hair. *Mi Reina* barely stirred under the sedative.

"I will never forgive you for what he did to her. What he did to him." He nodded toward me, but her eyes never left his face. "Leave."

"I can't offer you your old job back," Trish replied, sounding nonplussed, as if he hadn't spoken at all. "But I can offer you contract work. Your skill set and—"

"I've heard of your intelligence, Agent Stanhope, but I see the rumors are untrue." Disregarding my predicament, I spoke up, done with the callous disregard of the trauma she'd forced her top agent to endure.

Her attention snapped to me, and a brief flicker of anger filled her expression. Still, I continued. "We do not forgive betrayal. You are not wanted here, and you are not welcome in the future. Leave."

"You don't have a leg to stand on, Aaron Rodriguez." Her harsh glare was callous, but as empty as the fish stare she was named after. "I allowed you this luxury." She waved her hands around the hospital room. "Me. Your little stunt with Carmen Delgado means I lost a key witness in this case. I'm not welcome? You'll be welcomed with open arms into prison when I try you for her murder."

My gut had not failed me. I'd known this moment was coming. My penance was due for my rash decision to kill the woman who'd harmed mine. The muscles within my stomach clenched, but I drew in a slow breath to dissipate the cramping, refusing to break eye contact as she continued.

Her laugh was a bark, aggressive and rough. "There were a dozen witnesses, and you want to talk about intelligence—fine. I'm sure Alvarez would love to get his hands on you when you share the same cell."

Kellan stiffened beside me, his entire body emulating a stone gargoyle.

"Trish," he stated slowly, as if working hard to maintain his patience. "Leave. Now. I have so much evidence against you and how you operate, the media would destroy you in days, and I am done playing around. Fuck. Off.”

The severe woman’s glower rivaled a laser, but she filled her lungs and squared her shoulders, stealing our air as we stole her dignity. Without uttering another empty offer or loaded threat, she turned on her heel and strode toward the door without a backward glance.

Before she turned the handle to walk out the door and out of Kellan’s life, she cocked her head, leaving us with a final thought.

“Antonio escaped our capture. I thought you’d want to know.”

She left us in stunned silence as her heels left a resounding melody along the hallway. Antonio Carlos was still a threat. Kellan wasn’t yet free from the burden of his birthright.

Our fresh start was still a dream, perhaps never realized. That thought was the most depressing of all.

CHAPTER 24

Lauchlan

"Come on, come on," I chanted under my breath, as I wiggled my hands behind my back with just the right amount of counter-pressure. It'd been a long time since I'd wormed my way out of a pair of handcuffs. The challenge would have been a fun one if I wasn't worried to feck my family was dead in a torture chamber somewhere.

Da was dead. Shayna was dead. Ma might as well be dead because she was no more of a mother figure than Mother Teresa was to me. The only people in the world who knew the real me were already gone.

Except that was as big a lie as the ones I told pretty old ladies whose pockets I was looking to get into. I had a new family now, but I had no feckin' clue if they were dead or alive. If they were dead, I'd rather rot in the misery of an American prison than have to live a life outside without them.

I'd tried not to think about it in the last few hours with no one but myself to talk to. The guard at the end of the hall completely ignored me after I'd told him my best Irish joke about a priest and a leprechaun, and I'd counted every single floor tile in my sights five hundred times, just to be sure there were actually 312 tiles. I'd write up a report about the poor grout quality for the Carlisle police later, just to close the loop and feel good about my contribution to the hard-working police force that locked up retired con men instead of nasty murderers.

Gits.

A nice little layer of sweat coated my skin as anxiety and I became good pals. Fidgeting with the cuffs was my last line of defense before sinking into madness, and the mechanism released just as I was about to give up and start again.

Before I could bask in my elementary skills, heavy footsteps tramped down the hall. I snapped my head to the alcove to see the guard with zero sense of humor. Weston Williams, in all of his glorious, manly beauty, followed, which hopefully meant I was out of here.

And… Joey?

Wasn't gonna look a gift horse in the mouth. "Hi, folks," I exclaimed brightly despite my exhausted brain and starving belly. "I'm going home?"

"To the hospital." Weston stated with a grimace while the guard opened the door and glared daggers at me when he discovered my handcuffs were unlocked.

I tossed a wink at him and scooted out of the cell before anybody could change their mind, too eager to—

Wait—the hospital? Of course, they were in the hospital. Blondie had been half-dead the last time I saw her, even though I'd blocked that image in my mind and replaced it with the one of her between Aaron and me just to keep myself sane. I stopped in my tracks and turned on a dime, panic rocketing through my chest in a wave strong enough to make a lesser bloke puke.

"Weston, you'd better tell me they're all alive with that kind of segue, mate. They made it? They're okay?"

The smooth nod almost brought tears of relief to my tired eyes. Thank feck. Thank *Epona*, and every god and goddess in the universe, and thank feck blackmail was still the most effective bartering chip known to man.

"Ms. Lane has just been released from surgery, but we don't know her exact prognosis yet." The handsome man completely burst my bubble of hope with that one sentence. "Joey's going to take you to them."

Fear sat in my belly like I'd just swallowed a watermelon. Blondie had been hurt bad enough to go through surgery. But she was alive—I had to hold on to that fact. They were all living, breathing, tough-as-feck machines, and I had to get to them right away.

The guard escorted us through the front doors of the precinct and into the chilly April air. Weston caught my shoulder. "And I'll be visiting later to discuss where you would like to go from here with legal action. They have nothing tangible the FBI can charge you with, so you should be in the clear, but we'll explore all possibilities when I come by."

"Sounds good, mate."

I tossed him a salute with a heartfelt thanks and hopped into the front seat of Joey's waiting vehicle, one free of bullet holes and shattered windows. We'd destroyed an entire fleet of vehicles these last few weeks. I still mourned my M&M sports car.

Anxiety be damned, I practically squealed with delight at the massive bag of Skittles in the cup holder.

"Ms. Lane wanted you to have a treat when you got out," Joey said as she pulled out of the parking lot and onto the highway. "It was one of the few instructions she left me before going into surgery."

Bless that lovely woman's heart. I ripped into the bag and let the artificially flavored, artificially colored candy coat my tongue with its tingly artificial goodness. If she had thought of Skittles, she couldn't be close to death. Right?

The colorful candy renewed my hope, and a giddy anticipation worked its way through every one of my bones, like I was a horny teen who'd glimpsed his first tit. They were alive. They were alive. They were alive. With any luck, everyone else was dead and buried in a crater somewhere, and we could figure out the rest of our lives as a foursome.

That was now the only thing I wanted—them. My Blondie, my Barbarian, and my Daddy Roboto. I had no place to call home, but I'd make one with them if they'd have me.

Joey dropped me off at the front entrance, and I practically raced up the steps at the hospital, a ward hollering after me to slow down when I almost took them out. I shouted back an apology, but I didn't stop until I stood in front of the guarded private suite on the top floor.

I didn't have a lick of ID on me, but one guard, a brutish woman with black hair and green eyes, opened the door for me without a question. They must have had my picture, because even I wasn't charismatic enough to have doors opened for me without a word of my charm.

I rushed into the room to see the three of them in side-by-side hospital beds. Blondie looked disheveled and ghostly pale, sipping some gross-looking concoction through a straw, but alive. Kellan wore a too-short hospital dress and a whole lot of dried blood and bruises, but he too was alive. And Aaron, stiff and stoic as always with his arm wrapped in a sling—alive.

"I've never been so excited for a foursome in my life," I joked as I took in the three of them, the relief cresting over me in tidal waves. I sank to my knees, every emotion I'd blocked out in the last several hours bashing me over the head like a mallet in a *Looney Tunes* cartoon.

I hung my head in my hands and let the tears fall, unafraid to be the crying bloke in front of the people I loved. When I looked up through the watery stream, a large hand was extended toward me, inviting me up.

I took Kellan's palm and rose to my feet, wrapping my arms around his enormous body in a crushing hug. He smelled of sweat and antiseptic spray, and it was the most delicious smell ever.

"Good to see you, Conan," I muttered into the crook of his shoulder. He squeezed me back, his arms the most comforting blanket of strength and calm.

"Good to see you, Lucky."

I froze in his hold. He'd never called me Lucky. It was Blondie's name for me, but no one else's. I loved it coming from her, but I *really* liked it coming from his mouth.

He pulled back from me, and a tiny smile cracked the fierce pout of his lips as he interlaced our fingers and gently pulled me forward toward the other hospital beds. My heart melted into liquid when he brought me to the foot of Hillary's.

Her hair was gnarled into matted clumps, and a purple welt marred the left side of her face, swelling one of her eyes closed. Her lips were as cracked as the bottoms of my feet—and she was the most beautiful sight I'd ever seen.

"Hey, Luck," she whispered, her voice raw and strained. Those dry lips formed into the gentlest of smiles, and my melted heart became whole again, just to beat for her.

"Welcome home."

CHAPTER 25

Hillary

Tears, inescapable, never-ending tears soaked my cheeks and chin as I stared at the last man in our foursome, finally joining us after we'd escaped hell.

Hell we escaped because of him. I don't know how he did it, and he would surely brag about it later, but for now—for now, all I needed was to hold him.

I didn't need to ask. He was on me in a second, wrapping me tenderly within his arms, peppering the faintest kisses all over my forehead. I melted into his embrace and released the breath trapped in my chest until I saw him again.

We sat that way for a long moment. Aaron, Kellan, and Lucky all murmured softly while I snuggled into his chest and listened to the steady thrum of his heartbeat, the irrefutable proof he'd survived along with us.

Through Kellan's determination not to break, and Aaron's submission to be a sacrifice, my inability to let evil win—even at the cost to my body—and Lucky's ingenuity to get us out, we'd survived together. We were here, ragged and raw, holey and whole. I held on to the fine wisps of happiness as they swirled around me, determined to make them last before they vanished.

I'd been down this road before: the private rooms, the years of therapy, the never *actually* healing from trauma. Life was giving me a second chance to fix my damage, and I was damn well going to take it, with all my men at my side.

"Whatcha thinking about, lass?"

Lucky's smooth Irish lilt broke through my thoughts. Shaking away the thick clouds of contemplation, I gave him a serene smile and squeezed the hand that hadn't left mine since he'd entered the room.

"The road ahead," I said simply, stroking my finger over the calloused skin of his palm. I eyed the thick white bandages all over my arms, the puffy gauze catching on the fibers of the hospital blanket.

Lucky cocked his head, gaze lit with tentative curiosity. He chewed on his lip for a moment before softly muttering, "Am I included on that road?"

My eyes widened in surprise. After all we'd gone through—did he still not think he belonged?

"I'm the new guy," he quickly amended, as if afraid to hear my answer. "I came in, led you on, tried to steal your painting. I think I convinced you lot to put up with me." He nodded to the other men lying in their beds beside mine, who quietly observed the conversation. "But I know I'm not a part of the group—not really. I'm a great fuck," he joked, though the laughter in his tone didn't meet his eyes, "but I know I fucked up, and I—"

It was Aaron who moved before I could, shifting his weight off the bed to stand at Lucky's side. He placed two hands on his shoulders, stopping him mid-sentence and forcing his attention into the deep, penetrating eyes only Aaron had.

"*Rojo*, you are childish and you speak too much. Your impulsiveness is reckless. But you are brilliant, and kind, and your bravery saved our lives. It is a debt I will never repay."

He lowered his head, placing a gentle kiss on Lucky's lips. When he pulled back, a soft smile I wasn't used to seeing on Aaron's handsome, stern face tugged at his cheekbones and lit up my heart.

"You belong with us."

Lucky sat in stunned silence for a second before his face brightened with a toothy grin. "Well, that's one way to shut me up," he admitted with a light chuckle.

Kellan grunted on my opposite side, and we all turned to see the uncomfortable Viking watching the display with his brows crinkled with conflict.

"I don't want you to leave." He cleared his throat as if this admission was a challenge, but the ferocity swirling in the dark blue of his eyes clearly belied his intentions. "You drive me crazy, but I don't want you driving anyone else crazy... but me." He drew in a breath and blew it out loudly between his teeth. "Us," he amended.

"I won't promise not to be the overbearing pain in the ass I know I am"—Aaron and I both snorted and smirked at each other as Kellan gathered his thoughts—"but I learned my lesson. I'm not leaving. Whatever comes next—we'll deal with it together."

The declaration sobered my blossoming mood. Antonio was still out there—in hiding, according to Weston—and the FBI and the DEA were slowly dismantling every part of his operations. But Kellan, all of us, wouldn't feel any semblance of safety until he was buried deep underground.

"Thanks, Kell-Bell." Lucky's response held a muted teasing cadence, playing at the edges of the rueful smile on his lips. "I really like you too."

An intensity burned in the room between them—of attraction, of emotion. They might "like" each other now, but it had been steadily growing into something more— something fiery and tender—and maybe one day, they'd be able to admit it.

Our Irishman's attention fixated on me. The calming sea-glass of those stunning green eyes searched my soul, and I knew I had to tell him. I needed to hear the words myself, not just whispered in a torture chamber when I thought I'd never have the chance again.

"I love you, Lucky." I slowly leaned forward and brought his knuckles to my lips before holding his hand against the flushed skin of my cheek. "Not just because you saved our lives, but because of who you are. You are all the things Aaron said you are—and you balance us in a way I don't think anyone else ever could. I don't want to have survived hell to not have you on the other side with us."

The mattress creaked beneath Lucky's weight as he pulled his hand out of my grasp and moved off the bed and sat in the small space beside me. He lowered his face to mine, and the fruity scent of Skittles washed over me as he stared at me so hard, I thought he was counting the pores on my forehead.

"I think I've loved you from the first moment we met." He was so close, I could count every dainty freckle across the bridge of his nose. I loved every single one. "Didn't know it, because I didn't know what the feck love was, but Blondie, you're it for me. I love you so fucking much."

Supple lips enveloped my mouth with forceful passion, and I melted under their touch, infusing every feeling I held for him in my heart into the kiss: desire, appreciation, playfulness, care. He caressed my tongue with delicate laps of his, tempting and teasing me with their intoxicating flavor, melting me into a pile of—

"Ms. Lane?"

A guard broke the magic of our kiss, peeking his head through the door, a concerned frown on his face. "There's a woman here to see you, a"—his head disappeared behind the door, and we heard muffled murmurs before he popped back in again—"Winter Wallace? Do you know her?"

My heart jumped in my chest like a jackrabbit, adrenaline mainlined directly into my bloodstream. My best friend was here, after I'd spent months being a shitty friend to her and avoiding fessing up at every opportunity. News of our capture, then rescue had been the major headline for days. Principally, all anyone cared about was my stock value, not me—and I hadn't even thought to call her to let her know I was alright.

Hot shame followed the adrenaline spike, but I swallowed it down under the many other layers of buried shame my therapist was going to have a field day with, and managed a tight smile.

"Yes," I said, dipping my head to the guard, "please let her in."

Two seconds later, Winter Wallace in all her glory, barreled into the room with two of her husbands in tow—Cam and Travis, Kellan's family.

Lucky hastily stood and backed away from his previous position mid-kiss. "Let's go for a walk and stretch these legs, Daddy!" He hoisted Aaron off the bed, guided him into a wheelchair, and wheeled him to the doorway before I could say another word.

Kellan also got the message. "We'll give you some privacy," he muttered, leaving his bed and placing a firm hand on his nephew and brother's shoulders. "Let's go to the cafeteria so we can chat."

I didn't bother saying anything about his appearance. With how terrifying Kellan looked in the tiny hospital gown with dried blood all over him, no one else would breathe a word either.

Once the three men strode through the threshold, Winter and I were alone, the silence between us so thick it coated my tongue.

"Winter, I—"

Before I could offer an apology, an explanation, or beg her forgiveness, she leaped at me like a cautious spider monkey and wrapped her compact frame around mine in a bruising hug. It was painful, but I welcomed the warm embrace.

The lump in my throat grew from a small pebble to a clogging boulder as I pulled back to stare at my best friend, the woman who'd seen my soul and loved me anyway.

"Hey," I managed to get out through the massive stone sitting on my vocal cords.

"Hey."

Her eyes, a calming blend of blue and green, roved over me carefully, as if I would shatter if she stared too hard. They lingered on my bandaged feet, and she scrunched her nose and her eyelids closed, catching the shimmer of tears collecting on her lash line.

"Oh, Hill." Her voice broke, and she closed the distance between us again, this time gently wrapping me in her arms. I buried my nose in her hair and inhaled the familiar concoction of vanilla and lavender. It instantly soothed the ache in my chest.

She backed away and sought my stare again, shinier this time. "I am so sorry you've had to go through this. Kellan told us a little, but I know there are a lot of gaps in there."

She stroked a hand down my arm and grabbed my hand in hers, settling it in her lap as she took the space beside me Lucky had occupied just minutes before.

"Are you ready to tell me the real story?"

Winter had a subtlety in her softness that could easily be misconstrued as weakness. It wasn't. Where I was a calculative bull, she was an observant mare, tactical and shrewd when she had the right information.

Her expression was open and nonjudgmental. She waited out my timid silence, her patience far more cultivated than mine. It was her greatest gift, and today I cherished its grace instead of being annoyed by it.

I'd never shown her my true darkness. She'd been exposed to my shadows but never the demons that lurked within them. I wasn't afraid of her reaction, but more afraid of how she'd view me after the fact. A victim, on a crusade because I'd allowed someone else to break me. The vulnerability of being seen so clearly was scarier than any of the predators I'd ever faced.

She wouldn't hate my darkness—I knew her well enough for that. But I'd lied to her, withheld important information about my life and my whereabouts for years, not the actions of a true best friend. Could she forgive me? Would I be able to live with myself if she didn't?

Nausea hit my gut with a powerful punch at the thought of losing her because I had valued protecting her over trusting her with my deepest secrets. I was Kellan in this scenario, and I'd hated the way he'd made me feel for years, all under the guise of protection. Did she feel the same way about me?

Despite these reservations pushing bile into the back of my throat... it was time.

The need to move on from the hell of my own making superseded my fragile ego. I wanted Winter and her family to be in my life until the end of time, and that meant some brutal, tragic honesty.

So, I opened my mouth for the greatest confession of my lifetime. One the police would never hear, but would salivate for. I allowed a cautious smile and concentrated on the freckles on top of her cheeks, larger than Lucky's and a different shade of brown.

"When I was in college, I fell in love with a woman named Isabella..."

I allowed the emotion of the story to overtake me, sobbing through Isabella's death, Alec's involvement, and everything I had done to avenge his crimes. How I let it consume me, how it consumed me still—how even after the torture we endured, Antonio was still alive. How I'd found three men to love, and I had no idea what to do or where to go next. How that was potentially scarier than the cartel king with a price on our heads.

She laughed along with me when I admitted how Lucky and I actually met and I had pegged him as a challenge. She sobbed her own tears when I spoke of Isabella's downfall. She clutched me harder when I recounted, in less graphic detail, Carmen's assault and our near-death experiences. Winter had her own encounter with gunpoint trauma at the hands of Antonio's dead son, and we commiserated over the Carlos family, thankful Antonio hadn't outright ruined the men we loved.

"I love you, Hill."

She'd laid down beside me, her head snuggled into the crook of my neck, arms loosely wrapped around my abdomen. I rested my chin on the thick mop of auburn hair and let her heartbeat set mine, more grateful than ever for her presence in my life. My men filled a hole no one else could, but Winter's friendship was my most precious gift.

"I love you, Sweets," I returned, favoring the nickname I'd given her all those years ago. "I'm sorry I didn't tell you any of this sooner."

"Well," she teased, "that would have been one hell of a text." Her fingers trailed a soft outline along the pattern of my hospital gown. "But I know why you didn't."

She shifted to look me in the eye, an unsettling sincerity in her stare. "You realize this changes absolutely nothing, right? I mean, I'm probably going to worry about you more now, at least until someone finds Antonio, but this changes nothing. I've always known you are a badass—you've just confirmed it."

Fresh tears of relief formed, and I smiled fiercely through them. "Don't go thinking this means I can't protect you—Shane's going to have hell to pay if he ever hurts you."

Her obnoxious snort drew a snicker from my chest. "Why is it always Shane with you? Not even Logan gets under your skin the way he does."

"He has a talent."

Her grin sobered, and her tone turned serious. "Do you think you'll stay in Carlisle?"

"I don't know," I answered honestly. "It's no longer just me I'm considering. But the things that used to matter to me just... don't anymore. I can't see myself wearing polyester soon but... maybe I need some time to reevaluate."

"Then take it." Winter's declaration held all the authority I was used to commanding. "Seriously, Hill. What better time than after your entire revenge empire closes out and you survive a bit of torture?"

More softly, she added, "You've lived most of your life for someone else—to avenge them, to honor them, even to measure up to your aunt's inheritance expectations—please, take the time."

I didn't respond. I had little to say. The future, for the first time in my life, was a looming question mark of unpredictability and possibility, a new game where I didn't know the rules. I squeezed her as tightly as my bandaged arms would allow before she had to leave me to return to her own life—one she'd fought hard to build with her own men.

My thoughts swirled above our heads as we fell silent, taking comfort in the quiet strength of her company while we still had this time together. The boys would be back any minute, and our moment would be lost.

I allowed the faintest prick of resolution to pierce my heart as I mulled over her words. The game had changed. I didn't know the board or the players involved, but I knew me, and I knew my men. And when you had a royal court, it didn't matter which game you played, the odds would be in your favor.

After all, I was still the Queen.

CHAPTER 26

Hillary

Two months later

"Laney ... are you sure about this?"

Marty's dubious expression pulled a laugh from my throat. I'd asked myself the same question many times over these last three months as we'd strategized our next moves. Eventually, I landed on "yes, fundamentally, categorically sure."

We were seated in my office for likely the last time. Me at my desk in a baby pink cashmere track suit and Louis Vuitton sneakers since my feet were still undergoing a strict rehabilitation regimen, with Marty and Weston seated opposite me, dressed in suits, as usual.

They were perched in front of piles of documents organized by color-coded folders, each reviewing the many sets of directions I'd agonized over. Every detail had been written out with the most explicit instructions of what was to become of my company now I was leaving.

"I just... I can't believe you're leaving. How can Lane Enterprises exist without a Lane to run it?" My assistant's crestfallen face tugged at my heartstrings, but it wouldn't change my mind.

"I promise you, I have the perfect replacement in mind." I placed a hand over his and squeezed it lightly, my lips quirking into a placating smile. "But we'll get to that. Weston?"

Weston shuffled the papers in front of him. "Yes, okay, so first—the endowment."

He whistled through his teeth, clearly seeing the amount of money put into a secured trust for Roberta's Foundation. It was the only way I'd accept walking away from the mission that had consumed my life for the better part of a decade. If I wasn't getting my hands dirty, I could leave a sizable gift to the kind hearts who protected the most vulnerable in our state.

Thankfully, Alvarez and any low-life ties associated with his operations had been completely shut down, and the FBI had dismantled much of Antonio's illegal businesses even though they hadn't been able to track him down across three countries. Sequoia citizens were likely the safest they'd ever been from soulless predators, but human nature would continue on, and eventually another evil person no doubt would move in to take their place. I couldn't single-handedly fight them all.

"Yes, the endowment. I'd like that one to remain anonymous, please. No named buildings or anything like that. Just make sure they have access to the funds annually to keep up with their needs."

"Okay..." Marty chewed on his lips but flipped the page to the next item: stock options.

"So, you're giving one million dollars worth of stock options—*your* stock options—to a Gertrude Baker?"

A small grin pinched my cheeks at that request from Lucky. Trust my previously opportunistic, now kind and sappy Irishman to want Gertie to be taken care of for life for her part in Alvarez's incarceration. I was happy to do it, and had already hired her as a new assistant as one of my final duties. Lane Enterprises was going to need one.

"Yes, and double the amount will be left to Josephine Horton, Winter Wallace, and Noble Wallace—the latter set aside in a trust until he turns twenty-one. Of the rest of my options, I'd like them divided up among all staff in my immediate companies—the details are in there." I pointed at the yellow folder at the bottom of the pile; Weston pulled it out to see the details for himself.

His deep tone broke through the noisy din of paper rustling after skimming the first page. "That's over five thousand employees."

I nodded. "It is, yes. As for Aaron's company that I inherited after his fake death, the Board has agreed to buy me out entirely. We'll sell the shares over time to maintain the stock value, but I want them all liquidated before the end of the year. That's my retirement money."

Weston dipped his head in acknowledgment and turned his attention back to the folder, his eyebrows raising every few seconds at the figures listed there. Being a billionaire was no joke—and most people couldn't fathom how much money it actually was. By the time I was done here, I'd have only a fraction of that wealth, but still more than enough to live off of.

My heavy shoulders felt lighter with the release of that burden.

"Retirement," Marty mumbled as he thumbed through in a mild fugue state. I felt bad I was throwing this all at him at once, but if I knew anything about Martin Williams, he could handle the load.

"Does it say anywhere in here who will be my new boss?" he muttered grumpily. Weston kicked him under the table, and I stifled my snort while waiting patiently for him to flip to the last page.

When the light gray of his stare finally met the blues of my own, eyes widened in shock, I couldn't help the wide grin from creeping across my face.

"Laney, I—what—really?!" he spluttered. Weston peered over to view the instructions. Another whistle pierced the air, and he placed a large palm on the back of his husband's shoulder in a congratulatory squeeze.

"Really," I confirmed, unable to control the light giggle on the tip of my tongue. "I've already enrolled you in a CEO mentorship program so you can feel comfortable in this role —but Marty, that's a formality. You know this business inside and out, and I trust your instincts."

He and Weston shared a loaded look—the kind only couples who have been together for years can communicate with—and when he turned his attention back to me, a beaming grin showed off every one of his beautifully straight teeth.

"Yes, yes, one thousand times yes!" he exclaimed dramatically, leaping off his chair to wrap me in a bear hug. "This is just—I mean, I didn't expect this and—Jesus, this is a crazy day."

He pulled back from the hug and rubbed his hands over his face, smiling sheepishly through them. "Sorry. I can't imagine how crazy this must feel for you. The Philippines? What in the world are you going to do in the Philippines?"

"Hopefully, a whole lot of nothing." I shrugged nonchalantly, as if leaving my entire life behind for a tropical island on the other side of the world was the most practical solution there was. "You can't buy an island there, but you can lease one for 75 years, and I'll be long dead by the time that number comes up. I'm ready for a simpler life."

Simpler. And safer. Antonio was still out there—his kingdom was in ruins and he'd gone off the grid entirely— but until he was dead, I wasn't risking the safety of anyone else around me. We had eyes and ears everywhere across several countries. It was only a matter of time before we found him. But I had learned the hard way time was too precious to waste.

I would miss Winter more than life, but her words had really struck a nerve, like an uncomfortable cleaning with a poorly trained dental hygienist. I'd built my empire, and I was proud of everything I had accomplished, but none of it had ever been driven by what *I* wanted. She was looking forward to visiting my new tropical paradise, claiming my new home would become her permanent Christmas vacation destination. I'd build an entire wing onto our new home just for them.

"I hope the simple life is ready for *you*." Marty's teasing smirk lit up his eyes, and it brought a pang of sadness to my heart. I'd spent so much time with him, late nights brokering mergers, early morning meetings to build better and brighter futures for our people... I was going to miss him dearly.

Like the incredible assistant he was, he sensed my mood, and immediately wrapped his arms back around me. This time, the hug was a soothing consolation rather than exuberant excitement, and he stroked a palm down my spine in a calming motion.

"Thank you for trusting me, Laney," he whispered with a squeeze. "I'm excited for you to live your new life."

I gently shrugged free of his hold and stood, truly ready to leave this entire part of my life behind. "I'm excited too. Take good care of her for me."

Weston stood, dropping all the folders on the mess of a desk in front of him to stick out his hand. "It was a pleasure doing business with you, Ms. Lane." I returned his grip, my gratitude for his role in our escape placing him on the Lane loyalty list for life.

"You're one hell of a lawyer, Weston. If I ever need one again, I'll be calling you. But I'm really hoping my life gets quite boring from here on out."

His chuckle vibrated through my arm before he let go. I offered one last smirk then turned on my heel. Donning my purse and sunglasses, I hobbled out of the building I'd once called a second home.

Walking out of my office for the very last time on my own two feet—something the doctors hadn't believed likely—I felt the summer sun on my face and welcomed the warmth licking against my skin, the simplicity of the feeling settling the unease of the new life ahead of me.

"Oy, Lass. Need a lift?" Lucky called to me from the roadside, his window down and his obnoxious Chad sunglasses perched on the bridge of his nose like a frat boy, matching the suggestive wiggling of his eyebrows perfectly.

I giggled at my boyish man and slowly ambled toward his brand-new bright orange Mustang GT. "In honor of my favorite Skittle," he'd said when he brought it home off the lot. He'd received his payment from The Six once Camden received the forged version of my stolen painting, and insisted he was shipping it to the Philippines, even if it was the most impractical vehicle for a tropical island, ever. Now officially retired, he was leaving his entire life behind to join me on our next adventure.

Aaron's parents had gone into hiding, and I'd been positive he would pursue them before he'd be willing to leave them behind, but I was wrong. *"I trust that Karma will take care of them, Mi Reina. Or perhaps I will in another life. I too am ready to move on from this life."*

Kellan had already declared his intentions in the hospital room before we were released, and he'd stayed true to his word. It was now the four of us against the world, on a private island, figuring out who we all were when we didn't have outside expectations dictating our next moves.

Lucky patiently waited at the curb until I finally opened the door and settled into the buttery leather seat. When I'd gotten the go-ahead to walk on my own two feet, I very clearly threatened every one of their lives if they tried to baby me, and it only took a few light stabbings for them to get the message. When I was safely buckled, he placed a lingering and longing kiss on my lips, the soft, pillowy skin promising me more for later.

"Come on, Blondie. Let's get you home."

CHAPTER 27

Kellan

Three months later

The cool Colombian mountain air grazed my heated skin as I stalked the trail up to a tiny cabin, in search of the prey that had long eluded me.

Despite the "clean life" we now all lived, thanks to Lauchlan's ability to hack into camera footage worldwide, and Aaron's connections through the dark web, I'd finally found the man who'd tainted every part of my soul, and it was time for his reckoning.

My Killer had insisted on coming with me, and I'd staunchly refused, not that it mattered. As much as my new family all wanted their piece of flesh from Antonio, I'd wanted—*needed*—to do this alone. Apparently however, being a part of a unit of equal power meant we all got a say, even when it wasn't *their* father. I'd been overruled, three to one. No longer being the leader had some perks, but I was not a fan of our new voting arrangement.

Aaron had his own agenda, wanting to search for his parents, rumored to have landed back on Colombian soil, and he couldn't be swayed to take my side, no matter how many bribes I'd offered him.

As a compromise, I was *allowed* to take the reins on the planning. I'd chartered a private plane to make the trip from our new home to Antonio's old stomping grounds in the Eastern Andes.

On our second day, Aaron had tracked down his parents to an old relative's compound, and together we'd placed several bullets in their brains after uncovering their newest venture: child trafficking. His revenge on Veronica and Vicente was swift and violent, and I was reminded once again he was a formidable ally, lover, partner, and friend, but as an enemy he was fucking terrifying. I'd witnessed the very definition of depravity many times in my life as an agent and with the cartel, but when Aaron unleashed his darkness...

He was behind me now, protecting my back as we hiked up the uneven rocky path to the small one-bedroom hut on the hillside. After six days lying low, Lauchlan had determined my dear father would be staying at this cabin tonight thanks to—well, however it was that man knew things. Ten months of getting to know him and he was still an enigma, but an enigma who had my back and brought light to my dark. He and Hillary were coming up another path toward the rear of the building, armed to the teeth with enough firepower to erase it from the landscape entirely.

I wasn't taking any chances. I wanted the man to die a miserable death, but I didn't need vengeance enough to risk the people I loved. Not again.

We'd set up camp a few miles from Antonio's location, just in case we needed a backup site. There was no telling how long this mission would take us, but I had hope we'd be back in our Alaskan king on the other side of the planet by midnight tomorrow.

The rugged mountain valley was beautiful in twilight, but the setting of my homeland was lost on me. My mind was still and focused, my training kicking into full force on the precipice of battle.

I raised my right fist in a stopping motion once we made it over the ridge. The tiny cabin sat on the crest of the hill beside a narrow riverbed, looking as innocent as a fairytale illustration, complete with a thin trail of smoke rising from the brick chimney.

"It is a shame we must cover it in blood, no?" Aaron mused idly as he stepped up beside me. His sweeping gaze assessed our surroundings. "We will return to the mountains when we are not on killer missions. I would like *Mi Reina* to enjoy our country."

Before I could reply with my agreement, my satellite phone buzzed in my pocket, the signal Hillary had arrived at their destination, just beyond a smaller ridge less than a quarter mile away. We'd all worried the hike would be too hard on her feet, but the woman's stubbornness could rival mine, and she wouldn't listen to a damn word we said. She wouldn't complain even if she were in pain, just to prove the point, but I'd be checking her over later—whether she liked it or not.

My companion adjusted the Velcro of his Kevlar vest and spun the silencer onto his favorite pistol, but the plan was not to need it at all. I too had Old Faithful locked and loaded with its own silencer, but the last thing I wanted was a quick bullet to Antonio's head. If my luck held tonight, the man would suffer.

"Ready, *compañero*?"

Rough fingers interlaced with mine, the grip of his familiar hand solid and warm. I gave it a firm squeeze, letting its comfort wash over me before dropping it.

"Ready," I confirmed, and the fierce heat of incoming retribution rose to the surface of my skin. I tapped out a quick message to the other half of our team—the signal we were going in.

We moved in unison, maneuvering down the rocky terrain on quick feet, using the limited cover to hide us within the shadows of dusk. When I reached the small wooden door at the front of the cabin, I waited until Aaron was directly behind me with his pistol cocked before bursting through the door.

Before I could blink, a bullet rocketed into my Kevlar right at chest level. I stumbled backward to the ground at the impact, my chest burning with the hit, even though the force of it had been mostly absorbed. Angry shouts flew over my head as Aaron's returning fire elicited a male scream from somewhere within the cabin. My gaze darted to the bald man—his favorite guard—now dead on the floor from a perfectly clean shot right between the eyes.

My body begged me to catch my breath, but there wasn't time. Antonio stood at a two-person dining table, dressed in a casual linen shirt and a pair of chino shorts, eyes widened in a rare expression of surprise. He spun in place, gaze searching for a weapon of some kind. I spied a steak knife on the counter. I wouldn't let him get the chance. This man wouldn't hurt another person I loved—another person ever —again.

Before he could grip its handle, I summoned the energy to aim my gun at the soft, fleshy tissue between his thumb and forefinger, and fired.

Blood spattered from the wound, and trails of thick viscous liquid oozed down the front of his shirt as he cradled his hand against his chest.

My father's scream of pain echoed through the open door and into the mountains, disturbing nature's peace. It would be the first of many.

"Check the bedroom," I ordered, and Aaron rushed past me with his gun raised to kick in the small door to the left of the kitchen. I aimed Old Faithful at my father's head and glowered at the miserable sack of shit.

"Sit." I waved my weapon toward the vintage teak and leather chair in the center of the room. Antonio's returning sneer spewed visceral hate, but with the threat of a bullet in the brain, he reluctantly sat, dark eyes calculating how he would work his way out of death, but he refused to say a word.

Aaron returned a moment later, a pretty dark-skinned woman draped only in a towel on his arm.

"She says she is a prostitute from a nearby village." He spat in disgust, but not at the woman's job title. Antonio's incessant need for sex and dominance couldn't even be curbed on a remote mountainside in Colombia. The man was truly pathetic.

The woman cowered in terror, shaking within Aaron's loose hold while muttering prayers of forgiveness in Spanish.

"Let her go." I nodded my head toward the door we'd just entered through. "We don't need any more blood on our hands today."

Aaron led the woman to the threshold and released her into the twilight. She stumbled off in the direction we'd come, her sobs of thanks to her god echoing over the mountain.

Without needing my direction, Aaron stalked to Antonio and wrenched his arms in front of him, ignoring the latent scream of pain as he intentionally gripped the gaping hole in Antonio's palm. Blood dripped down Aaron's hands as he quickly tied Antonio's arms to the wood of the chair legs in front of him with cable ties, the awkward angle hinging him forward.

I maintained my stance, aiming my gun at Antonio's temple, while Aaron reached down to tie each ankle to the legs. Then, he removed four thin razor blades from a clear container in his pocket and inserted them beneath the ties, right at the junction where his veins met plastic.

As he stood, he brought his lips to Antonio's ear. "Should you choose to move, *Carechimba*, you will create great pain, but it will take hours for you to bleed out."

Sweat beaded along Antonio's brow, but he clamped his lips shut, motionless for the moment.

I whipped around at the sound of rustling behind me. "We're coming in, Viking!"

Hillary and Lauchlan strode through the open door, guns raised and on alert, dressed in Kevlar and blood.

"We ran into a few goons on the way up," Killer explained with a casual shrug. "Took us a second to throw their bodies over the cliff." She assessed our surroundings with a shrewd stare, the blood spatter on her face making her look like a Viking Queen coming from battle. As much as I didn't want her here for this, that look—the fiercely protective one for the people she loved—tweaked my heart with gratitude. This woman never failed to have my back.

"Heavy fuckers," Lauchlan grumbled good-naturedly, eyeing up Antonio's position in the chair. He let out a low whistle. "Nice one, mate," he said, nodding at the razor blades against our victim's skin. "You're a sick feck, aren't you?" His grin toward Aaron said the opposite; he enjoyed Aaron's darkness as much as the rest of us.

Lauchlan turned his attention to me. "Set up two cameras just now. If we get any company, we'll know it. So you can"—he gestured toward Antonio's mute form—"do all your murdery stuff without interruption."

"How thoughtful," Aaron deadpanned, walking over to stand with us at Antonio's front. They were waiting for me to take the lead, none of them fully knowing how I was planning on ending the man who'd caused so many to suffer.

Luckily, the chair Antonio sat in had a low enough back to give me the access I needed.

I'd fantasized about killing this man for all of my adult life, and most of my childhood. Death by hanging, by mutilation, by firing squad. I'd even considered flaying him alive after seeing Aaron in action with Alec. A bullet wasn't enough. Neither was a knife.

I sucked in a fortifying breath of stale cabin air and allowed each molecule of oxygen to hit every muscle in my body before speaking. The black pits my father had for eyes bore into me, challenging me to be the brutal man he'd raised, even as he faced death.

A good man would dig into himself and find a way to forgive, or at least a way to move on. I was not a good man. I didn't need that label to feel good about my life or my purpose.

I needed Antonio's fresh blood to run between my fingers and stain my skin—then, I could forgive whatever godforsaken forces had given me to this man, and move on with my family.

"You ruined my mother," I said, the acknowledgment still a stone in my throat all these years later. "But she still lives in my body." I waved at my blond hair, blue eyes, large stature, and at my gun still clenched in my grip. "I am far more of a Viking than a *Guecha*."

I handed Old Faithful to Aaron and brandished the sharpened machete hanging from my belt, raising the blade in the dull glow of the oil lamp light. "In Norse mythology, there is a particularly brutal form of execution, reserved to avenge the killing of a family member."

I stalked closer to Antonio's seated form, unable to hold back the smirk as he shrank back into his chair, small trickles of blood trailing from his ankles and wrists with every movement.

"It's known as the Blood Eagle. Have you heard of it?"

Apparently, he had. His eyes widened in horror, but he still refused to speak, his pride outweighing his fear, if only for the moment.

"You killed my mother," I repeated, circling the chair to stand at his back. "You tried to kill my family." I pointed the machete past his head toward Hillary, Aaron, and Lauchlan as they observed in silence. "You've destroyed thousands of families for your own greed."

Sweat poured off his skin now, and the stench of his fear filled the cabin, masking the metallic scent of the blood dripping from his limbs. But his ego was his kryptonite, and he couldn't help himself from speaking.

"Your mother was weak." His scornful scowl was as bitter as battery acid. "*You* are weak. I spent my life training you into a man, but you are nothing but a boy in man's clothing, believing your ideals are above the empire that could have been yours. *Patético.*"

I lowered my head to his, so close I could see the blood pumping furiously through his jugular from his heart. The man was terrified and struggled to hide it.

"If I am so weak, why do I scare you so much?" I murmured, my tone soft and coaxing. "Why do you cower while I claim your throne? *Patético.*" I echoed back at him, unable to control the taunt. His gaze stared forward, refusing to look at me, so proud he wouldn't beg for his life. I'd expected as much.

I could draw out his torture for days, bleed him out slowly, starve him, burn him. I didn't want any of that. The people I loved waited on the other side of his chair, and we had a full life ahead of us. After tonight, Antonio wouldn't take another moment of my peace.

I stood to my full height and eyed every one of my lovers, each of them staring back at me with solidarity and care. The amber in Aaron's eyes showed his understanding—he knew firsthand the peace that would come from my vengeance. Hillary's cool blue eyes were as dark as mine in this light, but they shone with wicked intent—she relished this kill almost as much as I did, but she stayed on the sidelines, so I could give my version of justice. Lauchlan's—*Lucky's*—sea-glass stare held nothing but curiosity, like he was enjoying learning this last little bit about me.

I dipped my head in a solemn nod, acknowledging their presence and recognizing their place in this part of my life. In sickness and in health, in darkness and in light—this was us.

I shoved my father forward, exposing his back to the open air. Muttered curses escaped him as Aaron's blades cut harder into his skin.

I sheared his shirt off his back, exposing the sun-kissed skin beneath. His back vibrated with shudders from his ragged breathing, and still... no sound.

If he wouldn't beg for his life, it was time to hear him scream.

"*Ge tillbaka för gammal ost.*" I declared and shoved the eighteen-inch knife beneath his shoulder blades until it hit air on the other side, then sliced it upward along his spine. Forcefully, I pulled it back out and stabbed along the other side, breaking the ribs and puncturing his lungs, widening the hole that would bring the Eagle's wings to life.

His gargling screams enveloped us all in the small space, high-pitched and unbearably shrill. I soaked them in like music as the blood frenzy took over me, fully immersed in the supposed animalistic ritual of my people.

I reached my hands into the opening to grip his broken ribs from behind and yanked them back, the reverberating crack of bone snapping melded with Antonio's sobs.

I turned to my three observers, each one of them put in harm's way by my father.

"Come." I beckoned them forward with a tissue-covered hand. Not one of them hesitated, moving in sync to stand beside me.

I pulled a bone through Antonio's skin until it stood upward outside of his body. I pointed at the rib with a savage smile. "Be my guest."

Lucky's eyebrows hit his hairline, but he was the first to move, reaching into the cavity to haul a rib up to meet the other. "You fucked with my family, you miserable teet." He spat. He grabbed another for good measure, and didn't shrink when Antonio's screams vibrated through the bone. His willingness to be a part of this ritual, the least violent of the four of us, stirred something within me, and I vowed to show him just how much it meant to me later.

My Killer reached in after him, her trademark ferocity darkening her angelic face into one of brutality. Dainty hands brought up two ribs, one after the other.

"There are no words for you, other than 'good riddance.' Fuck everything you stand for." Blood dripped down her porcelain skin, and she was the most beautiful she'd ever been to me.

Aaron took his time, letting Antonio's blood flow across his skin like water. He pulled two ribs to the surface, the sadistic look of pleasure across his features another reminder of how dangerous our man could be in the right circumstances.

"You will haunt him no more," he said, but it was enough. This violent, romantic man was more than enough for me.

Together, we stared down at Antonio's mutilated form, bones jutted out of his back like the wings of a bird in flight, admiring the picture of a broken man bound as a broken eagle.

Thick, hot blood coated my arms, up to my biceps, soaked the front of my pants, and flecked my beard. I welcomed the scent of iron on my skin, savoring the release of its significance.

Vengeance was mine.

Rough gasps of air faded to whimpers as my father—my mentor, my torturer—pitched forward, dead bodyweight tipping over the chair onto the dirt floor. I watched him with a growing lightness in my soul as the evil remnants of him leached into the soil.

We all watched in silence as he took his final breath, and held the quiet for another moment longer. Finally, I moved around the carcass and out the door into the darkness of night.

"Leave him to rot," I called behind me. "He'll be a warning to whoever comes to find him tomorrow."

The stars lit up the mountainside so brightly, it was as if we could just touch the Milky Way. I ignored all of its beauty and tore off my Kevlar and all of my clothing, then bounded to the river to rinse off the remnants of my father's demise.

Fully naked, I dove into the cool water, relishing the soothing balm against my heated skin.

The man who'd raised me to follow in his footsteps had hoped I would become fucked up beyond repair. Considering the way I'd just mutilated his body, he'd succeeded, but it didn't make me loathe myself like many other actions I'd taken in his name over the years.

He'd used and abused me, damaged my soul and scarred my body. But for all his efforts, he'd failed to break me. I was still here, bonded to three other broken people with shitty parents and decades living for something other than their own wants and needs.

Antonio's death didn't just bring peace. It brought fucking hope. The target on our backs was gone—we could build a life without the fear of it all being taken away. I'd forgotten what true freedom felt like. I'd probably never had it. But tonight, I could taste its sweetness on my tongue.

Soon, three naked bodies glided into the water alongside me, their splashes the only sounds breaking through the hoots of owls in the distance. I dug my hands into the riverbed, using the sand and small rocks to exfoliate away the blood and debris on my arms, my hands and my face. Then I hauled my ass out of the rushing water to sit on the bank.

When Hillary waded out of the water to sit beside me, I roughly grabbed her by the forearm and pulled her into my lap. Her soft, wet skin glided across my crotch and instantly hardened my cock to stone. Fighting and fucking worked on the same chemical level, and the adrenaline coursing through my veins needed another outlet besides murder.

She turned in my hold to stare into my eyes, but I wasn't in the mood for talking. Gripping her chin between two large fingers, I closed my mouth over hers and demanded entrance with my tongue, combining the sweet taste of freedom with the sweetness of her.

The soft moan in the back of her throat spurred me on. Her hands wrapped in my wet hair, and I released my grip on her chin to palm her ass, lifting her to straddle my lap and tease her heat with the thick, angry head of my erection. Warm arousal dripped onto my cock as she squirmed against me, desperately seeking friction against her clit.

I needed this woman more than I needed air to breathe. My partner, my lover, my Queen.

The sensation of being watched made the hairs on my neck stand on end, but not in fear. I cracked open one eye. Aaron and Lucky watched us from the river, lazily stroking their cocks to the same rhythm as our bodies.

I pulled my mouth away from Killer's, the urgent need to fuck and fuck hard superseding every other rational thought. "What are you waiting for?" I called over the soft rush of water. "Come join us."

Hillary twisted in my lap to face them, breasts and bare pussy on full display, as they scrambled to kneel in front of us.

"Not really the time or place," she let out on a groan as I reached out to tweak a pebbled nipple, "but I want to fuck every one of you tonight." Another gush from her pussy soaked the inside of my thigh, and I shifted our positions to wedge my solid cock between her ass cheeks. She shivered in my hold, bucking up into nothing, desperate to be touched.

I'd touched this woman almost a hundred times this way, but tonight, it felt as fresh as the first time. New and exciting, like I hadn't truly fucked her before now. Maybe because this time *was* different. I wasn't just fucking her, I was *loving* her, giving her everything I should have given her all these years. My body, my heart, and my demons on full display.

"I want to fuck every one of you tonight too," Lucky admitted, his eyes never leaving the pink flesh of her hot cunt. Without warning, he lowered directly in front of her open legs, sticking his tongue out to lick her wetness; he sucked every drop from her clit to the edge of her puckered hole.

I banded my arms around her to hold her in place while he enthusiastically sucked her dry. Aaron and I watched, impossibly hard, but too into her pleasure to stop it for our own gain. Her whimpers and pleas erased Antonio's screams. I wanted to hear them all make those noises tonight.

When Lucky came up for air, Aaron knelt on his knees before him, his thick cock jutting upward for Lucky's lips. The Irishman didn't hesitate, opening wide and hollowing his cheeks with the sticky sweetness of Hillary still coating his chin.

Aaron plunged into him, gripping the sides of Lucky's head to fuck his mouth. He took no prisoners as he pounded against his tongue, his body shuddering with each thrust. I pressed into the crest of Hillary's ass to release some of the pressure, bringing my hand around to gently rub the swollen nub of her clit while we watched the show.

These two men were beautiful in their own right. Strong and fierce, yet each embodied their own softness and didn't apologize for it. They worshipped Hillary with the same devout spirit I did, and now I could see they worshipped each other with the same care.

Saliva dribbled down Lucky's chin as he took each invasion without complaint, until Aaron pulled out entirely and hauled him upward into a passionate kiss. Their tongues collided like they were in the middle of battle.

I hadn't let myself be taken care of since my mother died. When she was gone, there was no one to take care of me, and the more Antonio controlled my world, the more my shield solidified until it was completely impenetrable.

Could I let *them* take care of me?

"Fuck, that's hot," I grunted, rutting harder against Hillary's backside as I watched them. The two men stopped their kiss and moved closer, sitting down beside us on the grassy knoll.

Aaron's hands skirted up Hillary's thighs and dipped into the heat of her pussy, brushing past my fingers on her clit. When he removed the two fingers, they glistened with a thick coating under the moonlight. He licked off her arousal, closing his eyes to savor the flavor on his tongue before dipping them back into her, curling and thrusting them against her walls.

"Fuck me," Hillary moaned, as we worked her over, sandwiching her between us in a three-way pet. I nipped at the soft skin beneath her earlobe while Aaron leaned in to press his lips against hers. Lucky moved closer beside us, massaging her breasts, all of us commanding her attention from all sides.

Aaron's lips moved from hers to mine, and I got to taste the fading remnants of her lust on his tongue. The bittersweet tang rocketed a violent need through me harder than a hit of cocaine. I wanted everything from these people. I wanted every experience, every possibility. I wanted to take care of them, and be taken care of, for as long as they'd have me.

For the first time in my life, I wanted to be soft for someone. Adrenaline was one hell of a drug because it even made me want—

"I want you to fuck me."

Everyone stopped in their tracks like I'd whipped out a gun instead of this admission. All eyes turned on me, even Hillary, who'd arched her back against mine to shoot a questioning look my way.

"To whom are you referring, *compañero*?" Aaron asked.

I nervously chewed my lip but, fuck it, I'd said it, and after murdering my father, what better time was there for another first? He'd threatened it in the closet all those months ago, and now... I wanted to know what it felt like to completely surrender to someone who would never hold it against me.

"You." I replied simply. "Will you do it?"

The request hung heavy in the air between all of us, but I waited. Lucky's crestfallen face was cute as hell, but our dynamic wasn't something I wanted to play with. He was my brat, and I was his Dom ... I couldn't release that part of me with him. But maybe I could with Aaron.

My entire existence had been an exercise in controlled settings and controlling people. It was time to let a little of it go, and I trusted my *Guapo* to deliver it.

His pupils dilated, and he licked his lips as his eyes roamed over my naked body with only Hillary as my cover.

"I will do it." Then he turned to the sexy Irishman on his left. "And you will take me."

"I—uh—okay?!" Lucky spluttered, rendered speechless for probably the first time in his life. He quickly recovered. "Fuck yes, I will," he declared with a triumphant grin. "I even packed lube!"

Of course, he did. I snorted in amusement and relief, anxious about this new experience. Before I could make a move, Hillary slid off my lap. The lascivious grin dancing on her lips shot electric sparks into my balls. I loved it when she looked at me that way.

She laid down in the soft bed of grass beside me and opened her legs wide in invitation. "I guess that means I'm the bottom. Come here, Viking, and fuck me."

Cock throbbing and desperate for the heat of her pussy, I rolled on top of her, holding my weight off her body with my forearms while I notched my head at her entrance, teasing us both with the contact.

She wound her arms around my neck and thrust her hips up, forcing my cock deeper. I drove the rest of the way into her, as deep as I could hit, relishing her moan against my skin.

Hillary Lane. My Killer—she'd always fought to protect me as much as I had her—and tonight, she'd watched me avenge my childhood without a single blink of judgment. She wasn't my sword or shield, but she was my safe harbor beyond a violent shoreline. I couldn't love her more.

The tight sleeve of blissful heat strangled my cock as I thrust harder and harder, pistoning my hips to hit her G spot while my pelvic bone rubbed her clit. The frantic motion only halted at the cool drip of lube against my ass. Aaron's low tone was barely audible over the sound of our lusting, ragged breaths.

"I will make your first time good, *compañero.*" He smoothed a rough palm over the swell of my ass and I clenched my cheeks at the unfamiliar intrusion. Hillary squirmed under me, soaking me with her desire while she waited for me to move.

"Relax, Kellan. You will soon know what *Rojo* is always begging you for."

I forced my muscles to loosen as he massaged the gel into my hole and blew out another breath when he slowly inserted a single finger. It was a natural impulse to resist it, but as he lightly circled the inside of my hole with a gentle pressure, heat trickled up my spine. I rode out every swirl of his index finger, the heat building until the uncomfortable pressure became a delicious quake of pleasure.

"There you go." Aaron's voice dropped an octave into a potent sensual lull. "You are doing so well for me, baby, just relax."

Aaron Rodriguez, a tormented man who'd found peace in letting go. He could have been a brother in another life. Instead, I'd been given him as a lover. His patient nature and devotion to Hillary had taught me love didn't need to be perfect, but it had to be honest. It was a bond I'd never be able to replace.

He inserted another finger and curled them against my walls, massaging the so-called mythical P spot over and over while I held myself still inside of the gorgeous queen under me. A tremor hurtled through my entire core, every limb jolting at the contact, my dick jumping inside Hillary's tight pussy as stars showered behind my eyelids.

"Ohhh, do that again." She squirmed against me with a moan of lust, arousal dripping out of her and coating my balls. I gritted my teeth to stop myself from flooding her with my cum right there.

The cool air against my ass jolted me out of the pleasure.

I mourned the loss of his fingers and wasn't above begging for them back when I felt the persistent pressure of a heavily lubed cockhead pressing at my entrance.

"Are you ready for me, *compañero*?" His thick head wedged slowly into the thick ring of muscle, burning with the stretch. "I will leave an imprint of my cock inside you so that you never forget this moment."

Aaron wasn't a pencil-dick. He was girthy and long, and

—

"Fuuuuuuuuuuuuck." I groaned when the burn turned into liquid pleasure, every tensed muscle in my body melting into his as he slowly burrowed deeper into me. He lowered his body with every small thrust, and the warmth of his torso covered my back like a blanket, his hands covering mine as they dug into the earth next to Hillary's head.

Is this what I'd been missing? The most vulnerable I'd ever been, but the most whole. Complete. Safe and taken care of. He bottomed out inside me, his sharp intake of breath letting me know how much he enjoyed the feel of me too. I clenched my cheeks, causing him to mutter a strangled curse, but he still didn't move.

"Your turn, *Rojo*." He issued the command through slow breaths. "Do not go easy on me."

A rustling of grass and loose pebbles came from behind as Lucky got into position.

"My pleasure, Daddy."

Lauchlan O'Donnell, the irritatingly likeable shit who never took "no" for an answer and usually ended up being right. Chaos personified, he was the perfect antidote to my callous nature. I'd never have picked him, as a friend, a business partner, or a lover, but thankfully, we didn't have to wait for my slow ass because he picked me. Now that he'd latched onto my body and mind like a playful parasite, I'd have to keep him. I couldn't give him up even if he hadn't.

I waited with bated breath for what was to come, gently pulsing my cock into Hillary's soaking core and clenching Aaron's cock deeper into me. Their shudders against my body told me as soon as Lucky took charge, we were all going to come in mere seconds, too wound up to care about the fast fuck.

I could feel additional pressure as Lucky worked his way into Aaron. The Colombian bit into my shoulder blade as our Irishman sunk deeper into our blend of bodies. My veins sang with the sting of his lips against my skin.

"Fuck, Daddy, you feel so fecking *delightful.* I haven't taken a man's tight hole in forever, but you can bet I'll be taking yours daily from now on."

Aaron grunted, a frustrated sound laced with amusement. "It is I who will take your hole, *Rojo.* Fuck me."

With that order lingering in the air, Lucky moved, and fuck, did he move. Pounding thrusts vibrated through Aaron's body and into mine, each push into him shoving Aaron's thick cock impossibly deeper into my ass. Sensation surrounded me. Aaron and Lucky's movements filled me as Hillary's tight pussy took every rut like she was frantic for it.

As if reading each other's minds, Aaron and I each lifted a palm from the grass to knead Hillary's breasts. She responded with a guttural groan of pleasure; I thrust my pelvis up against her clit as Aaron hit my P spot, and her walls clenched around me with a heart-pounding scream of release.

Fuck, that sound was going to completely unravel me.

"I'm not. Going to. Last." I gritted out. Sweat beaded across my hairline and spine as she milked my cock with her aftershocks, coaxing me to explode.

A hand—I wasn't sure whose—reached underneath my body to massage my balls, and it was the very end of me. My head spun, white flashed behind my eyelids, and all sounds dimmed the moment my orgasm ripped through me, my cum exploding into my greedy Queen's cunt.

Aaron rutted into me like a deranged animal, so hard I was sure I'd have that imprint he threatened me with. Then the burning bliss of his cock stretching me wide was replaced by the hot sensation of his cum flooding my ass in angry spurts.

Aaron went limp against my back, but the pounding continued. "Yes, yes, yes," Lucky chanted with breathy moans before his strangled cry overshadowed our ragged breaths and he found his release.

We collapsed into each other, a naked pile of sweat, skin, and sin under the stars in the Colombian night. I brushed an errant strand of hair out of Hillary's face and kissed the tip of her nose before pulling out of the pile and laying on my back to see the night sky, truly seeing the beauty of the stars in the Milky Way for the first time.

A year ago, my life had looked vastly different. I had been caught between two worlds with nothing to give me hope of a different life. Yet now, here we were, the most oddball family in existence, freshly fucked and free of our burdens.

In an instant, sharp emotion completely overwhelmed me, the adrenaline and lust finally dissipating into an oxytocin-fueled love-fest. I cleared my throat before it could clog up my words, words I needed to say.

"I love you all." Fuck, my throat still felt like I'd swallowed a boulder, but I pressed on. "Thank you, for—being here tonight."

"Always, Viking." Hillary's satisfied smile melted the ball of anxiety in my chest. She rolled over and snuggled into my side, pressing a delicate kiss on my pec. "I love you."

"It is an honor to witness your new beginning, *compañero*." Aaron's words were solemn. His hand slid into mine, the squeeze soft and reassuring. "Love does not describe the bond we share."

"This is where we all belong, Kell-Bell," Lucky piped up cheerfully, gaze still on the sky above us. "There's no place I'd rather be. I got to show Daddy Roboto how much I loved him tonight, but I'll show you just how much I love *you* later." He turned and shot me a suggestive wink over Aaron's head.

"Not a chance." I laughed, shaking my head. "I don't bottom."

"I don't think you're that guy anymore, Kellll-Bellll." Lucky sing-songed, his cheeky grin taunting me. "You kiss, you shake hands, you bottom... you're a changed man."

I couldn't smother the tug at the corners of my mouth, a wide smile replacing the surly frown I was going for. When I laughed, the booming, free noise echoed across the river and down the mountainside like a roaring clap of thunder announcing its presence.

I was a changed man. These three people had changed me and every part of my existence. After tonight, nothing on this earth could hold me back from building the life I'd never even dared to dream of. I didn't want to waste a single second of it.

I knelt in the grass and gently pulled Hillary up with me, our two men following suit.

"Come on," I directed, pulling on my pants, leaving my dirty shirt to rot in the sunshine of the following day. "Let's go back to camp. I want to get home."

CHAPTER 28

Hillary

"We have one more stop to make," Aaron informed me when we stepped onto the chartered plane. We'd spent three days in the Colombian Eastern Andes.

The pilot conducted his checks as we settled into the small Cessna that would take us out to a main airfield, where we could get on a larger plane to cross the Pacific Ocean. At least, that was the original plan.

"Where are we going?" I asked, not overly interested in the answer. I was tired, the emotional toll of a torture trip finally hitting me with a smashing headache and achy limbs. The high altitude and rough terrain hadn't been kind to my out-of-shape body. My feet were unbearably tender, but I would carry that complaint to my deathbed. It had been hard enough convincing Kellan we were all coming on this mission. I wouldn't give him the satisfaction for all his hovering.

"Brazil." My head shot up to find Aaron's liquid amber eyes staring through me in challenge. "This is a trip of closure, no? We shall get closure for you as well."

My spine stiffened at his intrusion. "Aaron! That's not your—"

"I'm afraid I have sworn to take care of you, *Mi Reina*. It is very much my place."

The distinct rumble of engines coming to life interrupted us, and I glared daggers at him over the noise.

"I agree with Aaron on this one, Killer."

Kellan folded his massive body in the small seat, eyebrows raised as if taunting me to test him. Lucky, on the opposite side of him, lifted his hands in surrender.

"I had nothing to do with this, Blondie. But for what it's worth—aren't you ready to let go of everything? A true clean slate?"

Burning tears gathered in the corners of my eyes, but I held onto them for dear life. I wasn't ready to see her again, even after everything I did to honor her name and bring her justice. Quick, shallow breaths burst out of my nostrils. I needed time to plan. I needed to think. I needed—

Sensing my rising panic, Lucky unbuckled his seatbelt and sidled past Kellan to kneel in front of me, his sea-glass stare searching mine with the clearest sincerity.

"I can't pretend to know what you're feeling, lass." He reached up to stroke my cheek with the soothing kiss of his thumb. "But I know how I felt when I visited Shayna's grave for the first time. Her body wasn't even in it, but it was the sentiment, you know?" He shifted on his haunches, swallowing hard. "Musta cried for an hour like a bloody baby, but when I left, I felt better. Renewed, even. I want you to have that too."

His tender tone and kind delivery did me in. Rivers formed along my cheeks, and their drying streaks remained when we arrived at the *cemitério* one fuel stop and several hours later.

Our driver dropped us off at the gated entrance, and the four of us stood at its opening staring at the vast expanse of white-washed cement pillars and monuments, hundreds of rows stretching far into the distance.

Aaron wrapped a powerful arm around my shoulders as I stood frozen on the threshold. Every exhibit of my failure to bring honor to her name, to avenge the dishonorable way she died, unfolded in front of my vision in a blurry mirage through a barrage of fresh tears.

Had she forgiven me? Could I move on with peace in my heart and still preserve her beautiful memory, the piece of me she became?

My *caballero oscuro* turned me into him, cradling me within the heat of his body and soft notes of sandalwood and vanilla.

"*Mi Reina*," he crooned, "*Es momento de despedirse.*"

It is time to say goodbye.

I felt Kellan's broad form close in against my back. He rested the crest of his chin on top of my head, and enveloped the two of us in a tight embrace, exuding stability and calm —classic Kellan.

"Come on, Killer." He released his hold and walked one step ahead of me before turning to hold out his hand. "We're here with you."

We're here with you. Through it all, they had been. As much as I was terrified of this moment, they stood beside me, offering the sanctity of their strength and the light of their love. They knew what I needed, and had made the arrangements to give it to me, even when they knew it would be painful. These men—my men—didn't coddle me, but they cherished me.

Love swelled in my chest so deeply, my heart ached with the wealth of it, so powerful it replaced the fear wreaking havoc in my brain. It was time to introduce the new loves of my life to my very first—the woman who'd unknowingly changed my entire world, and eventually, led me on a path to them.

Lucky joined us on Aaron's other side, a tender smile gracing his lips as the four of us walked down the narrow trail to her gravesite beneath the shade of a willow tree. They held back while I tentatively approached the stone, anxious energy mingling with a wash of euphoria now I was finally here.

I caressed the cracking concrete under the blistering sun. A light breeze picked up as I sat down next to the headstone, as if her spirit felt my presence and was saying hello.

I drew a slow breath, blew it out in one rush of air, and smiled.

"Hey Bella," I whispered, "It's been a long time…"

EPILOGUE

Hillary

One year later

"Holy feck, have you seen this?!" Lucky crowed in triumph as he read a news article online while we all ate breakfast.

Well, Kellan and Aaron were eating breakfast—they'd fallen in love with *almusal*, the standard breakfast of the Filipino—eggs, fried rice, and a cured pork thing they swore was delicious, but I wasn't sold. I was drinking my standard green smoothie, with fresh fruit right off our trees on the island, and Lucky was munching on dessert, aka the Philippine Nestle equivalent of *Count Chocula*.

We were seated in the solarium, a beautiful room of floor-to-ceiling windows overlooking the surf on the beach side of the island. The sea was still today, the azure water beckoning me out for a skinny dip.

"I would guess that we have not seen it, *Rojo*," Aaron stated dryly after a mouthful of coffee. "Feel free to share."

"Oh, you're going to *love* this." My redheaded lover cackled as he stood from his seat and bounded toward me, shoving his phone in my palm. "Looks like our parents finally did themselves in!"

I put down the dregs of my smoothie to read aloud the article he had up on the screen.

"An American man and woman have been charged with fraud after attempting to sell a forgery of 'Reclining Nude,' by Amedeo Modigliani. Camden Lane, one of the accused, claimed his wealthy daughter, Hillary Lane, previous owner of Lane Enterprises, had gifted him the painting before she took a leave from her company. Camden Lane is no stranger to the police, after being sentenced to house arrest for insider trading less than a decade ago. Marcia Davidson, his alleged accomplice, is not known to American police, but further investigation yielded ties to The Six, an alleged "for-hire" network of thieves with bases in six different countries. Sentencing is underway for the pair, but ten years' imprisonment is the likely verdict. Hillary Lane could not be reached for comment."

"Did you know about this?" Kellan inquired after another mouthful of rice.

"I didn't." I handed the phone back to Lucky with a gleeful grin of my own. "But I counted on the possibility. I figured they would dig their own graves, so why should I waste my time doing it for them?"

I'd already sold my painting, the legitimate original, via a private deal, and it was safely sitting in a very secure vault of the Japanese buyer's private collection. I'd walked away from most of my wealth when I removed myself from

Lane Enterprises, but the painting's proceeds, along with Lucky's "little" nest eggs of several million dollars, had financed this island property and our lifestyle moving forward. I wasn't sailing away on a yacht, but I hadn't resorted to polyester, either.

Shrugging smugly, I grabbed a mug from the cupboard to make my morning cappuccino.

"That's my Blondie, fecking smart, she is." Before I could grind the fresh espresso beans, Lucky pulled me into his arms and smacked a wet, obnoxious kiss on my lips. "Always believing the worst in humanity, and half the time she's right!"

"Hey!" I protested, pointing the filter into his chest. "That's not true. I believed in Blackbird's innocence, didn't I?"

Marco Alvarez had finally been sentenced to prison a few months ago—with his father, Alejandro, and his brother, Daniel, along with him. We all had to fly back to the US to testify against him, and a lifetime in prison with no chance for parole had been the final verdict. Kellan leveraged a connection with a gang member loyal to him for years, and when Alvarez was finally cornered by multiple men with shanks, they'd drawn some truths out of him before they bled him to death.

According to Mad Dog, whoever the hell that was, Blackbird had originally been on Marco's payroll when I'd hired her, acting as a double agent between us for several years. Somewhere along the line she'd changed her tune— maybe she hadn't realized what Marco was actually up to when he'd hired her. Maybe she had a sadist kink and decided she liked the way I conducted torture more. But she'd switched allegiances to me and jumped on board to help Lucky hack into his company. When Marco discovered her betrayal, he had her killed, and sent me the warning.

I sat with that betrayal for a long time. I'd considered her a friend, but she'd played me all along, right under my nose. Still, without her help, we wouldn't be sitting on our private island watching the birds on the shoreline at breakfast, all our enemies vanquished.

Walking the line between light and dark was complicated.

"You did, *Mi Reina,*" Aaron agreed with a small smile playing on his lips. "And her true actions were most unfortunate. But you nearly gave the pool boy a heart attack when you thought he was paparazzi."

We'd had a few uninvited visitors to the island in the last few months, and I'd reached the end of my patience when I'd seen Angelo out on the pool deck like he belonged there.

Apparently, he did.

"How could I have known Kellan hired someone new?" I complained before turning the grinder on to drown out the sound of their chuckles.

"You tackled him into the pool," Kellan deadpanned, one scruffy blond eyebrow raised in challenge. "Extreme, even for you, Killer."

We'd mostly enjoyed our privacy on this side of the world, but I'd developed a bit of notoriety being one of the few billionaires on the planet who'd walked away from it all. Some said I'd developed an expensive drug habit and was shutting myself into rehab for the foreseeable future. Some theorized I'd "found Jesus" and I was "walking my path to redemption."

Accurate, but not in the way they were thinking.

I issued my best death glare at the bronzed Viking God seated at our breakfast table. His hair was even longer now, hanging past his shoulders to well below his shoulder blades. He'd sometimes put it in a ponytail on the top of his head and braid it down his back, in a very effective move to obliterate all of my defenses and have me on the floor under him in minutes. I was a sucker for his version of Uhtred.

"I said I was sorry and sent him home with a fruit basket. My *best* mangos, Kellan."

"Her best mangos, Kellan!" Lucky sing-songed. When my glare turned on him, he blew me a kiss. "How about I get a taste of your mango before work, Blondie?" He wriggled his eyebrows suggestively and winked, the lascivious grin telling me exactly which mango he was referring to.

"Nope, we're headed to work." I tossed a nod toward Kellan as the steamy espresso hit the bottom of my coffee cup with a satisfying hiss. "Maybe you can taste Aaron's banana."

Aaron's face crinkled into one of disgust. "Please do not refer to my manhood as a banana." His beautifully pouty lips pursed, rich and pink against the dark stubble along his jawline. "I am a jackfruit, at the very least."

Lucky burst into laughter, and I held back a snicker when Kellan stood from his place at the dining table, trying, and failing, to hold back his own amusement.

"Enough cock talk," he ordered, ever the commander. "We're taking the plane into Manila, and headed to Bangkok. Should be a short assignment. Do you guys need anything while we're there?"

We'd purchased a small biplane to island hop quicker than the boat, and we'd all gotten our licenses to fly it, but Kellan enjoyed it the most. Since we'd taken on a few side jobs, the plane was our most useful tool for travel.

Our other two men didn't miss a beat. Their assignments were likely waiting for them in their inbox.

"Ooooh, some Red Rubies, please." Lucky smacked his lips for emphasis, his love for the Thai treats on full display.

"I will take some chai tea, *compañero*." Aaron answered thoughtfully. "And some more soap. They are pretty."

My tender, romantic killing machine. My heart.

I poured the steamed milk into the waiting espresso and made myself a pretty picture of a heart before downing the hot liquid in three large pulls. Kellan was right. We had a busy day ahead of us, and time was not on our side.

Placing the mug in the sink, I strode over to Aaron's still-seated form and kissed him hard. "I love you, *caballero oscuro*. See you soon."

"Be safe, *Mi Reina*. I will love you when you return."

"Love you, Blondie." Lucky smiled at me when I came over to give him his farewell kiss. "Give them hell."

"Always." He kissed me gently this time, a slow promise of what was to come when I returned. When he pulled back, I was breathless and disheveled, just as he'd intended.

"Brat," Kellan admonished, standing behind me to claim his own kiss from Lucky. "She can't be thinking of you when she's pretending to be married to me." He leaned down and took the lead on his goodbye kiss, leaving Lucky gasping for air and palming down his half hard cock when he pulled away.

"I'll see you later." He smirked victoriously before stalking off to the bedroom to grab our packs for the trip.

"See you..." Lucky stared dumbly after him, bested at his own game. Aaron and I indulged him, but Kellan enjoyed his power over his pet more days than not.

I followed him to get myself ready. It was time to become a Queen.

The plane ride from Manila to Bangkok felt shorter this time. It was only our third assignment, and our second to Bangkok, but each trip spiked my adrenaline and rehydrated my thirst for blood.

Several months ago, the four of us had been struggling to adapt to our new lifestyle. After years of holding powerful roles of authority and living lives filled with stress and activity, the island life hadn't sat well with any of us—at least, not the way we'd been living it. The peace was a beautiful change of pace, but it had lost its meaning when we had nothing to contrast it with.

Lucky had finally admitted it one night under a star-filled sky as we all lay on the beach after a fantastic foursome session: "I'm a miserable feck for saying I'm a bit bored, aren't I?"

Turns out, we all were a bit bored—a bit *too* secure. That admission turned into a strategy session. What was it the four of us could do, and do well, while still maintaining our tiny plot of paradise?

Aaron and I didn't want to run Fortune 500 companies anymore, and the thought of opening a small business in a foreign country hadn't appealed to either of us. Lucky's skills in software engineering could garner him a job somewhere, but the man would never commit to a 9-5 anything. Kellan had only known two jobs in his lifetime: law enforcement and cartel enforcer.

Serendipitously, one of his Interpol contacts reached out to him a few weeks later, asking for his consultation on a human trafficking case out of Southeast Asia. We'd all jumped at the opportunity to help, and our insight had been so effective he was asked to consult on another one in Cambodia, then another one in Vietnam. Our proximity to the hot-bed of human trafficking in the world lent itself to some in-person missions, and after several successful consultations, Kellan was asked to "bring his team in" for a chat.

We didn't work directly for Interpol. We'd formed a subcontracting unit they discreetly hired for specific jobs, and we took on the assignments we could manage. We all took different roles on rotation, and tonight, Kellan and I were the contractors of choice.

So, here we were, attending a high-profile fashion event in the heart of Thailand. Interpol had received a tip-off several people would be trafficked here under the Royal Thai Police's nose, and we were here to intercept the bad guys by acting as a rich American couple in need of Thai silks and Tibetan lamb furs.

I'd been true to my word. I wasn't getting married again in this lifetime. Besides, how could I choose which person to marry of my three men? Our commitment to each other was stronger than a ring or a promise in a church. We were blood bonded. Bonded through our histories of trauma. No other single soul in the universe could capture my attention like Aaron, Lucky, and Kellan. They were all I wanted, and all I needed. I slipped on the fake wedding band to go with our costume, anyway. Playing dress-up was fun, at least.

"Ready?" Kellan draped his arm around me as we stood at the entrance of the Siam Paragon. He was dressed in a navy fitted suit and crisp white shirt with his hair tied back in a loose bun, looking every bit the handsome Viking King.

"Ready," I repeated, my silk pink mermaid dress trailing behind me as I walked up the red-carpeted stairs, donning a brilliant smile to play the part.

Tonight, evil would meet its match once again, and its match was me. The board was set, the players were ready. A King and Queen ready to be crowned the victors against the worst kinds of sins.

"Somchai," my handsome companion called over the din of the crowd, beckoning our contact over. "Allow me to introduce you to my wife..."

Game on.

To Claim a King

About the Author

Cora Flynn is a Canadian Indie Why Choose/Reverse Harem author with a penchant for cliffhangers and crafting characters that will equally excite and exasperate you.

When she's not writing, Cora attempts to manage the chaos of a two-toddler household with her extremely patient husband, while maintaining a job in "the real world."

She loves reading as many books as she can fit on her Kindle, her bookshelves, and her nightstand. Worlds with multiple men will always be her favorite.

Join the fun on Instagram and TikTok by following @coraflynnauthor.

Books by Cora Flynn

Cascade of Lies series
- (prequel) Winter's Song
- Days of Winter
- Nights of Winter
- Winter's End

All the Queen's Men series
- To Catch a Rook
- To Curse a Knight
- To Claim a King

www.coraflynnauthor.com